BOMBAY

BOMBAY

Soumitro Das

Vitasta

Published by
Renu Kaul Verma
Vitasta Publishing Pvt Ltd
4348/4C, Ansari Road, Daryaganj
New Delhi-110 002
info@vitastapublishing.com

ISBN: 978-81-19670-90-1

First Edition 2025
MRP ₹450

This novel is entirely a work of fiction. Names, characters, events and incidents are entirely imaginary. Reference to real places, actual regions, institutions or community practices has been made in a fictitious manner. Any resemblance to actual persons, living or dead or actual events is purely coincidental.

Edited by Vichitra Goel
Typeset & Cover Design by Somesh Kumar Mishra
Printed by Vikas Computer and Printers, New Delhi

PROLOGUE

As far back as my mind goes, I have had difficulty saying the word 'Love' to another human being. Something would get stuck in my throat, and my body twisted out of shape with unimaginable, untreatable and tortuous expressions whose purpose, as I came to realise later on, was to undermine any reality that this word could express. I first said the words 'I love you' at the age of five to a girl at whose house I and another friend of mine would go to play every evening. I had told this friend about my caper, and he agreed with me, saying it would be a wicked manoeuvre on my part. That's how he saw it. So we went up to the terrace apartment this girl stayed in with her parents, and I took up position behind a water tank, waiting for her to appear. I found myself torn into two—nervous and ready to give up, yet determined. I really loved that girl; she was, at that age, a pretty specimen of humanity. So, as soon as she emerged out of her terrace apartment, I walked out from behind the water cooler and, with an exaggerated and perverse gait that represented the cross-fertility of cultures and the danger of what I was aiming to do, I said, 'I love you, Shalini,' two or three times in quick succession. I was swinging laterally from my hips outwards, and my voice had suddenly discovered a bizarre tremolo. My friend and the girl laughed at me as if it were all a grand little joke. The next day, her mother told us that the girl was ill and wouldn't play with us anymore. Just like that. After this episode, my friend and I would go to her house once or twice, and each time her mother would turn us away. I surmised that it had something to do with my little act of derision. Once, the girl herself opened the door and told us she wouldn't play with us anymore.

The memory of that fiasco must have stayed with me because, for the next 15 years or so, I remained terrified at the idea of revealing my feelings in front of girls, even though there were several in my school who roused me sexually, if not romantically. This was in West Delhi, a particularly tough neighbourhood full of machismo and sexual arrogance, where young boys instinctively understood the place they should occupy in a girl's life.

Another big problem that inhibited me was my parents, in particular, my father. They had been brought up in a puritanical atmosphere where nobody ever made the mistake of falling in love for real. Love as fantasy was acceptable to them as long as it was kept to oneself without burdening other people with useless and pointless emotional drivel. So rigid was the boundary between what was permissible and what was not. I was too young and inexperienced to defy them, but I was biding my time, even as I devoured books written for boys by Englishmen such as Frank Richards, who spoke of a boarding school life full of adventure, love and happiness. I wanted to live that life but didn't know where to find the right landscape, the appropriate friendship and, above all, the love interest. My parents let me run wild and didn't notice what I was consuming in the form of paperbacks and what was running through my mind. As long as it didn't impinge on their reality, I could run around like other kids in the neighbourhood between 3 and 6 in the afternoon.

At home, there were no books, music, or TV, but that was not unusual in our milieu. Television was a luxury in those days, and those who had it would find their houses invaded every Sunday evening with the rabble off the road because they would run a Hindi film on that day. My father, an airline pilot, was frequently absent, but when in Delhi, he would come home around 7 pm and immediately engross himself in the morning paper. There was no conversation, entertainment, adventure, or anything that would teach one how to behave with the opposite sex. It was only much later, when I had started reading Freud, that I recognised the contours of the ferocious sexual repression that my parents jointly represented. And they were not alone. Every house in the neighbourhood suffered from the same apathy and neglect when it came to the word 'sex'. Again, it was only with the help of Freud that I realised my upbringing had crippled me sexually. I was incapable of saying 'I love you' to a girl in a healthy and sober manner despite going to a school that firmly opposed gender segregation, and which frequently put us in the awkward position of choosing a partner in a game or a dance. The dog collar of puritanism was worn crudely around my neck. Sex was not something you discussed with your parents; you knowingly joked about it with your, largely, male friends and masturbated like mad with the onset of puberty. At the right age, your parents would find a suitable girl, someone as repressed as yourself, or, in some cases, even more, and you would bungle through a marriage, blind and deaf to everything beyond your class, community and, above all, religion. The only advantage I had was my ability to recognise the enemy early. Bitter recognition.

1

So, I came to Bombay, the city of skyscrapers and tinsel love, when I was fourteen.

We stayed in a posh locality, Nepean Sea Road, where my father had rented a 7th-floor apartment from where I could see the rain advance like a wall of water over the sea before making landfall. It rained abundantly and torrentially for hours at a time. People in other localities would complain about being flooded, but we never had such problems. It was also during the monsoon that my heart would ache with love for women out of my reach, mostly models and film stars. I frenetically masturbated several times a day, which meant I was almost always in a state of taut sexual tension. However, I was not out of control yet (that came later).

There were problems in finding me a school, but thanks to my father's connections, I was finally admitted to Bombay Scottish, in Mahim. The school wasn't top-notch and had many children of famous film stars of the time, but that was okay with me. Even at that age, I did not let myself be bothered by people's social pedigree.

In my class, Shahid Hossein and Simple Chopra, son and sister of famous Hindi film personalities, graced the front benches while I dozed off in the rear. I was not impressed by them, and vice versa. And then there was Angelica de Silva, a beautiful Goan girl, who made my heart thunder with, what I would later identify as, intense sexual longing. She was mercilessly abused by a group of charlatan chauvinists who banged their desks and made spitting sounds the moment she entered the classroom. I wanted to tell her that she was too pretty for them to handle, that she was far above the gangsterised insults she had to face with so much courage and forbearance. But something would get stuck in my throat.

Not the fear of being on the wrong side of the abusers—I did not care two hoots for their practised meanness—but something that came from deep within whose only expression in the outer world was crucified love. I did not dare to take a stand in public. One day, I pretended to drop my keys on the floor next to her desk. I looked her in the eye but saw no love in return. I could not go up to her and say, 'Listen, I don't agree with these hoodlums, I am on your side.' I was too timid for that. Besides, I would end up showing my softer side and I wasn't saint enough for that. What I did do was drop my keys in the aisle right next to her desk and fumble to pick it up. I don't know whether the rest of the class had cottoned on to the manoeuvre and at bottom I didn't care. The act was ambiguous enough to be interpreted in different ways and so, I felt safe. The message though had gotten across to Angelica, I was pretty sure about that.

It was around this time that I grew aware that I detested ganging up with people, no matter what the excuse, because it was an abdication of the heart and base. I knew I loved Angelica, but would never be strong enough to break through the myriad layers of taboo, prohibition and self-exile that would inevitably break over my head if I showed the slightest intention of showing my emotions in public. In short, I was a coward. As a result, in the two years in Bombay Scottish, I did not utter a word to Angelica. I realised that I had no goal in life. I wouldn't become a lawyer, doctor or engineer, and, therefore, my marital purchasing power was mostly speculative. This further inhibited my capacity to love and be loved. As someone told me years later, I was not husband material. It meant I was going to be a vagabond or a good-for-nothing. With what right would I love Angelica? 'Put money in thy purse,' said Iago.

In school, I naturally fell in with a group of boys, including Amin Ismail, Ashraf Jamal and Bharat, who were cavalier spirits, regularly bunking PT and never completing their homework. It was while chatting with them that I noticed Ravi Motwani, a quiet cynic, who devoured pulp fiction like nobody's business and couldn't care less for academic excellence. I made a discovery right then—I liked loners. One day, Amin and Ashraf were involved in a heated discussion of *Woodstock*, the movie, specifically the inaugural songs by Richie Havens. Ashraf said Havens was emotionally charged, but his music was monotonous. Amin said he had a style of his own, unique and, above all, a true representative of Black power (those were the days when Tommie Smith gave the Black Power Salute of the Black Panthers at the Olympic Games in Mexico City). Coming from a small provincial neighbourhood in North India, I knew nothing about race politics in the USA and even less about Western pop culture. But I easily made friends among people who didn't instinctively follow the herd. Amin and Ashraf were both upper class and could have been pack leaders if they wanted to, but, they were hard-core rock and rollers who believed that the family was the primary site of social and cultural contestation and that the *enemy* was their parents. I disagreed with them, but being ignorant, I held my tongue.

Motwani came up one day and said, 'Hi, I am Ravi.' I shook his extended hand shyly. A tiny uncomfortable pause followed. 'What's your name?' said Ravi. I told him my name. 'It's got five syllables,' said Ravi. That was the beginning of my self-awareness. 'I'll call you Sam if you don't mind,' said Ravi. The name stuck with me for the remainder of my days in Bombay—I would introduce myself with my first name and then follow it up with, 'You can call me Sam.'

'Where do you live?' said Ravi.

I told him where. Some more conversation followed.

'Have you read this?' asked Ravi. He held up a book. It was *The Prize* by Irving Wallace.

I said no.

'Would you like to read it?'

'Definitely.'

He handed the book to me, and we became friends.

After school, we'd often walk to his house nearby, a ramshackle old building and a dilapidated, congested apartment. His mother would make us delicious vegetarian Sindhi food that I would tuck into with relish. We spoke about Hindi films, politics, teachers and girls. Ravi did most of the talking, and I would just interject with a yes or a no.

Ravi spoke to me at length about his father, a self-made man, a refugee from Karachi, who had started out by selling garments on the footpath in Colaba. Eventually, he saved up enough money to buy the shop in front of which he had his stall. He was making serious money then, but Ravi told me about his difficult years when he didn't have enough money to pay for a movie ticket. I loved these stories. Ravi was also very religious, but that didn't prevent him from saying that he considered the act of making love to a woman, any woman, even his sister, to be above sacrilege. I didn't agree, nor did I find his views shocking. He would often be rude to his sister in my presence, saying, 'I know you are wet in your panties because of Sam; stop staring at us, go and study.' But, Laila—that was her name—would shyly smile and cling on to the curtain with even more desperation. She wouldn't say a word, wouldn't smile or anything, but just stare at us pointlessly. Ravi and I would often talk about the girls in our class, but I never told him or anyone else what I felt for Angelica de Silva. I instinctively knew that doing so would be like a breach of etiquette and that the news would get around and rebound on me in the form of ridicule or outright hostility. Even though Bombay Scottish was a co-educational school, the laws of sexual segregation were practised rigorously among the pupils. The girls sat bunched together on the right side of the class, while the boys occupied the rest of the room. Talking about Angelica would be like transgressing omertà, the law of silence binding us in one macho community, united against femininity as a concept. Those were the days before the word 'rebellion' had entered our vocabulary. While talking about girls, one had to think, first and foremost, about one's family identity and pride. The idea of sex was a filthy idea meant for sissies and delinquents. So, we spoke about Mumtaz instead, and how gorgeous she looked in one of her films. We talked about her because she would never become a part of our day-to-day reality; she was tinsel, and it was as a tinsel that we loved her. No concrete arrangement was needed.

One was allowed to love one's parents, especially, our fathers. I rarely spoke about my family—my sister and elder brother, who was studying to be an economist at Elphinstone College, whom I admired beyond measure, mainly because he had been an outstanding athlete and an elegant left-handed batsman in the school cricket team notching up a few centuries and mentions in the newspapers. He was an aloof and remote presence in my life, somebody who was part of the parental group in the family but beyond intimacy and brotherly camaraderie. He also had a girlfriend called Anjana, who wore figure-hugging jeans and let her hair hang loose over her shoulders and the small of her back. My father was flying Airbuses to Delhi and Calcutta thrice a week. We were affluent and had enough money to live comfortably on Nepean Sea Road.

Ravi and I would occupy the backbenches of the classroom—he, with the latest paperback under his nose, and me, spread-eagled over the desk, snoozing away without anyone bothering to even notice. I never learnt anything at school. All I knew was that one had to memorise the prescribed textbooks and regurgitate the contents during exams. I would rarely do my homework. I didn't shine in my studies, neither at games nor in any other self-advancement avenues provided by the school. I went along with the herd, but I kept my eyes and ears open. It was at Bombay Scottish that I discovered a strong streak of scepticism in me. During PT and recreation, I would hang around in class with Ravi, Ashraf, Amin, Bharat and Dipankar, people who had no heroes and were not heroic, neither in their ideas nor in their aspirations. Amin and Dipankar were into music and girls, real girls, not celluloid creatures, who lived in their neighbourhoods and one had actually gone and squeezed a girl's breasts during a melee at the school fiesta.

We had become the big bad boys of the class. This was also when I rapidly grew taller. During the morning assembly, I would take my place at the end of the row, dominating the proceedings and peering anxiously at Angelica and her smooth waxed legs. We were not supposed to pay any attention to the girls and anyone doing so would be quickly expelled from the inner circle where only hardened machos reigned in frozen horror over a desolate kingdom peopled by those who could not shrug off public opinion, such as it was. We watched Hindi films where the hero approached women, sang songs, won their heart and presumably lived happily ever after having defeated the villain and gaining social acceptance by defying impossible odds. Everybody understood that only special creatures, who spoke Urdu and bantered immodestly with the heroine, had the right to free love. The movies were deliberately unreal, an idealistic fantasy where iron moral values were upheld even as the hero danced and chased the girl around the vegetation. Who is a hero? A hero is above all, alone, commanding impossible heights, yet predatory, chasing women, breaking through the walls of prejudice and taboo, single-handedly destroying obstacles placed in his way, until the heroine succumbs to the objective assessment of the hero's quasi-divine status. It was much later when I had started questioning everything, that I realised these stories were derived from mythology in which the hero was, more often than not, a god in disguise, to whom the ordinary rules of social conduct, especially among the sexes, did not apply. If anyone actually embarked upon a project to woo a girl as depicted in Hindi movies, harassing her to death, sometimes literally, he would instantly be rejected as a madman. However, it was also true that, whether we watched Hindi movies or not, we harboured deep within our hidden selves, the heroic ideal as an ambition, as a kind of Utopian conduct that demanded dangerously high levels of courage and, even, recklessness, denied to ordinary mortals. Secretly, we all wanted to be heroes.

The saddest part was that most of us would obey the verdict of reality and accept the commonness of our souls by marrying the girl our parents would choose for us. The heroic ideal, derived straight from our epics, especially from the story of Rama, was planted deep within us and was manifested only through certain socially acceptable domains—cricket, Hindi movies, politics and, of course, religion. Its immediate impulse was recognised as a mastery over the self. The autonomous individual, a routine entity in the West, was a summit that had to be conquered in India. The alternative was to renounce and retire to the Himalayas to meditate, aided and abetted by mind-altering drugs, on the Absolute and the gift of a rhetoric and a discourse through which shone forth a divine centripetal force that placed the subject above and beyond the concerns of dailyness and attracted lay followers, sometimes in their millions.

Anyway, all this analysis, and its deep insights, lay in the future. For the present, we, the tall boys of the class, except Ravi who didn't grow at all, had our own bohemian rules that laid down what was acceptable and what wasn't.

The satire that I wrote about our history teacher

and affixed, in a moment of Lutheran callousness, to the school noticeboard was read and ignored by the entire faculty but created a buzz in class, though only among the boys. They had no respect for poetry but thought I was one of them and agreed that humanities did not have a future except for juvenile delinquents. History? Who wanted to study history—the study of a past in which nothing happened except humiliation, defeat and sorrow, where one learnt the wretchedness of people, which outfitted the man with useless knowledge that wouldn't buy him bread or win him a woman. People who studied history were people of low IQ, such as women. All I knew was that I didn't want to study science and mathematics; I did not want to be a doctor, engineer, lawyer or, for that matter, an airline pilot. I had no idea what I wanted to do in life; it could lie in wait for me for the rest of eternity for all I cared. I asked Ravi if he knew.

'I have no idea,' he said. 'I suppose I will sit in the shop and sell fabric.'

I asked him whether that was a considered plan or a knee-jerk reaction. He shrugged and said, 'My future has been written. Nothing stirs but by his will.'

He was talking about God, of course. Though I couldn't fathom his reasoning, I thought that was better than not knowing who one wanted to be.

'And you?' asked Ravi.

'I don't know,' said I.

'What do you mean you don't know?'

'I guess I'll get a job and try to become the best that I

can,' I said, but indifference had already spoken through my words.

'You want to be just like everyone else?'

'Yeah, just hide in a crowd and not get noticed.'

'What was the lampoon about? You write fine English. You can be a journalist or a writer of some sort. You could be the next Irving Wallace, Sidney Sheldon or Robert Ludlum…'

At night, I would look at the stars through the window in my room and think heroism couldn't last forever. Would Alexander be remembered for all time to come? For billions of years? Somehow this thought left me depressed. It meant that my father was leading the perfect life—earning a living, raising a family and securing his future. But, I had no fantasies, no ambition, nothing. I wanted to make love to Angelica; and be a boy with a girlfriend, like Dipankar; I thought that would be glorious, putting me a notch above my peers. Sometimes, I would think of spending the rest of my life in a small town, living an obscure and contented life with a woman I loved, sitting in the sun in winter and just basking in the glow of the eternal.

The traffic thundered through Nepean Sea Road at night and the construction of a skyscraper continued apace opposite our tower. I had no critical faculties; I just swallowed what was written in books and was won over to the outlook on life they represented, until I read the next book. I remember reading Leon Uris' *Exodus*, Herman Wouk's *Youngblood Hawke* and Ayn Rand's *Atlas*

Shrugged. I could write a book, I thought, but that didn't lead me anywhere because no one around me knew how to become a writer. Nobody, in those days, thought one could go to University and study to be a writer. It was akin to seduction, totally mysterious, without any rules or an open channel of career, fortune and fame. Moreover, there was something shameful about wanting to be a writer, an ambition that couldn't be openly expressed. Why? Because it involved some cultural transgression, declaring oneself outside the centre of society, religion and nation? Because it would place one above the family, above my parents? Fame. I secretly wanted to be famous. Secretly, because there was some megalomaniacal madness in it. I would sit in my balcony and stare at the night sky, wondering whether my life was a cruel joke.

Anyhow, I got invited to a stag party thrown by Ashraf where, except for me and Ravi, everybody guzzled quantities of chilled beer to wash down the wontons, cocktail sausages and cheese balls that came along with the drinks. Ravi and I quietly sipped our lemonade and sat in a corner, listening to Frank Zappa and the Mothers of Invention.

'Sure you don't want a beer?' said Ashraf.

I said, 'No, I can't allow myself to lose control.'

Ashraf smiled and said, 'You don't have to; a glass of beer isn't going to turn you into a sex fiend.'

'Where are the girls?' said Ravi.

'Girls?' said Ashraf. 'Who wants girls around? Are you some kind of romantic sissy?'

I blushed pink at that.

So, it was all about toughness—the booze, the music, the male gender. I didn't know the meaning of the word 'misogyny' back then.

Ravi smiled at me and said, 'These people don't know where to put their cocks.'

That made me laugh.

'Any girls you like at school?' he asked.

I momentarily thought about what to say, and then said, 'No, not one of them.'

I was protecting Angelica from the unwanted attention of a loser. Had I been a science student, searching for and finding a career full of money, glamour and promise, I would have been less ashamed of wanting the most beautiful girl in school.

But I had really low self-esteem, hidden somewhat desperately behind a cold and aloof air.

'What do you want to be, Sam?' asked Amin.

'I guess I'll go to college and then find a job,' I lied.

'That's all? What kind of job?'

'Some job. Maybe a banker's job.'

Amin would go on to be a hotshot software developer in the US. But that was far in the future. I asked him about his plans.

'Engineering,' he replied vaguely. I don't think he knew what that meant and what he would get into. We were drifting in a sea of jelly that thickened around us and cut us off from parental expectations.

At home, they wanted me to study science, of course,

but they knew my views on it. My father was a quiet, soft-spoken man who rarely communicated his thoughts to his children. He had recently bought a car, an Aston Martin, which one of his higher-ups wanted to sell. He paid Rs 20,000 for it, a princely sum in those days of the planned economy and import substitution. He cut a figure driving up and down Bombay in the snazzy vehicle, looking important and prosperous. I always sat in the front seat while my mother would constantly give directions to him about tackling the traffic. My father loved cool cars and eating out. All his money went to food and his car. He would give me Rs 50 per month as pocket money that, even in those days, was just enough to pay for the occasional Coke and samosas at the school canteen. He was born in 1920 and hadn't noticed that the world had changed. He had the mind of a peasant; he thought his sons, both of them, would follow in his footsteps and get a job, after which mother and he would find suitable girls for us to marry. My elder brother was clearer about his future than I. My sister, two years older than me, wanted to be an air hostess, and my father approved of her ambition. It was only me that everyone was worried about. I was an average student and didn't seem to have any special skill or talent. I read a lot of books, but that was a side activity and wouldn't possibly count in any professional calculation about the future. At that point, as I said, I wasn't even sure one could be a writer in the way one could be an engineer, doctor or lawyer. The only kind of writers who made money that we knew of were journalists and screenplay writers. My parents loved watching Hindi movies, but I instinctively knew that they didn't respect movie people. Journalism was respectable, but it wouldn't be suitable for a person who was painfully shy and withdrawing at any public occasion. Plus, I had no handle on politics; I didn't even read the newspaper properly—I would usually skip the politics section and just read the sports pages. However, my parents didn't worry much about my future. They expected me to find a suitable job and marry the girl of their choice, and that was that.

'What kind of music do you listen to, Sam?' asked Bharat.

I told him. That seemed to stun him and Amin a bit. They hardly considered Engelbert Humperdinck to be a musician; if you weren't into rock 'n' roll, there was something seriously wrong about your ability to embrace adulthood. Big boys listened to Pink Floyd and Bob Dylan. My favourite tune was *Popcorn by Hot Chocolate*. Everybody laughed at that except Ravi. He came from the same unartistic, philistine background that my parents approved of tacitly. I knew I couldn't play that awful, noisy, hippy stuff at home; they would think I was turning into some socially suspect freak. Given a choice between buying a music system and a television, my parents stolidly stumped for a TV; the music system would come later. I wasn't unhappy with the choice. One could watch cricket and Hindi movies for free. Music—real music—could wait.

Amin and Bharat were seriously embarrassed by my taste in music, and they made fun of it.

'Boney M!' they exclaimed. 'You listen to Boney M?! That's dance music; that's meant for the cows.'

I said, 'That's all I get to hear on the radio,' I said, secretly ashamed of my lack of any big boy experience.

Everywhere, I could see boys my age becoming adults at a frenetic pace. But nobody could talk about books the way Ravi and I did. We would often meet in a half-done flat belonging to one of Ravi's father's business acquaintances. It was on Malabar Hill and gave us a fine view of a house which, as I learnt later, belonged to Jinnah and was being claimed by the Pakistani embassy for their consulate in Bombay. It was a beautiful old villa whose grandeur stood out even though it badly needed a paint job and the lawn overrun with weeds.

I told Ravi I want to live in that house on growing up. Ravi took pictures of it and gave me a few copies which I cherish to this day, like a dream never forgotten. All our time was spent talking about one thing or the other; I don't remember a single complete conversation with Ravi, but I recognise that it impacted how I approached adulthood. Like Ravi, I eschewed the idea of indulging in intoxication or flirting with girls. Real men didn't think about girls; they *did* them. On fifty bucks a month, I could only dream.

As I said, the woman that I loved and hopelessly pined after was Mumtaz, and she was a film star. I liked her lips and eyes and how she smiled and carried herself.

I would often spend my time drawing her picture from a photograph in *Stardust*, the film magazine my sister subscribed to. I was careful to hide this from my family because they thought I was too young and precariously poised in life to think seriously about women. So, instead, I put up a poster of Rajesh Khanna, the superstar whose films I had seen and was reasonably mad about.

***

The school had organised a trip to Singapore on a luxury liner. Ravi had signed up for it and asked me to do the same.

I said I knew the answer would be no; my father wouldn't allow me to cross the seas on a trip from which potentially I might never come back.

'But it's an educational trip,' said Ravi. 'Singapore is the new emerging hot spot! Do you know that their crime rate is almost zero?'

'That wouldn't impress my father,' I said.

And, it didn't. When I told him, rather tentatively, that Ravi was going on a cruise to Singapore, he pooh-poohed the idea.

'What does it have, that piddly little country on the tip of Malaysia?' he said. 'If you really want to go abroad, you should go to New York! On your own money!'

After a pause, he said, 'We will be making a trip to the South, Kerala and Goa. Those are really interesting places with some beautiful architecture and beaches.

You'll enjoy that.'

I said, 'Going on a holiday with the family is no fun.'

'You are too young to go on a holiday on your own,' he said, cleaning his pipe with abrupt, irritated gestures. 'They'll be serving alcohol and god knows what else. Do you want to turn into a drunkard?'

My father was a teetotaller, somebody who had never touched a bottle of booze in his entire life.

I said we would be supervised by our teachers.

'Nothing doing,' said my father. 'I know how children get into all kinds of mischief when backs are turned. I cannot allow my son to be exposed to all kinds of decadence at such a young age.'

I said Ravi would be going too.

'Can we stop discussing this?'

The talk was just going round and round.

So, I didn't get to go to Singapore on a cruise ship. Angelica would be going. In a way, I was relieved she wouldn't get first-hand knowledge about the state of my family's morality; it would have thrown me beyond the pale of schoolboy romance and bring the guillotine down on my fantasies. I spent the second rainy season at Nepean Sea Road, whose high point was Rajiv Gandhi, the Prime Minister's son and my father's co-pilot on his long haul flights to Kathmandu, visiting our house. He came with his wife, Sonia, and his two children, Priyanka and Rahul. Priyanka spent her evening chatting with my sister, while my brother and I had a conversation with Rahul, who seemed to be an average boy with an average intelligence. They had no airs about them, despite their being grandchildren of the country's Prime Minister, whose reputation after the Bangladesh War was sky-high. My father was a rigid right wing conservative and positively hated Indira Gandhi, mainly because she had nationalised the banks. He took care though, to hide his political views from the Prime Minister's son. Indeed, they spent the evening without discussing any politics. Rajiv Gandhi was not a public figure, and he seemed to understand that a political discussion would immediately strike a discordant note in the evening's proceedings. They all seemed to appreciate the dinner that my mother, an excellent cook, had rustled up. Also, during that memorable visit, I learnt my awkwardness in formal social gatherings. When my brother left our room to attend to his duties as a host, Rahul and I would relapse into a tense, uneasy silence.

'That's a radio?' Rahul said.

'Yes,' I said.

'That's really interesting.'

'Yes.'

Another tense pause followed. He was as shy as I was and had as much difficulty sustaining a conversation with me as I had with him.

'Which brand?' he said.

'Murphy,' said I.

'Ah.'

Again, a pregnant pause.

'It looks really old,' he said.

'It is,' I said. It belonged to my grandfather.

He was only five years old.

After they had gone, my father said, 'Nice family'.

My mother nodded in agreement. 'I was so afraid they wouldn't like the food. Especially the fish.'

They had, in fact, made it clear that this was their first experience with our family's brand of cuisine, and they relished every bit of it. That my mother was a chain-smoker didn't seem to bother them in the least.

So, we went South after that, straight to Thiruvananthapuram, where my sister and mother got themselves caught in the *chakravyuh* of dancing, mantra-yelling, half-naked priests. My mother hastily put a 50 buck note into their copper vessel, and she and my sister beat a hasty retreat, vowing not to step into another temple in Kerala again. After that we went to Kanyakumari where the food smelled of coconut. The smell made me sick, and for two days I lived on toast and eggs for breakfast, lunch and dinner. My father tried telling me about the rock in the middle of the ocean where the Hindu revivalist Vivekananda had meditated on the Absolute. I was bored. It was just a silly little rock. Eventually, we pulled out of Kanyakumari and headed North to Goa.

I loved the place despite my parents and their insane schedule and the idiotic hotel they put us up in. The food was fabulous, and the trip to Old Goa was worth every penny. The ride from Dabolim, the airport, to Panjim, the state capital, was heavenly. The hills plunged into the sea, and the lagoons sported a fairy-look with sea gulls. There was practically no traffic in that early hour, and the car whizzed past several superb pieces of Latin architecture that my philistine father didn't bother asking the driver about. We were lodged in Mandovi Hotel, an ugly monstrosity run by the State administration facing Panjim harbour. However, the hotel was spick and span—luxurious by Indian standards—with razor-sharp air conditioning and served us our meals on dot. The food was delicious; I gorged on Xacuti, Recheado and Pomfret Balchao. I constantly thought about Angelica and pictured myself spending the rest of my life in one of the cute little Goan villages with their distinct Latin look of tiled roof houses and pretty little squares. After Goa, we returned Bombay, and I swore that that would be my last trip with family. I was not my father's son anymore; I was someone else.

I plunged straight into my textbooks, preparing for my year-end Senior Cambridge exams. Ravi, Amin and Ashraf had returned from their trip to Singapore, full of stories about the amazing discipline of the local population. It was illegal to spit on the streets, and you were fined $ 50 if you threw even a toffee wrapper on the road. They saw several young teenagers picked up by the police and taken away in black Marias for a haircut. Long hair was banned in Singapore. The cruise ship was fabulous, with three swimming pools and a casino. Amin had used his talent for math and picked up a couple of hundred Singapore dollars at backgammon. Ashraf, too, had won $ 60 at the slot machines. How could they run a casino if they lost trifling sums of money to people who were not hard gamblers? Angelica returned looking even more beautiful than usual, and had had her hair styled wearing it short. The look suited her. Of course, I didn't exchange a word with her. I didn't know what to say to her, except that I loved her dearly and that it was impossible.

It was about this time that the police landed up in our house one morning. The Aston Martin my father had bought with his hard-earned money was a car stolen from Jabalpur and belonged to the President of the Congress, Shankar Dayal Sharma. Also, there was news from Calcutta: my grandfather had died on his way to collect his pension from the post-office. My father just crumbled when hit by this double whammy. The Aston Martin had cost him a small fortune, and he was proud of his car and its in-built comfort. My blood froze one night when I opened my eyes on a spur and heard him sitting in front of the portrait of Ramakrishna Paramahamsa and sobbing piteously about the frame of his mind. He was seeking forgiveness for his sins. What sins? He was mumbling softly about his car and his father. I heard him crying, and I went stiff all over, paralysed with abject fear. Fathers weren't supposed to cry; they were supposed to take it on their chin and move on to the next thing. I heard him mention the luxury flat he had bought in Calcutta, where he intended to settle after retirement. He was sobbing like a child. This, after my resentful trip down South, further confirmed my impression that I was alone in the world, that depending on this man—financially, emotionally and physically—was not a given. I would have to redraw the inexistent map of my future. I would have to take my own decisions and fend for myself. It was during these nights of horror that I promised myself that I would get a job after college and move out of my father's house, wherever it might be.

I sat for my exams and, as a humanities student, I came out with flying colours. I had secured an aggregate of 80 per cent, which was a lot in those days of illiberal marking. I scored 95 in Geography and English. In those wicked socialist times, this was good enough to secure a place in any good college in Bombay. I saw Angelica one last time at the annual school sports held in a stadium in Worli. She still had short hair and wore a colourful little dress that suited her to a tee and dark goggles to hide her beautiful eyes. At first, I couldn't recognise her, but then she smiled at me, and I shyly raised my hand to greet her.

'You're looking good,' I said.

'Thank you,' she said.

I sat down next to her. She wore Coriander, a French perfume that enhanced her sex appeal.

'What are your plans for the future?' I asked.

'I have applied to be an air hostess,' she said.

'Ah,' I said, blushing furiously. 'That's glamorous. Suits you completely.'

'Which airlines?' I asked, my heart pounding as I tried to come up with an unrehearsed remark.

'Air India,' she said.

'That sounds pretty good.'

'What about you?'

'I don't know. I don't have any plans. I guess, I'll study commerce.'

'Have you decided on a college?'

'Sydenham?' I said, unwilling to frighten her with my aimless drifting.

'That's fantastic.'

There was a lengthy pause.

Then I asked her, 'Can I have your phone number? We could catch a movie one of these days if your father doesn't bring out his service revolver and shoot me dead.'

She laughed.

She was practically the first woman whom I had moved to laughter. Her father was in the Army. She gave me her number. She stayed in Juhu as the only child of her parents, who doted on her.

'She likes you,' said Shetty, watching the joust a few rows away with Ravi, Amin, Ashraf, Ashok and the rest of the gang.

'Women make you weak,' said Ravi.

'Maybe,' said Amin. 'But you can't do without them.'

'She's in love with you,' said Bharat.

'*Shush*' I said, 'she can hear you.'

Eventually, I never got around to calling her up. As I said, with fifty bucks, all you could do was dream. Also, my father was a puritan; he would never allow me to have a girlfriend. She would just be a distraction, take me away from my studies and generally spoil my future.

Two months after the dinner with the Gandhis, the Bitch (as my father and many others called Indira Gandhi privately) declared a state of Emergency, effective throughout the country. The leaders in the Opposition were rounded up and jailed; the Press was censored, and the thugs in uniform were to be the arbiters of our daily battle against stupidity. On my part, I took this personally, even though I had no plans about being the next Irving Wallace. Now, I think that free speech and expression were an integral part of the ideological make-up of the middle-class; it allowed them to believe in the fiction that India was not a third-world country, reeling under a dictatorship, without any hope of redemption, putting up with Sanjay Gandhi, who seamlessly moved from being a garage owner to heir apparent to his mother. My father called from Delhi to tell us to be careful when talking over the phone and discussing political matters in public. He didn't seem particularly bothered about what the Emergency meant; he just wanted to protect his family. I discovered that the family fortunes didn't matter as much to me as the route to the truth being cut off. How could one be famous in the climate of pettifogging, miserable hypocrisy that we were all being subjected to in my first year in college?

2

My first day in Sydenham was spent in a classroom that could accommodate 150 students, boys outnumbering girls by 50:3. I was a tiny speck in the background. The first lecture I attended was by Afzalpurkar, who taught us commercial geography. He had a high-pitched voice and turned every singular noun, including place names, into plurals. I can't take this seriously, was my first thought. In school, we were taught by professionals who spoke the right kind of English—the public school variety. I felt disappointed and lonely.

After the class, two girls came up to me and introduced themselves.

I said, 'Hello,' blushing furiously.

'Hi,' said the darker of the two, 'We just wanted to get acquainted with you.'

'Why?' I said, narrowing my eyes in suspicion. 'What marks me out from the rest of the crowd?' My tone was rude and contemptuous.

They looked away in embarrassment and walked away. The truth was that I was uncomfortable with girls. It took a hell of a lot of courage for me to bare my emotions in front of them. Talking to Angelica had been the highest point in my love life, despite having studied in mixed schools all my life. I was timid to the point of ridicule. Plus, I had no money to take them even to Satkar, the neighbourhood Udipi joint, for a dosa and coffee. 'Put money in thy pocket.' It took me little time to realise I was not cut out for commerce. The only interesting lectures were those by Ms Zebunnissa Qazi, Mrs Hemmadi and Ms Kulkarni. They all taught English literature. However, I was careful not to tell my parents about my academic life. I was going to spend four years in Sydenham, I told myself, doing what?

I saw a notice on the noticeboard in the college lobby, announcing an inter-class debating championship. I don't remember what I thought and felt then, but I decided to put in my name. There were so few names that I was chosen to lead the debate for my first-year class against the second-year seniors. The topic was: This house believes that India is united in diversity or something to that effect. I wrote my short speech and memorised it. At the appointed hour, I and my three classmates took the stage in a classroom and debated furiously for an hour or so. I was surprised at the militant tone and the complete lack of political inhibition on both sides. More importantly, the debate was presided over by Vikas Kasliwal, a scion of one of the wealthiest families in the country, a handsome six-footer with blue eyes, who puffed away all the while choreographing the question round.

He beckoned to me after the debate—which we won again to my surprise—and asked me if I would join the college team. Nervous and exhausted from my effort in the inter-class first round, I said I didn't know if I could handle the pressure. He told me that Sydenham had been a champion for the last six years running, that I would get ample time to prepare and that he had been impressed by the way I navigated through the question round. Diffidently, I said okay.

And that's how it all started, the rollercoaster stag jamboree of quizzes, debates, elocution contests and, last but not least, theatre.

The first time I met The Gang or elements of it was on a trip to Delhi, to the Shri Ram College of Commerce (SRCC), to participate in their youth festival. We were a five-man squad made up of Dharen Chadha, Nero Gomes, Ram Bhonsle, and Franco Davis, called thus because his father was a Syrian Catholic from Kottayam, Kerala, while his mother was a Gujarati bania from Ahmedabad.

On the first evening I spent in the deliciously cold premises of SRCC, the weapons of war were brought out and displayed—2 bottles of Old Monk and a good fat stick of hashish. When the bottle was passed around, I grabbed it and put it to my mouth, and went glug, glug, glug, my Adam's apple going up and down as I did so. In a few minutes, I was both drunk and stoned up to my gills. I went and looked at myself in the toilet mirror. I was expecting a graphic alteration of my features, but no, my eyes were shot red, and that was all. After about an hour of back and forth between the hostel room and the toilet, I crashed out, unconscious.

The next day, Dharen, who had just sipped at the rum and had turned down the joint, and I, rocking gently from the after-push of the last evening, took the stage against St Stephen's and a few other local colleges. The motion was: This house believes that pigs have wings. We won hands down. I felt strange; victory felt strange. All eyes were on us, yet I've never felt so lacking in self-consciousness in life at any point after that. That was just the beginning. Ram and Franco, both sky-high on beer, won the quiz again, hands down. Nero won the prize for elocution; I don't remember the topic, but he was one of us, and I was one of them. Never have a more decadent lot won as many trophies as the merry band from Sydenham. Next thing you know, we were mingling with girls from Miranda and Lady Shri Ram at the Miranda House festival.

Our fame had spread all over the campus and beyond. I remember talking to a girl called Sheba, a beautiful Kashmiri with amber eyes who shyly looked up at me and laughed at everything I said. 'You're a funny guy, Sam,' she said. It was night, and we walked down the road to the nearest dhaba and had cups of steaming tea. We spoke about this and that, and before I knew it, I was holding hands with her and kissing her lightly on her lips. I didn't know how to kiss properly; I didn't know you had to prise open the other person's mouth and explore it ravenously with your tongue. Eventually, Sheba, who was as stoned as I was, hugged me for comfort, and thus we made our way back to SRCC, where we separated—I to Room 122 of the SRCC hostel, and she back to the Miranda House hostel.

Ram and Nero were waiting for me.

Ram was smoking a joint, and Nero was laughing at nothing.

'You really hit the bottle yesterday, man,' said Ram.

I smiled.

'You're growing up real fast,' said Ram. 'Got a lovely girlfriend, too. High time you got laid.'

I blushed. I was shocked beyond words. I thought love was all about whispering sweet nothings when together and aching for the person when separated. I had seen too many Hindi movies in my life.

'Make it short and sweet,' said Ram, passing me the joint.

I inhaled and immediately felt my senses dilate and pacify my nervous system.

'You really chewed up Stephen's,' said Nero, nursing a drink.

I blushed and smiled. I was socially awkward and charas was not doing anything to help.

'Yeah,' said Ram. 'Brilliant. But now is the time to reap the rewards and get laid. You need a condom?'

'I don't think I am ready for sex,' I said.

'Jesus, man, you are eighteen years old, legally an adult, with impossible erections at night, and you believe in some claptrap about romantic beatitude? You've been watching too many Hindi movies, you know.'

'Have you kissed her?' said Nero, smiling benignly.

'Sort of,' I said.

'Which sort?' said Ram. 'Rural UP or upscale Manhattan.'

'I don't know,' I said. 'This conversation is getting me down. Let's change the topic.'

'Okay,' said Ram. 'How cool is your dad?'

'He's not sex and drugs and rock 'n' roll,' I said.

'He's into milk and *The Times of India* and Akashvani, is it?' said Ram.

'Sort of,' I said.

'Bad sort, man,' said Ram. 'He's not going to like your girlfriend. He's going to explode. He's going to send your friend a questionnaire designed to pinpoint her socio-economic status.'

'That's true,' I said timidly. 'But, I am not marrying Sheba.'

'She's called Sheba?' said Ram. 'Don't say "sort of".'

I nodded.

'Come on, man,' said Nero to Ram, 'let him be.'

'Just asking,' said Ram.

'You're jealous,' said Nero.

'Not really,' said Ram, 'don't finish that joint all by yourself, kiddo; pass it on to me.'

Nero brought out his cassette player and played a tune called *Around Midnight* by someone with an impossible name.

'Thelonious Monk,' said Nero.

'Great stuff, man,' said Ram. 'Pure Afghani. I am talking about the hash, not the music.'

Franco tottered into the room.

'Three bottles of beer,' said Franco. 'Mostly vaseline and spirit.'

'Want a smoke?' said Ram.

'No thanks,' said Franco. 'Don't touch that evil stuff.'

Some guys from SRCC barged into the room. One of them looked at me and grinned.

'Delhi girls,' he said. 'All honey and milk.'

'You guys are getting stoned too,' said another.

'We've got a lifestyle to think about,' said Ram.

Then, we went for some food. There was talk about going to Karim's, the Mughal cuisine joint behind Jama Masjid. Dharen and his girlfriend joined us for dinner. We had puris with *chhola paneer* and mixed vegetables. Dharen was invited to read a poem he had written about life in Sydenham that everyone found good. It gradually dawned on me that these guys had genuine respect for me; they considered me a brother and it felt great to be in their company.

Something was happening to me. I began seeing through the hollow moral shabbiness and pretence of the English-speaking middle-class in the country. Yet I couldn't tear myself away from it and repudiate its banality. I was having strange thoughts about my parents. My father wouldn't touch alcohol with a barge pole, and my mother smoked intensely but would be ready to look for a bride for my brother when the time came for it.

They wouldn't put up with nonsense about girlfriends and might die of a heart attack if they found that I was into booze and charas. As for me, I really liked intoxication. It gave me an insight into paradise and, thanks to Nero, serious literature. It was Nero who first spoke to me about Kafka. When we returned to Bombay, he lent me his copy of *The Trial*. I took it home and started reading it. I couldn't put it down; I was totally absorbed by it. It was a kind of intoxication, too—the intoxication of high art. It was well past midnight when my mother woke up, saw the light in the living room and came to find out what I was up to.

'What's that stuff you're reading?' she said, angrily. 'It's one o'clock. Go to bed.'

I wanted to throw the armchair at her. I had never known such anger in my life. I refused to stop reading. She put out the lights. No sooner had she returned to her room than I put on the light again and returned to reading Kafka.

This world, I said to myself, is nonsense, but it backs the nonsense with a lot of power. I didn't want to go to the room I had begun sharing with my brother. I was rising to the spirit of the Occident. I felt close to that spirit; I let it define and regulate my existence. It was four in the morning when I finally put down *The Trial* and went to bed.

Sheba and I had parted on a friendly note.

'Can I write to you?' she asked.

'Of course,' I said, 'I'll call you, too.'

So, we exchanged as many coordinates as possible except our GPS locations. Sheba said she would write to me. She cried a bit, but it was nothing dramatic. I could see I was the first love interest in her life. I felt tender, too, but there was no question about having a steady girlfriend.

Back in Bombay, I sat at The Table in the canteen, which was informally reserved for The Gang (no one sat there except the Gang members). I got introduced to Roger Camoes, Nero's cousin, Mayank Shah, whom everyone called the Shah of Iran, Chandra Junior and Feridoon Cama, both of whom financed some of our outrageous orgies of music and booze interspersed with bouts of deep drunken metaphysics as we pondered over the origins of the Universe and our own future. A typical morning session would go something like this:

'Hey, Sammy boy,' said the Shah of Iran, 'you bohemian dog, let's buy a bottle of booze and fall down somewhere.' So, we went at 8 in the morning, got ourselves a pint of Old Monk, and walked down Marine Drive, smoking, drinking and chatting—the Shah of Iran mostly about girls in the abstract and me with my drunken pseudo-metaphysics. Shah was mostly into Henry Miller, reading whom he went giddy. He said it was possible to live like that even in India. I, already in a drunken stupor—couldn't yet hold my drink—pointed out that it was difficult to hold hands with a girl in public, let alone try the capers one saw in English movies. But, I was enthusiastic about the camaraderie and went along with Shah's crude elaboration of a life lived in the shadows and on the margins where possibilities existed if one's parents were wealthy enough to be utterly ignorant of their children's conduct.

'Love is not the answer to my question,' I told Shah.

'Then, what is?' said Shah.

'Not money, either,' I said.

'Now, you are getting complicated, man, there's life outside Sydenham too, y'know. You see all these cars whizzing by? They are all thinking about one thing and only one thing—how to make money and more and more money. You've got three years in Sydenham to play around with, to enjoy Freedom as she is meant to be enjoyed, and then—curtains! The show begins, and you must play your part as it figures in the script.'

'You really believe that? All that nonsense about Fate and rebirth and the rest?' I asked.

'I am saying, I don't know,' said the Shah of Iran. 'And I'm saying, let's not trouble ourselves any longer with what the Universe may or may not be about. I am saying, let's buy a bottle of booze and see what the world really looks like.'

Shah's father was a player in the stock market, and his son would follow in his footsteps. They were not filthy rich, but they were reasonably well off. Shah lived in a handsome two-storeyed house in Khar, next to the railway tracks, and we often had to curtail our conversations due to the din.

'I am saying,' I said, smoke coming out of my ears,

'why is there something rather than nothing? This is what Heidegger gave one of his courses on; I think it was *Introduction to Metaphysics*.'

'Heidegger? What's Heidegger got to do with two bad boys from college drinking themselves silly early in the morning? You shouldn't be reading that kind of stuff; you are too young for it.'

'Doesn't it make you wonder?'

'Doesn't what make me wonder?'

'The existence of the world, the only we know of among the billions of galaxies out there.'

'Yeah, so God heaped all this on our heads, only He knows why.'

'You believe in God.'

'What is the alternative?' said Shah. 'There's this girl in front of you who wants to be grabbed by her buttocks, and you are talking to me about the Universe. Let's focus on what we have, rather than grow melancholy about what we don't have.'

Shah was seeing Heather, who lived in Bandra, in the old Portuguese quarter right before Bandstand. She was an awful-looking bitch with short hair and an even shorter temper who exploited Shah's gullibility and his money and gave him a little illicit sex in return. I couldn't understand the deal. Shah was reasonably good-looking and, unlike me, well-dressed and soft-spoken when the occasion demanded; his father had money, he could have had a much better deal than a 34-year-old hag from Bandra. But on people's choices, I had no comments to make. Each to his own.

My first short story came out in the college rag called *Rapport*, edited by the late, lamented Parag Trivedi, who wasn't into booze, hash or women, but only karate and Gujarati vegetarian food. The story was called the *Fate of the Pig* and was meant to be a frivolous parody of the battle between Man and Nature. Nimy, who was from Seychelles, came up to me and said, 'Man, I am disappointed. I was expecting better from you, not this drivel.' I was embarrassed, to be sure. I would do better the next time around. He was invited to the stag party at Chandra Junior's house on Pedder Road.

And that is how my struggle against parental, mostly paternal, authority began.

I told my father I was invited to a party at my friend's place, and that I would spend the night there with the other boys. He put his foot down, and so did I mine. Two strong wills confronting each other—a story repeated across the country, in millions of households, of people who did not want to live like that anymore.

'Okay,' he finally said. 'Give me the phone number and address of your friend and be back before midnight.' I lied and said I would.

The Gang was out there in full strength. There was also Mehrunissa, who lived in the same building and was smitten with Chandra who, in turn, was running after Nisha Pillai, a stunning girl from Sophia College, who always carried several sachets of the finest Kerala Grass in her stylish leather bag. I landed up there around 10 pm and everyone, except Chandra, Shah, Nero and Ram, was already stoned and drunk out of their cheap little wits and had crashed out wherever the booze had caught them napping. I saw Aziz sprawled out under the dining table, Feridoon, who had been dropping mandies, snoozing off with his arms around his girlfriend on the big divan-cum-sofa. It was the music that blew me away. It was the first time that I was listening to the blues. I asked who the artist was. It was Taj Mahal, a giant of a man, who could play the harmonica like Orpheus bewitching the animals. It hit me in the body—this music of the Blacks that I heard for the first time in a super-posh neighbourhood of Bombay, calling out for love and rebellion. I hit the bottle of single malt that stood right in front of Nero, and before you could say Union Jack, I was gliding along a wave made of my lungs, heartbeat, guts, and brain—every part of my ultra-thin frame was involved in this music of wakefulness, exuberance and pain, all at the same time. I downed two pegs of Scotch, and the slow magic of the blues kept me alive to my surroundings. I felt like yelling for joy. Somebody had lit a joint, either Ram or Chandra, and the stuff was passing around the living room. Chandra's parents had left for the US the same morning, and the flat was given over to debauchery and substance abuse. We were having a wild time. There was Dharen, sitting at Mehrunissa's feet and telling her that it could be over between him and Reshma at any time, and this was plunging him into black despair. Somebody turned the music system—a Thorens Turntable, a Denon amp and two tall JBL 200-watt speakers—to concert hall levels, drowning all conversations.

I told Nero that Sheba had come to Bombay and wanted to continue from where we had left in Delhi.

'Women are tenacious bitches,' said Nero, smiling benignly as usual. 'Go for it, man. She really loves you.'

I said I didn't love her, and what happened in Delhi was just a silly little interlude of no consequence.

Within two months, I had discovered the two most important vectors of decadence in my life—the blues and literature. The fact that we were living under a dictatorship and that people spoke in whispers everywhere didn't seem to matter.

Ram joined the conversation, joint in hand, as usual.

'How are you, Sammy boy?' he said.

'I am doing fine,' I said.

RSS (Rashtriya Swayamsevak Sangh) guys had thrown some pamphlets in the lobby at Sydenham that morning.

'I hope the Bitch gets it in the neck sooner rather than later. They've begun cutting off people's pricks in the countryside.'

Ram was talking about the forced sterilisation in the countryside. He belonged to a political family linked to the regime and knew what he was talking about.

'I heard on the Beeb that Sam Manekshaw was about to mount a coup and overthrow the Bitch,' said Nero.

'There's no way of confirming that,' said Ram. 'Everybody is scared stiff.'

'They say trains are running on time, and there are no

demonstrations anywhere,' I said, repeating what I had read in the newspapers.

I was reading newspapers because of the situation in the country. How could I live free with the government breathing down my neck all the time? I hadn't decided on a career yet but instinctively felt that the Emergency concerned me, my very soul and that I couldn't grow in this country that had thrown its weight behind all forms of authority, both legitimate and illegitimate. It had thrown its weight behind people like my father, who openly welcomed the situation.

'Everybody is focusing on the job at hand,' he had pronounced at the dinner table one evening. 'That's rare in this country. If we continue like this for another 10 years or so, we'll be able to beat Germany in productivity.'

I said nothing. He had already warned us to be careful of what we said over the phone.

***

I was irritated by the phone call I received at Chandra's place that evening. It was my father.

'When are you coming home?' he asked coolly.

Never, I wanted to reply.

'Party's just begun, Dad,' I said, nervous like hell.

'There's a curfew at midnight.'

'I am just down the road, it will take me fifteen minutes to return. Can I enjoy myself a little?'

'You're sounding slurred. What have you been

drinking, young man?'

I said lemonade and that the telephone line was disturbed. There was a pregnant pause.

'All right,' said my father, eventually. 'I am expecting you back by midnight or I'll come to pick you up.'

I said we were all going down the Marine Drive to the coffee shop at the Sheraton and couldn't guarantee that I would be back by midnight.

'What's that music?' said my father.

'Pop music,' I said.

'It sounds really loud, even on the phone.'

The phone was on an extension in Chandra's bedroom.

'People are having fun.'

'Fun? You mean that you are blasting the neighbourhood to bits, preventing honest folks from getting some badly needed sleep, and you call it fun?'

'This isn't happening every day. Just once in a while.'

There was another pregnant pause.

'I think,' he finally said, 'you and your friends are up to some mischief. I am coming to pick you up immediately.'

'Okay,' I said miserably, 'I will return by midnight.'

'Make that sharp,' he said and put the phone down.

I returned to the room and found Feridoon squeezing Mehrunissa's healthily endowed breasts. Nero was relaxing on the divan, Ram was rolling himself another joint, Dharen had gone off to sleep, Shah was discussing sex with Chandra, and I had opened the living room window and, standing on the ledge, was peeing 20 floors down, right into the car park. There was nobody around, and we could see the smooth jet of urine falling pitter-patter on somebody's car.

'Okay, guys,' Chandra said, finally, 'let's go to Samarkand.' So, we all packed into two cars—Chandra's Audi and Feridoon's Vauxhall, driven not by him but by Nero (who didn't have a valid driver's licence) because he was the most sober person around. I got into the car with Chandra driving, stoned, drunk and happy. As the car turned into Marine Drive, Chandra stepped on the gas and the Audi just flew. Somewhere around the Gamdevi flyover, the car hit an old man, lifting him several feet up in the air, coming down with a thud a few seconds later. He, then, picked himself up and continued on his way without even looking at us.

'Jesus man, Chandra, take it easy, man, don't want to spend the rest of the night in a lock-up.' Chandra sniggered.

'There's no one around,' he said and continued driving at breakneck speed until we came to the Oberoi Sheraton. I was wondering what to order. But, these guys had a solution for that—it was called Cona coffee. You could have as much as you wanted, it would cost only Rs 10 per person.

'I don't have cash,' I said, sounding small and distressed.

'I'll pay,' said Nero.

'Sammy boy, you bohemian dog,' said Shah, 'just be cool, man, don't bother with the bread. We've got enough between us to feed three Doberman Pinschers up to their gills on filth.'

The coffee tasted awful, and there was no milk with it, but everyone at the hotel was sweet and polite, and never gave the impression that we were unwanted or anything. The name 'bohemian dog' stuck with me for the rest of my time in college. I was rather pleased with this nickname. I didn't want to be a manager or a chartered accountant and be someone with lots of money to throw around. I pictured myself as a folk poet singing the blues in a nightclub in Bombay.

From Samarkand, we got a panoramic view of the Marine Drive and the distant lights on Malabar Hill. Bombay lives at night; it seduces you, makes you generous, and liberates you. I've never felt as happy again in my life as I did with the Gang. And, the story had just begun.

When we returned to Chandra's place, my father stood at the gate with his official Ambassador parked right behind him. By that time, I had sobered off a little. I hated my father. He was turning me into an object of ridicule in front of my brothers. I hated the world he represented—the world of the affluent with their privilege and decorum, the taboos, the bans, the carefulness of tongue, the unfreedom of the mind, and the whole social jingbang. The fact that I was with rich kids did not strike me as paradoxical. I said bye to the others and went off with my father, back to the world of purposeless discipline.

3

Every Friday morning, the Gang would land up at Sterling to catch the morning show devoted to classics and art house cinema. That's where I first saw *Sleeper* by Woody Allen and *Taxi Driver* by Martin Scorsese. The films there blew me away. I could understand the impulses that led Travis Bickle to aspire to a better life, a life less lonely, battling with his demons and searching for innocence in the oddest of places—pornography and whorehouses. With Woody Allen, I just laughed and laughed and almost fell off my chair. These were the people who were cocking a snook at God, presenting an alternative Universe where the impossible became possible. I saw *On The Waterfront* and a movie by John Ford about Apaches being driven out of their homeland by the steady advance of progress. It was exhilarating. After the movie, we'd walk back to Sydenham, discussing the movie we'd just seen and how real they all looked. The last commercial Hindi movie I had seen in my life was *Sholay*, which was okay by commercial standards but didn't give me the high I got from watching the American classics. Friday morning would be my opening to the world away from my parents. It was teaching me dangerous lessons—lessons on how to dynamite my career prospects. A silence would descend on my soul, a primordial silence which welcomed the odd, the crazy, the whimsical about life, which was telling me about a life lived outside accountancy and balance sheets, a life in which I was not lonely because I was intellectually eccentric. This was because I was already laying claim to another world whose contours were understood only by those open to the idea of Freedom as it came from the West. I quickly grew to be a horrible example of the moral decadence and corruption of the West. And there was camaraderie, the opportunity to share one's thoughts and feelings with people who didn't see you as a freak just because you had gone off the loop as far as middle-class values and aspirations were considered. I never asked myself whether Shah, Chandra, Nero or Ram thought about the world the way I did or whether, despite decadence, you were a rebel or not. I never asked myself whether these guys understood the desire to overthrow the present order. It was enough that they liked what I liked.

But there was a problem. We got the drugs and rock 'n' roll right. But there was no sex. There were no independent-minded women in Sydenham who could understand us—why we stood aloof from middle-class values and why we were what we were. Chandra, Shah, Dharen and Feridoon had steady girlfriends, but they were not from Sydenham, and you couldn't discuss Kafka and Rimbaud with them. As far as I was concerned, the problem went a little deeper. Even before I started going to college, I was a nihilist. The world made no sense to me. There was no God to bail me out of my existential crisis and provide an answer to my fundamental query. The world was meaningless, and one had to live with it; there was no remedy. The worst thing was that reality was not consistent; things happened by chance, hazard reigned supreme and kicking a sleeping stray dog didn't invite immediate consequences. The worst of all, love was not the answer to my question.

So, where did that leave me as far as women were concerned? Perennially, unambiguously, ferociously frustrated. I couldn't tell a woman that the world made no sense to me and that love was not a healing property. Women were a part of the problem of meaninglessness. That is why I had reacted rudely, even boorishly, to the girl who approached me with a promise of friendship. I couldn't tell them that their feelings in the matter were nonsense; I couldn't tell them that there was no love in my heart and that I did not crave their attention, affection or whatever that impelled them to reach out to me. They were a part of the Nonsense.

But, I was desperate for sex—sex without emotional strings attached, without the exchange of hard cash, given over to silence and physical pleasure. Sex without the lure of a comfortable existence, procreation and belonging. I was not boyfriend or husband material. Tell me the meaning of my life, and I'll go with you.

The first girl to have really attracted me, both

physically and morally, was a beautiful Gujarati girl called Bhavna. She hung out with the Gang from time to time and smoked a joint or two once in a while. And she was equally attracted to me.

'Can I come along?' she asked Ram one Friday morning even as we were preparing to walk over to Sterling. Love is a pebble laughing at the Sun, said President Schreber, whose *Memoirs of my Nervous Illness* I was to read one year down the line. The fact that he was insane didn't matter much. Ram said okay if she knew what she was getting into.

'You mean freaking out,' said Bhavna.

'I mean freaking out,' said Ram. At Sterling, she manoeuvred her way into sitting next to me. It was *Woodstock*, a movie that was to change my life forever.

I was blushing pink when she sat on the chair next to mine. My heart was pounding, and it was not love that was doing that. I was squirming in my seat. I was terrified at the prospect of being taken away from my happiness and thrown into the emotional whirlpool of sexual longing.

'Hi, Sammy boy,' she said, with a radiant smile on her face.

'Hi, Bhavna,' I stammered back. Something in me was pushing me to respond to the interest this girl showed. I didn't know how this happened—I was afraid of making a fool of myself, of revealing my complete inexperience in these matters. My hands were shaking. Something was pulling me away from this girl. I was being asked to renounce my happiness and throw myself into a river of fire that would consume me. I was unnerved by the fact that this girl knew nothing about me, my eccentric values and my already active resistance to assimilation into a world without surprises—a world which would teach me how to be a lover and drag me towards an imaginary idyll where people lived happily ever after, or so I thought.

She held out a bag of popcorn in a way that I would have to touch her hand to help myself. I was standing on the edge of a precipice, seized with vertigo, not knowing whether I would fall on hard ground or another planet where Bhavna and I would be the sole inhabitants.

I muttered, 'No, thanks,' and that was that.

Love made no sense.

Once the movie began, I was engrossed. 'Sometimes I feel like a motherless child,' that was Richie Havens. The music hit me in the guts; I was struck by something akin to awe, by the sheer power of that song, of the unsentimental pain with which it was sung. I suddenly realised that the girl next to me was not responding to the music. She was busy eating popcorn and looking at the screen, totally detached, waiting for something to happen next. She could have been watching a spy thriller for all she cared. I had this stupid smile on my face. Between Bhavna and the movie, I chose the movie. I didn't want to be aware of her. For the next two and a half hours, I sat immobilised, enthralled by the capability of these musicians. 'It's happening,' said the boy with curly hair who was one of the managers of the concert. What was happening? People were tripping on acid, dancing to the music, roaring their approval, being swayed, viscerally, by this demonstration of raw power, transfixed before God who was allowing them to throw their weight behind musicians who spoke of love, war and generosity. But I was aware of the girl next to me, who had committed herself openly to me and to whose longing I had nothing to say.

As we walked back to college, Bhavna and I, I said, 'How did you find the movie?'

'It was brilliant,' she said, fiddling with her hair.

I didn't know what to say next.

She said, 'And, you?'

'Mind-blowing, literally,' I said.

I didn't know what to say after that. This girl, I realised in a sort of panic, was interested in me and not afraid to show it. This meant she was willing to stand naked before me. How could it be? I was embarrassed by my lack of feeling. I too wanted to possess her physically and pulverise her, but words dried up in my mouth when it came to talking to her. I didn't know how to mount a conversation that would be banal enough to reassure her that love was a normal occurrence. I was staring at the road, walking with my head bowed before the power of love to which I had no adequate response. I was waiting for the moment of confession to be over. We had spoken to each other, she, with love, and I, with blankness.

It was the beginning of the rainy season and I could see a wall of water advancing over the sea and whiplashing the tall buildings with their torrential fury on Nepean

Sea Road. It was then that I felt a surge of emotion for Bhavna. I longed for her; I wanted to hold her in my arms and kiss her passionately. Was this love? It lasted for a fleeting moment or so before blankness caught up with me again.

Anyway, when we returned to college, the Shah of Iran was waiting for me.

'Hey, Sam! Did you get laid, you dog?'

'He's blushing,' said Chandra.

'She's probably wet in her pants for you,' said Ram. 'Let's discuss this on the floor of the house.'

'Hey, guys,' I said, 'just leave me alone. I am not in love with anybody.'

'What's love got to do with it?' said Chandra.

The three of them, Shah, Chandra and Feridoon, teased me mercilessly for a few minutes before Feridoon brought out his guitar and played the opening bars of *Smoke on the water* by Deep Purple. This song became a sort of anthem for the Gang for the next three years. Bhavna joined us for some chai and samosas before she took out a packet of Marlboros and put a fag to her luscious lips. Since then, I have had a special fondness for women who smoke.

'Do you believe in God?' Bhavna asked, staring at me.

'No, but that's the source of the problem,' I said, blushing like a pig. 'If everything is to depend only on experience, there is nothing to prove that the next samosa I eat will not taste like orange juice. Experience varies. How long does an emotion last?'

'Two blue fucks for your philosophy, Horatio,' said Benny Pathak, scratching his mop of curly hair.

There was only lust in my heart and my heart was weak.

'An emotion can last a lifetime,' said Bhavna, coyly, not daring to look at me while saying that.

I shrugged. I was a tough guy. Tough guys didn't fall in love; they had mistresses instead. And God was a sadistic bastard.

She didn't have any competition, Bhavna; Sydenham had few girls around, most of them gold-diggers. I didn't see myself as husband material for any of them. There was the question of poverty. Almost everyone in our Gang had more money in his pocket than me, and that gave me a tremendous inferiority complex.

Which brings me to my father.

My father had a handsome salary that he spent wisely, leaving some apart for a rainy day. He would get a pension after retirement. However, it was his overall view of what a college should be that was problematic. You went to college to study, not blow money on chicks. Having money was like being able to succumb to all sorts of temptations. So he put us, me and my siblings, on a tight leash, teaching us about economic hardship and the scarcity of money in a poor country like India. My siblings had no problems with that because they were on the verge of launching themselves into well-paid careers, and their attitude towards our parents was dutiful. I was headed in the wrong direction right from the beginning.

I was interested in blowing things up, and planting IEDs everywhere in anticipation of a moment when I could press the detonator. I saw myself surrounded by gutless masses of people who had consented to tow the Bitch's line as a default response to autocracy. I heard on the BBC that they had shifted Jayaprakash Narayan to a state-run hospital in Chandigarh, and I thought they were going to kill him and that he wouldn't come out of the hospital alive. The Bitch's son, Sanjay, was running amok with forced sterilisations and rebuilding Delhi by firing on demonstrators belonging to 'a certain community' (Muslims).

In the college canteen, we discussed politics openly.

Ram, who found himself on the wrong side of history, was particularly vituperative in denouncing Jan Sangh, one of the constituents of the JP-led movement. When Nero recounted how he had been pulled out of the queue and shoved to the ground by a cop, with nobody in the queue coming to his defence, Ram said, 'I don't know whether the Bitch has given out specific orders to behave like this. They're just acting on the assumption that they can do this with impunity, the Bitch will back them when the time comes for redemption. The main question is whether these other guys in jail at the moment, will take us forward when their turn comes, which could take forever.'

'She has nationalised the banks,' said Chandra. 'How does that take us forward?'

'She has also made it illegal to have bonded labour,' said Nero.

'Okay,' said Ram. 'But her minions are going around telling us that we will be shot even if there is a whimper of opposition to her decrees. The press is gagged; people whisper sedition to each other on public transport. What about democracy?'

'I think the vast majority in this country cares two hoots for democracy,' said Nero, calmly sipping his tea. 'The guy wondering where his next meal is coming from is not bothered that books are being burned. And the politicians know this. The Bitch knows this. Which is why she sees the Movement as a historical irrelevance. They are worth so much shit.'

'If they are worth so much shit, why lock them up?' asked Ram.

'Just to be on the safe side,' said Nero. 'Everything is gone, as far as I am concerned. The only thing that will bring the Bitch to her senses is international opinion. The Third World will back her to the hilt because most of them are running banana republics anyway. So that leaves Western Europe and the US. And the Bitch doesn't depend on them for anything. She won the war in Bangladesh on her own...'

'...with Soviet help,' I chipped in.

'...with Soviet help,' said Nero, 'but ultimately she didn't have to call on their support, did she? I mean the Seventh Fleet never fired a single missile at us; they couldn't afford to be seen on the side of genocide.'

'Point taken,' said Ram. 'What I am saying is that the guys in the Movement are not spring chicken either.

I know Jan Sanghis who openly talk about murdering all the Muslims in their sleep and dropping the atom bomb on Karachi. And then there's this Hindu nonsense—cow slaughter, the religious demography, the guys who have crossed the border into India and are not interested in going back.'

'Freedom is a first-world luxury,' said Nero.

'Hey, you guys! Can we talk about chicks, for a change,' said the Shah of Iran.

'And they will put all the hot babes in burqas and veils, too,' said Ram.

'Chandra,' said Azam Khan, 'when you see Zeenat Aman playing badminton in your courtyard, is your cock subtle?'

'No, it is not subtle,' said Chandra, 'it is ironic.'

'Sam,' said Benny Pathak, 'why don't you go and get yourself castrated? If you are not using your God-given apparatus, throw it away, man.'

'There are ladies present,' I said.

'You mean, Bhavna?' said Pathak, 'She ain't no lady!'

'Do you mind,' said Bhavna giving Benny an elbow in the gut, smiling all the time.

I had problems being crude in front of women, even though I could see Bhavna enjoying the sexual attention.

'Look at her, Sam,' said the Shah of Iran, 'isn't she lovely. Look at her smile, her whole face lights up. And that Marlboro, man, it's so sexy. Sam, do something.'

I blushed and looked at Bhavna who hadn't stopped smiling.

'Actually,' said Bhavna, 'I was following the politics on this table...'

The bell rang and everyone headed for their class, everyone except the Shah of Iran and me.

'What's your problem, bohemian dog?' said Shah. 'This girl is clearly smitten. So what if she clings to you.'

'She terrifies me,' I said.

'How?'

'She's open and blasé about it. I can't handle her emotionally.'

'Grab her and fuck her.'

'Where?'

'We could make a trip to Lonavala. My dad's got a house there, rotting in the hills. We could drive over one weekend with the rest of the Gang and you could use the master bedroom.'

'Everyone will know.'

'So?'

'She'll devour me.'

'Man, you got a problem with chicks, as far as I can see.'

'That's right.'

'Anyone else in your place would grab the chick first and ask questions later.'

'It's my father.'

'What about your father?'

'He thinks I am too young to throw away my life for the sake of a chick.'

'That's a problem. Girlfriends are expensive, especially

when you live in the poshest part of the town.'

'It's all show.'

'Fifty bucks won't buy you a dosa at Satkar's.'

'There you are. Besides, I am not in love with her.'

'Who's talking about love?'

'My dad reads the paper, and is afraid for his children in the world. You know how he turned up at Chandra's place and picked me up in front of the rest of the guys. He thinks love in college is all about teenage pregnancies.'

'You don't have to tell him.'

'I can't keep late nights. He gets paranoid. He starts pacing up and down in front of the house in panic.'

'Talk to him. Tell him you're growing up and you need your freedom.'

'He won't understand that. He thinks the world is waiting to devour his family.'

'You've got a problem, bohemian dog.'

'Plus, there's me.'

'What about you?'

'The world doesn't make sense to me. Women confuse me. They make you weak.'

'So, you want to be a hero?'

'No! I don't know where to place women in my scheme of things. I have only lust in my heart.'

'That's okay,' said Shah, pulling on the joint he had just lit up. *'Goli maro'* ('forget it').

I took the joint from him and inhaled deeply, powerfully.

'She asked me if I believe in God,' I said. 'That's the

first step towards matrimony.'

'You are scared, man,' said Shah.

'You bet I am.'

'Why don't you discuss the problem with her?'

'Are you crazy? I don't want to reveal myself to her, just like that.'

'You are scared that you will make an utter fool of yourself.'

'That's right.'

'That's a risk you've got to take with women.'

I shrugged.

'I am not in love with Bhavna,' said I.

'Okay,' said Shah, crushing whatever remained of the joint on the pavement outside Sydenham. 'I'll give you a book to read.'

The next day, the Shah of Iran walked up to the table where we were sitting and handed over a book with a black cover to me.

'*Tropic of Cancer*,' I said, 'by Henry Miller.'

'This will kick open the doors that are blocking your mind about the opposite sex.'

I promised I would read it promptly.

'You're plying children with pornography, Shah,' said Ram.

'On the contrary,' said Benny Pathak. 'Grow up, kiddo.'

I was captivated by the book. Not as strongly as with Kafka, but powerful enough to make me see that sex is an ordinary part of the human experience in cities like Paris.

Two days later, I told the guys what I thought about the book.

'We're not in Paris,' said I, 'this is Bombay. You can get arrested for holding hands in public with a girl.'

'It's not about Paris only,' said Chandra. 'It could be true for Bombay, too.'

'I don't see how,' said I. 'You could starve to death in fifteen days if you tried to launch yourself as a writer in Bombay. There are no support systems, no English literary magazines, no writers in residence programs, and no fellowship between writers to help you out.'

'I'll introduce you to Adil Jussawalla and Arun Kolatkar, if you want,' said Nero. 'What's all this about, Shah? Trying to indoctrinate Sam? He thinks this is a Hindi movie and you're supposed to frolick around trees and bushes without touching anyone.'

'Has Bhavna read the book?' said Ram.

'That's the key question,' said I. 'What does she think romance is all about? What are her mental constructs?'

'You've got to wash your prick in her cunt,' said Chandra giggling naughtily, 'that's Mao Tse Tung, by the way.'

'It's all about caste, income and skin colour,' said Ram. 'Hey, Sam, let's go to Lamington Road this evening.'

'My father will kill me if he found out,' said I.

'How will he know?' said Ram.

So, we landed up in a seedy little brothel, full of 50-buck whores. Nero sat on one of the chairs and immediately had two or three women slobbering all over him. I chose a tall, dark girl, who turned out to be Bengali.

We retired to one of the dimly lit rooms along a long dark corridor. It was like fucking your maidservant with make-up. I discovered that I had a foreskin problem. There wasn't enough. It stretched to a tearing point when I shoved myself into the girl. It bled. I said I can't do it. We talked for about 10 minutes after which I came out.

Nero had a broad grin on his face.

'So, you got laid, Sam,' he said.

I nodded, a little sad in the knowledge that I wouldn't be able to screw the babes I wanted to. I had to have an operation. That would cost money. How would I explain it to my father?

4

Bhavna and I slowly drifted apart. She was in her final year and deep in her books. I was increasingly spending more time sitting on the wall of the building outside Sydenham, smoking, drinking and talking about my lack of a future with the Shah of Iran and Chandra. It was around the time that Shah, Chandra, Nero and I made a hair-raising trip to Lonavala in Chandra's car, and that Nero handed me his copy of *Waiting for Godot*. It took me a couple of hours to read one rainy evening. Somebody had taken hold of the foundation of my being and given it a good shake. What was Beckett doing all my life, I wondered. Two tramps waiting on a country road with a tree in the background, waiting for Godot who never turned up. It was about the structure of desire and its existential outcome on planet Earth. I joined the British Council library during the summer vacations and devoured everything I could find on Beckett. I found Martin Esslin's Theatre of the Absurd, whose central thesis—that suffering is meaningless—bothered me like hell, but to whom I was grateful for having enlisted all the playwrights who followed the groove ploughed first by Beckett. I read the *Myth of Sisyphus* by Camus and was once again blown away by the extraordinary cruelty about a man perpetually condemned to roll a boulder up a slope only to see it roll down again when it was about to reach the summit. All this bred in me a cavalier attitude towards death. Life was not a precious gift from God, but a sentence to be served out. In this world, money had no value nor did the capacity to acquire things. The only logic that stirred me up was indiscriminate self-destruction. No amount of praying could deliver a human being from the essential desolation of his soul.

So, Shah and Chandra turned up one evening, stoned, and asked me to join them for a trip to Lonavala. I asked my father if I could go, and he said yes, God knows why. We went over to Nero's place in Byculla and picked him up. Nero brought with him a bottle of Dimple scotch and we packed into the car and headed for the Bombay-Poona expressway. Soon, Chandra, overcome with exhaustion and intoxication, began dozing off at the wheel. Nero and I maintained a steady conversation with Chandra to keep him awake and aware of his surroundings. On the highway, large trucks trundled by menacingly. It was just a matter of time before we were hit by one and died senselessly. Climbing up the ghats was a nightmare with Chandra fumbling for his brakes. It was exhilarating. Nero told me about Graham Greene who had played Russian roulette every day for about a year or so and survived, after which he converted to Catholicism. Nero had briefly been part of the Catholic congregation called the 'Illuminati', whose sole endeavour was to establish the reign of Jesus on Earth. But nothing happened except moments of self-discovery that could be achieved just as well outside of the Catholic faith.

We somehow made it to Lonavala and to the Shah of Iran's summer retreat. Shah and Chandra crashed on the sofas in the living room, while Nero and I, fortified ourselves with a single malt and listened to some Jazz, Coltrane and Herbie Hancock if I remember correctly. We had a long discussion about the blues. Intoxication made sense inasmuch as it denoted a refusal to participate in life, to swallow whole the values and the belief systems of our parents. I said I did not want to retire to the Himalayas and meditate on the Absolute, until and unless I had concrete evidence that a guru whatsoever could provide coherent answers to my question. 'God is love' and 'work is worship' were not the answers to my question. That was at best a confirmation of the professional ethic of people with jobs. Then we listened in silence as Coltrane's saxophone came alive with a tune called *India*, which sounded like birds chirping their heads off at sunset.

'What about money?' asked Chandra in the morning as we walked unsteadily down the road to have some breakfast.

'What about money?' said I.

'You can buy what you want,' said Chandra. 'And be happy.'

'Happy?!' said I. 'You mean you can really be happy

knowing that you will gradually turn into a skeleton one day, without knowing where you are coming from and where you're going.'

'You can have sex,' said Shah.

I said nothing. The proposition didn't merit an answer in my opinion.

After some time, Nero said, 'We are playing with our lives, just like Graham Greene. It's a thrill, don't you think?'

I looked at him, not knowing what to say.

'I like getting drunk and stoned,' I said.

Nero said, 'So why didn't you get Irina (Chandra's girlfriend) and Brenda (Shah's wife-to-be) on the show last night.'

'Not to scare them shitless,' said Shah.

'Yeah,' said Chandra. 'That's a lame excuse.'

***

We woke up around 3 pm when Nero and I expressed a desire to return home. The Shah of Iran said he would stay back one more day. Chandra simply said he was too stoned to drive.

Nero and I took the train which, at that early hour, was mercifully empty-ish, and returned to Bombay. On the train, Nero looked at me with concern.

'What's the matter with you, Sam?' he asked.

'It's my old man,' I said.

'What about him?' said Nero.

Nero was older than me and had read, at that point, much more than me and was my mentor in all personal matters. I could talk freely with him without holding back anything. I knew he was someone I could rely on.

'Nothing,' I lied.

'Nothing?' echoed Nero.

'Nothing,' I lied again. 'Nothing.'

I could see from Nero's face that he was not convinced by my answer.

'Why are you looking at me like that?' I said.

'Because you are not telling me the truth. Your tongue is saying one thing and your eyes another,' said Nero.

I sighed.

'He's paranoid about his children. He thinks they will all end up murdered and raped if he loosens his stranglehold on their lives and especially my life.'

'But he's hardly in Bombay,' said Nero, trying to reason with me. 'Most of the time he is airborne.'

'You don't understand,' I said. 'He's more paranoid when he is flying than when he is at home. He calls up my mom, once every hour from 6 in the evening till midnight, and wants to speak to us to ensure we are at home and up to no hanky-panky.'

'What's his problem?' Nero asked.

'He thinks we are not yet ready for adulthood and the freedom it brings. He thinks of people who stay up at night as some sub-human, semi-criminalised scum. He goes to bed sharp at 10 pm after a glass of bitter gourd juice.'

'Your mother is a chain-smoker,' Nero said.

'That doesn't count,' I said. 'She backs him to the hilt as far as the children are concerned. She's conservative to the point of fascism.'

'So what do they expect you to do?' Nero asked, looking more and more concerned.

'Study, study, study,' I said.

'And what do you want to do?' Nero asked.

'Fuck, fuck and more fuck,' I said.

Nero laughed.

'Aw, c'mon man,' he said. 'You have women falling all over you. Why didn't you make it with Bhavna?'

'Look,' I said, 'I am looking for one-night stands, casual, no strings attached sex with normal girls, not whores.'

'Have you spoken to your father about this?' Nero asked.

'He'd kill me if I did so,' I said. 'He thinks if you want sex, you should keep your cock under control until you get married to a suitable girl he'll choose for me. That makes me depressed. My life is turning into a B-grade Hindi movie, y'know—son revolting against father in the name of love for which he is ready to pay the supreme price, at which point his father undergoes a spiritual conversion and forgives all and takes off for the Himalayas, leaving the hero and the heroine to live happily after. It's just incredibly stupid.'

'And you?' asked Nero.

'Me?' I said. 'I want to fuck the first thing that moves.

I dream about orgies and humping with several partners, each one of them more beautiful than the other. I have desperate fantasies, and I beat my meat like hell. I have a vivid imagination. That's what's keeping me alive.'

'You must live hidden, says Kundera,' said Nero.

I nodded, without knowing what he was talking about, fiddling in my pocket for the loose change that I would require to catch the bus home from Victoria Terminus.

The best thing about hash is that it doesn't smell or leave other tell-tale signs. My parents suspect nothing.

If you're looking for casual sex in this country, you have to belong to the right set and that usually means lots of money.

'The other thing about my father that gets my goat,' I said, 'is that he believes in God and is psychologically the weakest man I know. He has the mind of a child. I have heard him crying over his car, his father's death. He has no control over himself. When he is around, and if I am fifteen minutes late after curfew, he starts pacing up and down the street and berates me bitterly, as soon as I loom over the horizon. His brain is as brittle as stale bread. He just won't accept that his son has to turn into an adult at some point in time. Instead, he blackmails me and holds me responsible for the shape he is in when I am just trying to keep company with my friends. I mean, none of you guys seems to have a problem staying out late at night. He doesn't realise that it makes me look like a namby-pamby in front of my peers. It's hopeless. All I want after college is to get a job that will enable me to move out of my father's reach and live my life as I think fit.'

'Life doesn't make sense without a woman,' said Nero.

'I don't know,' I said. 'Nothing makes sense to me. Put me beyond my father's ken. At the moment, I am close to the Buddhist nihilists who think the world not only does not have a meaning but also persecutes people who try to look for one.'

Summer vacations were approaching, and I started reading plays seriously. As I said, *Waiting for Godot*, which Nero had given, hit me like an earthquake. In those tramps, I saw myself—a person waiting for meaning to show up. As I read Pinter, Ionesco and Beckett, I felt there were places on Earth where I would feel less of a freak and more like a person looking for answers to unanswerable questions. It was also after reading Beckett that I wrote my first play, *The Players*, about two men trying to wriggle out of a nonsensical world with only money as redemption. I showed Nero what I had written, and he was immediately taken by it. He took himself off our table for the afternoon and seemed to devour all the lurking insanities of the piece. He got back to me in a few days and said, 'Sam, we've got to put this up.'

I planted a notice on the College noticeboard inviting participation in an audition. A few people came around, but they were looking to enhance their CV, not the kind of people I was looking for—people who were in radical dissent with the universe of money. Ultimately, Cristobal Colon told me about Jiten Merchant and so we auditioned him. He was a plump, fair individual who was into Western classical music. I gave him my play to read aloud from whatever point he wanted. He was perfect. I told Nero about it and he was instantly enthusiastic, even though he hadn't met Jiten as yet.

The same night, my mind went blank. I had the dialogue and the tone down on paper but didn't know anything about the action. I stayed up all night pondering over the stage directions to flesh out the play before a live audience. Over the next few days, I had a reasonable dramaturgy at hand and I told Nero we would begin rehearsals in a couple of days. The Gang turned up to watch. Darshan Jariwala, the Bollywood actor Sanjeev Kumar's nephew, helped me with some complicated stage manoeuvres. And the Gang, well, they went crazy about it.

'Hey, Sammy boy, you bohemian dog,' said Shah, 'why aren't any girls on your show?'

'That's the point,' I said. 'There are no women when you really need them.'

'Let's have girls with miniskirts; your play will be a rage.'

'Girls with miniskirts?' I said. 'What should they do? Just hang around and be lusted after? What's the point? Girls are like a mirage—you see water when there is none and you are badly thirsty.'

'I get the point,' said Shah. 'This is a serious play.'

'You bet it is,' I said.

5

Meanwhile, Feridoon, Ram and Benny had organised a trip to the beach. Feridoon's father had a country house there. We went with two crates of beer and some cricketing gear. The idea was to have fun. As usual, there were no women around, except two sunbathing beauties who had materialised out of nowhere. After fortifying ourselves with some beer, we hit the beach with a vengeance for a game of cricket. I was asked to monitor the boundary from long-on. Behind me were the two ladies watching us without curiosity. Everything was fine until Ram came to bat. Ram was a good cricketer; he hit the first ball through the line and it came straight to me, passing through the legs to nestle safely between the two deck chairs that the women occupied.

As I went to fetch the ball, one of the women said to me, 'What have you been drinking?'

I said, 'Beer.'

'Hmm,' said the other woman. 'Makes you horny as hell.'

'I beg your pardon,' I said, not trusting my own ears.

'Never mind,' said the first woman.

'If you want to join the game, no problems,' I said with all the stupidity at my command.

'No, thanks,' said the other woman.

'Okay,' I said.

On the next ball, Ram hit through the line again to send it to the same spot he had the first time around.

This time, the other woman snapped at me.

'Hey, you whippersnapper smart alec! Where do you think you're going?'

'I-I am j-j-just here to collect the ball,' I stammered.

At this, the other woman got up from her deck chair.

'Stop staring at us like that!' she said. 'Haven't you seen boobs before?'

'I-I-I...'

I felt the blood rush to my cheeks.

The ball was delicately ensconced between the two deck chairs.

'Can I-I-I have the b-b-all, please,' said I. Even though I had done nothing wrong, I felt as if I had.

Ram and Feridoon came over.

'Is there anything the problem, ma'am?'

'Your friend is hunting for honey here,' said the first woman.

'I was just collecting the ball,' I said.

Feridoon looked at me with sympathy.

'I am sorry if we're bothering you,' said Feridoon. 'It's just a game of beach cricket, ma'am.'

'We've had enough of your excuses,' said the other

woman. 'The next time we see any of you sniffing around us, we'll call the police. Okay?'

Then Ram lost his cool.

'The next time we'll carry you off and take our pleasure,' said Ram.

'How dare you, you guttersnipe?' said the other woman.

She took her mug of soda and splashed it on Ram's face.

Nero Gomes and the Shah of Iran had joined us, meanwhile.

'What's the matter, ma'am?' said Nero.

'You guys are harassing us,' said the other woman.

'No, we are not,' said Shah. 'This is just a game of cricket.'

'Let the cops decide,' said the first woman, who hadn't left her deck chair.

'We'll shift the pitch away from this spot,' said Nero. 'If we've been importunate, we are sorry, but Sam here is a thorough gentleman.'

'Ha,' said the other woman. 'He can't take his eyes off our bikinis.'

I was close to tears. I'd never been so humiliated in my life.

'Sam, did you do or say something?' asked Nero.

'I was j-j-just collecting the b-b-ball,' I stammered.

'We're sorry for this incident,' said Nero. 'Guys, let's shift the pitch up further. Please don't call the cops, ma'am, I promise we won't bother you again.'

'Okay,' said the first woman.

So, we took our stumps to the northern side of the beach and I was placed on the gully, a few metres away from the sea.

'Hey, Sammy boy,' said Ram. 'Shit happens. Don't take this to heart.'

'I am cool, man,' I said.

For lunch, we went to a local bar where we were served beer by a dazzlingly beautiful Nepali woman. She was obviously available for cash.

'Come and sit with us,' said Shah.

'I can't,' said the woman in Hindi.

'Why not?' said Shah.

The woman looked at him and smiled radiantly.

'Nero,' said Shah. 'Why don't you take her in your lap?'

'Maybe we should let Sam get laid, for a change,' said Nero, grinning from ear to ear.

'What's your name, sweetheart?' said Chandra.

'Dimple,' said the Nepali woman, smiling sweetly at us, unafraid.

'Well, Dimple,' said Shah, 'Sammy, the bohemian dog, thinks you look great. Why don't you sit on his lap for 50 bucks?'

The woman gathered up her skirt and sat down on my lap. I immediately got a hard on; her soft pulsating buttocks were driving me crazy. The woman looked deep into my eyes and said, 'You're blushing.'

I was blushing furiously. I knew I had to do or say something, but the words wouldn't come to me. I was tongue-tied with terror.

The woman got up brusquely and said, 'Your friend doesn't like me.'

'Some more beer, everyone,' said Feridoon, enjoying the conversation.

'You don't like her?' said Shah.

'I don't know what to say,' I said. 'I'll have some more beer, then maybe I'll find the courage to say something. Plus, I am scared of getting the clap.'

'Hey, bohemian dog,' said Shah, 'what kind of a triangular pizza are you? She's asking for it, man.'

'I don't have the money,' said I.

'Don't bother about the money,' said Shah. 'We'll create a fund for you, impromptu.'

'No, no, I am not interested.'

I was thinking of my virile member and its insufficient foreskin.

'Okay, guys, let him be and let's enjoy our beer,' said Nero.

Then, the woman planted a kiss on my mouth and said, 'This is for free.' She smiled and went away.

I was red all over with embarrassment and shame. I knew I would have to explain my feckless conduct later; at that moment, I wanted to disappear from the face of this Earth.

For lunch, we had crab gratin, tandoori chicken and fried rice. We finished it off with some excellent Black Forest cake.

Then, we retired to Feridoon's cottage on the beach

to listen to something. I think Chandra's dad had just bought him an album by Howlin' Wolf called the *London Sessions*, with Steve Winwood on piano and Eric Clapton on guitar. Soon, the entire shack was vibrating to the sound of rhythm and blues. Howlin' Wolf was followed by BB King live at the Cook County Jail. I had never heard such beautiful, uplifting music in my life. From then on, every time I heard the sound of blues playing in somebody's apartment, I would switch off and immerse myself in the music—its rhythm, exuberant content, angry and smart melodies, and the clear rasping blues voice, triumphing over everything that stood before it.

I was carrying on a drunken conversation with Nero who knew the trick of remaining sober even after several large pegs of Scotch. I was telling him about the impact that Beckett had on me.

'Man,' I said, 'that guy just blew my brains away. He makes sense out of nonsense, just like Kafka, although Kafka is a classicist. Beckett speaks to your soul directly, without any foreplay. He just rams it up your snout, y'know, this is what the world is—a country road and a not particularly healthy tree. We are all tramps living in some desperate, forlorn hope that Godot will come, that he'll come and his coming is beyond hope, meaning and goodness, that the least he will do is to break this monotony, that there will be this oasis of eventhood in a vast expanse of shadowy dunes with no hope of being considered saveable.'

'You should read the novels,' said Nero, 'that's the real

deal. Incidentally, there is a presentation of *Waiting for Godot* at Prithvi Theatre next Friday, with Naseeruddin Shah and Benjamin Gilani.'

'Let's go for it,' I said.

'Okay,' said Nero, pouring another large dose of Johnny Walker Black Label into my tumbler.

'How's the Bitch allowing all this?' I asked.

'It's non-political,' said Nero. 'Or, so she thinks.'

So, the following Friday, Nero, Shah, Chandra and I landed at the Prithvi Theatre and bought our tickets for the show.

It was disappointing as hell. Neither of them seemed to have a clue as to how to respect the letter of the play, let alone its spirit. They made the whole thing sound trite, mystic, abstract and mysterious, whereas it would have been more apt to present it in the spirit of stand-up comedy—not just the high art of tragedy but the low art of vaudeville, as well. But then, English theatre in India was steeped in a particular kind of social and political theme-based drama. Even though, as I came to believe later, hopelessness was also political—not as in poverty, unhappiness and suffering, but as in wavering between the hollow misery of dispossession and the viciously uplifting savage irony of black humour.

'It was all wrong,' I said, as we came out and looked for a drinking joint nearby in Juhu. Shah knew a bar and we all made for it.

'How did you like the play?' Shah asked.

'Rotten,' said I. 'They should have got Mukri and

Mahmood to play Vladimir and Estragon. Shah and Gilani made it look respectable. Heroic. Bad, bad, very bad.'

'I don't know, man,' said Shah, 'it just went over my head.'

'You've got to understand the philosophy behind it,' said Chandra. 'You can't expect people on the fringes of Bollywood to understand what this play was all about. It's not abstract, as Sam pointed out, it's terrifyingly concrete.'

'What about Lucky and Pozzo who, I thought, were absolute disasters?' said Nero.

'It seemed pointless and absurd,' said Shah.

'Yeah,' said Chandra, 'it's about God and his creature.'

'The sadism of reality,' said I.

'Yeah,' said Chandra, 'Lucky is someone who has to be flogged to respond to reality. In return, the dog gets a bone.'

'Think, slave!' I said laughing. 'Beckett is a comic writer.'

'That's the point,' said Nero, 'they didn't get the humour at all. You have two guys struggling to survive with some hope and dignity and all they get is a sadistic lunatic and his cart-pulling idiot.'

'It was in Martin Esslin's book,' I said, 'where Beckett says in one of his novels that nothing is as funny as unhappiness. With him, it's a kind of primal laughter.'

Then, the discussion went off track, and soon Shah was holding forth on Henry Miller.

'Sex is not everything,' I said dejectedly, at a certain point.

'It's as good as everything,' said Shah.

'I don't think this can happen in India,' said I.

'I agree,' said Nero, 'Miller is talking about life in Paris between the wars and that's one of the most sexually liberated periods in history. You had the Surrealists and all kinds of avant-garde activities.'

'Hey, Sam, you bohemian dog,' said Shah. 'Why don't I look for a girlfriend for you? How long are you going to remain a virgin?'

I just smilcd and said nothing, but, surc, I was bothered by that, too. My penis needed a repair job, before it could even start looking for parking space.

Unbeknownst to me, things were moving fast and coming to a head.

6

The play was a hit. I was baffled by my success. How could such an abstruse piece of work designed to repel the audience end up being wildly applauded? A guy dressed in saffron came to me behind the stage and said, 'Everybody liked your play, everybody. It was beautiful.' I looked at him, slightly embarrassed at being recuperated by a religious person, but it was alright in the end because Kaikobad and his friends also came backstage and looked at me as if I was the eighth wonder.

And then, there was Isabella Gondola, who had just been admitted to Sydenham. She was the most beautiful girl I had ever seen. Tall, lithe and graceful, with cascading hair falling untidily over her shoulders, she accosted me outside the little corridor that led to the green room. She first congratulated Feridoon who had handled the dimmer and the special audio effects, and then, seeing me, stopped short and smiled. 'That was just great,' she said. I was tongue-tied; I was so taken by her slightly melancholy eyes that I didn't know what to say for a while.

'Can we meet?' she said.

'S-sure,' I said uncertainly.

'I'll be in the canteen tomorrow afternoon at 2 sharp,' she said. 'Is that okay?'

'Y-yes,' I stammered, afraid to move a muscle for fear of frightening her away.

After that, it was the turn of the literature professors who, surprisingly for a commerce college, were brilliant. There was Zebunnissa Kazi, Hemmadi and Kulkarni.

Kazi spoke first to Nero Gomes who had put up a brilliant performance.

'I didn't know there was so much darkness in you,' said Kazi.

'I didn't know it myself, ma'am,' said Nero, obviously pleased.

'And you, Sam, how did this happen in your dainty little head,' she teased me. 'Congratulations! That was just brilliant.'

'A bit Beckett-ish though,' said Hemmadi, archly.

I had this stupid grin on my face, at a loss for words.

'Must be all that weed you people smoke in the canteen,' said Kulkarni.

At this, I laughed.

'Great piece of writing,' said Hemmadi.

'Thank you, ma'am,' I said, finally getting a grip over myself.

Later in the evening, we went to Gokul's in Colaba, where we listened to some jazz and drank beer.

'I am foxed,' said I to Jiten. 'How did my play

become a hit?'

'It's a great piece of literature,' said Jiten, at whose house I had been going to listen to a studio recording of *Waiting for Godot* with Bert Lahr, the great American stage artist, as Estragon.

'What was that chick telling you?' said Shah.

I said, 'Nothing in particular. She just wants to have a cup of coffee with me.'

'I have a good feeling about this, man,' said Chandra.

'Basically, get over masturbation,' said Ram Bhonsle. 'For a virgin like you, it should be manna from heaven.'

I smiled and said nothing, basking in the glory of an unexpected critical and popular acclaim.

'Mood Indigo is coming up soon,' said Nero. 'We should put up the play there.'

'Yeah,' I said, 'let's do it.'

'Here's to *The Players*,' said Jiten, lifting his one-litre tankard.

We all lifted our tankards and said 'Cheers!'

'Sammy boy, you are now the Daad of Chad,' said Ram Bhonsle. 'The world lies at your feet.'

'Don't exaggerate, man,' I said. 'It's just a college play. Like *The Zoo Story*.'

'*The Zoo Story* is about big bucks, man,' said Shah. 'This isn't exactly Broadway, y'know.'

At night, I couldn't sleep; I was thinking about Isabella Gondola and her generous breasts all the time.

The next day, I was at the canteen waiting for Isabella Gondola. She came sharp at 2 pm, and we decided to go to the Shamiana at the Taj.

I got into her Volkswagen Beetle, and we drove through empty summer afternoon streets to the Gateway of India. She parked her car and we walked over to the coffee shop with a view of the sea on one side and the hotel lobby on the other.

As soon as we sat down, she took out a small writing pad from her handbag and started scribbling in it. Then she rummaged in her bag and took out a packet of Marlboros, slid out a cigarette and held it out for me.

I took the cigarette gingerly and put it to my lips. She flashed out a Zippo lighter from somewhere and lit my cigarette for me before lighting up hers.

She blew the smoke through the corner of her pretty mouth and said, 'Your play is great.'

'Thanks,' I said, blushing hot pink.

'More people should get to see it.'

'We could take it to the youth festival at IIT Powai.'

'I am thinking in terms of a more commercial venture,' she said, letting out a steady stream of smoke through the corner of her mouth again.

'That's an expensive proposition.'

'I'll pay for it.'

I swallowed hard.

'You have to hire a hall, do some real rehearsals and publicity.'

'I'll take care of all that.'

'That's a lot of money. I don't think my play is worth the trouble...'

'You leave that to me.'

'You are going to ask your dad?' I said, trying to play tough.

'My mom, actually, uh-huh.'

'Your mom is going to be okay with the script?'

'She relies on my judgement.'

'So it's going to be kept a secret from your dad?'

'My dad has other things to think about. Things like money. Just a sec…'

She scribbled something down in her notebook.

'You are taking notes?'

'Just stray thoughts that occur to me. Here, take a look.'

I looked at her neat handwriting and realised I was dealing with a person who was mentally tidy. It said: Call up Prithvi, ask for their rates, discuss with mom, 40 bucks a seat? Negotiate.

'Okay,' I said. 'Let's do this.'

She smiled and her whole face was transformed; she shone like the Sun dispelling all the darkness around her.

'Can I ask you something?' she said, lighting another Marlboro with the one she subsequently stubbed out.

'Sure, go ahead.'

'What do you think of the Bitch?'

'I hate her from the bottom of my heart.'

She smiled again. She looked so beautiful; I felt myself to be so unworthy of her charm that I sat there with a puzzled look on my face, I guess.

'You are puzzled?' she said.

I nodded.

'I don't see,' I said, verbally tip-toeing, 'how a girl like you can be interested in some avant-garde shit that some poor, dumb bastard has come up with, in a moment of insanity.'

'Your play is beautiful,' she said, deadpan once again. 'It's amazing, it's written with so much freedom, I mean given your class background and the fact that you are studying in an institution that gorges itself on big business. The bourgeoisie…'

I pricked up my ears at the sound of 'bourgeois'.

I must have looked stunned, because she said, 'Is something wrong?'

'No,' I said, gasping to recover my breath. 'I mean, are you a communist?'

'Sort of,' she said, casually blowing smoke away from me.

'Which sort?'

'Marxist-Leninist,' she said, without cocking an eyebrow.

'You are a—' I stammered.

She put a finger on her lips.

'You never know who's listening to what over here.'

'A Naxalite,' I whispered to myself. 'So how come you are having coffee with me at Shamiana?'

'I am subverting my class identity. It's no big deal. There are high-level corporate executives who are from the Party.'

'I don't want anybody waving the red flag at my show,'

I said, timidly. 'I don't want to send out any political messages.'

'This has nothing to do with politics. This is about my guts.'

I stared at her in utter disbelief.

'So what do you guys do?'

'Some of us are into blowing up things,' she said, smiling now.

'Such as?'

'Police stations, camps…the instruments of state oppression.'

'The Bitch nationalised banks.'

'That means nothing, the lower peasantry gets nothing out of that. Land has to go to the tiller. Why are we discussing this?'

'I don't want to be a toy,' I said, licking my lips nervously. 'If my folks found out, they'll lock me up in a lunatic asylum.'

'My folks don't know about my party affiliation either. Even though my grandad was a Hungarian communist.'

I suddenly noticed how beautiful she looked sitting there in her pink top and figure-hugging jeans. I was overawed.

I could do nothing but stare at her.

'The party might not like the idea of you being associated with a play like this,' I said, finally.

'This is none of their business.'

'I am a nihilist.'

'I understand,' said she. 'So was I two years ago. Then,

I went with this NGO to the Dandakaranya forest and–and that was it, I guess. Where I saw meaninglessness before, I saw people struggling to keep their self-respect and their land from grubby multinational mining companies. I had no struggle in my life. I always got what I wanted, yet that never made me happy. I was miserable being privileged, and the world seemed to make no sense to me. I mean, belief in a personal God and all that. I have been atheist from very young. But I had no focus. A godless world made even lesser sense than a God-ful one. It was like being caught between the Scylla of injustice and the Charybdis of thoughtlessness. Then, I met Jade, Jade Singh. He was a project coordinator for an NGO and worked with the tribals. He was a communist. It was he who gave me a book on psychoanalysis written by R D Laing and that transformed me. It dealt with deconstructing identities and looking at reality with as little of an ideological prism as possible. Jade would talk to me about Marcuse and Frantz Fanon and Bakunin. He had read a lot of books in his life and, as he spoke, the idea of revolution came alive. I told him my grandfather was a communist, Imre Nagy's right-hand man in 1956.

'Jade was not rich or anything. He came from a humble middle-class family. His father worked for the Railways, I think, but his extended family was into farming. Anyway, he never spoke about his family or his personal life. It was politics, art, cinema, literature—everything that was left out at home. Jade went on solo missions deep into the jungles to deliver supplies to villagers whom he knew to be actively sympathetic towards the Naxalite guerrilla. He would disappear for days on end and return unkempt and then tell us about life in the jungle with the tribal. Am I boring you?'

'No-no-no,' I said. 'This is interesting.'

'And then,' she said, exhaling a prodigious amount of cigarette smoke, 'And then, one day, I fell in love with Jade. But I found him emotionally blocked. He just couldn't talk about himself. No one ever saw him relaxing with his team which included me. He was always indoctrinating us with his Leftist ideas; I never got to know which sort of Leftist he was, Marxist, Marxist-Leninist or just plain old Communist Party of India. But he was a good talker. He would tell us yarns from his missions in the jungle, student politics in Bengal—he was a graduate from Presidency College, Calcutta—but never a word about his family, or about anything personal, women, friends, food and drink, his childhood, nothing. He was like a prophet, with the glaze of the divine over him and his hard metallic voice talking about his political friends and enemies. I was awestruck. He seemed to have no weaknesses at all. How could it be? So, I had this massive crush on him. But I was equally terrified of expressing any emotion in his presence. He expected us to do our job because of an ideal, a commitment to the cause, selfless dedication and not for some airy-fairy idea of revolutionary romanticism. So I did what many girls of my age did: I started fantasising about him. Sexual fantasies.'

'Why were the police after him?' I said.

'The police were after everybody dealing with the tribal. Everybody was watched, even lowly volunteers like us. Jade had formally told us to never be alone in any situation, but to move around with at least one person. So, we had to do everything in groups, including buying provisions and cigarettes and the occasional bottle of booze for end of mission parties. Anyway, I was so inhibited in my emotions that I never spoke to anyone about my feelings for Jade. But my emotional life revolved around him. The only saving grace was that my parents were totally cool about my extra-curricular activities. Politics kind of ran in the family. I had uncles and aunts who were communists.'

She lit another cigarette and continued.

'So, eventually, I asked Jade for author recommendations. The next day, he handed me a copy of *Capital*. It was awfully boring. I just plodded through it, chapter by chapter, not understanding his basic argument back then, that all profit was exploitation of labour. After much effort I managed to grasp what he was driving at but still couldn't empathise with it yet. He sounded terribly arrogant and cocksure of himself and his views, and I didn't finish the book. After a few days, Jade asked me how I was doing with my political education and I told him it was not too good. I said Marx was a lousy writer. He said okay, and that he would give me something else to read. He gave me another two books which were to change my life forever, *Soul on Ice* by Eldridge Cleaver and *On Rape* by Germaine Greer. He said he would give me some more similar books if I liked these. I opened Cleaver's book and was instantly hooked. I was totally ignorant of the history of Blacks in the US, and Cleaver's book spoke loud and clear on the condition of the black man in his country. It was so eloquent! I later learnt that he had been to prison for raping a white woman. But, he absolutely did not have the mind of a rapist. He came across as someone trying to look clearly, within himself and without. Greer's book was just as exhilarating and I wanted to read more from her. Jade always carried a certain stock of books with him. He would retire to his tent by 10 pm and stay up late reading newspapers, magazines—the *Economic and Political Weekly* among them. So, I read a lot on the conditions of Blacks in the US, thanks to Jade, and understood why he had given them to me to read. It was about oppression, oppression of subject populations, ethnic minorities, women, and I could relate every bit of what they said to my own situation in India. Thanks to Jade, I now understood that women and minorities would have to stand up for their rights against both the capitalists and the patriarchs and that the two struggles were related; there could be no freedom for anyone as long as women and minorities remained repressed.'

'So that is how you learnt to talk about revolution at the age of eighteen?' I asked.

'Not really,' she said, crushing a half-finished Marlboro in the ashtray. 'I give occasional lectures on feminism at the party's indoctrination cell, but that's all. I don't know half of what the others have read on the subject.'

'And then, what happened?'

'What happened? Jade Singh died,' she said. Her eyes grew sombre and she looked away.

'Died? How?'

'Three shots into his chest. His body was found in a ditch near the highway. The bore of the cartridges clearly showed they came from weapons used by the anti-Naxalite task force. There was a lot of hue and cry from the media; human rights organisations got involved and filed their own reports and the matter was even taken up by the opposition in Parliament. The authorities said Jade Sing had been eliminated by the Naxalites for being a police informer. That was laughable. Jade Singh was not beholden to anyone for his status among the tribal. It is true that he was sympathetic towards the Naxalite cause; they were fighting a common battle along with the NGO, but Jade Singh was too independent to fit into any rigid ideological framework. He was more of an anarchist than a run of the mill communist. He believed that every authority had to justify its actions ethically before being obeyed. Jade Singh was nobody's man. He walked his own path oblivious to rumours and propaganda. It later turned out that he knew some of the militant commanders in Dandakaranya, occasionally acting as a courier for them. But he would not join the organisation full-time.'

'So, what did you do?'

'Nothing. We just cremated him right there. The same night, while we were packing up our personal effects and dismantling the tents, we were visited by two men and a woman. They introduced themselves and said they were from the People's War Group and that they had come to talk to us on behalf of the organisation. They spoke to us about their ideology and their idea of revolution. We listened to them patiently. After the talk, they asked us about our future plans. We all sounded terribly vague. Some of us said they would continue to work with the tribal in the same NGO. Then a tall, thin man with a pencil-line moustache said they needed people in the cities to organise students and workers and prepare them for the revolution. Somebody asked when the revolution would take place at the national level. The tall thin man said within the next five years. A hush descended among us. It was absurd. How could an organisation living in the forests of central India spread its influence all over the country within such a short period of time? I felt they had said five years to keep up the morale of the group. But they looked serious, dedicated and willing to die for their cause. The tall thin man said there was no hurry; we didn't need to make our minds the same day and that they would contact us at our homes within the next fortnight to know if we would work for them.

'When I returned Bombay, I got a regular scolding from my father who forbade me from further NGO adventurism. I tried to explain that our area of work was perfectly safe—we weren't radicalising the tribal against the state, we weren't insurrectional, that these people needed somebody from the outside world to speak up for them and for their rights as equal citizens of this country.

But he just wouldn't listen. He slashed my allowance by 50 per cent and said that I would go abroad to study what I wanted to and would not indulge in philanthropy any more. I felt shattered. I was full of resentment, anger and rebellion. The other girls in my group had no problems convincing their guardians that the killing of Jade Singh was a one-off moment, that he never involved us in any kind of illicit dealing with Naxalites and that they could continue working for the NGO under a new, politically neutral leadership. In any case, the organisation was half-dead with Jade's death. So I was pretty confused and unhappy until I got a call from someone called Raman. He wanted to know if my answer was a yes or a no. "Yes," I said without thinking twice. He asked me to get in touch with a person called Romeo—I immediately understood that this was a pseudonym—at the number he was giving. I called up the number; it was answered by a deep, suave and an extremely courteous voice. "Romeo," I said and he asked me to hold on. A few seconds later I could hear the entire line resonating with Led Zeppelin's *Immigrant Song*. Then he was back on the phone. "Who gave you my number?" he said, without any belligerence. "Raman," I said. "Okay," he said. "Meet me at Mediterraneo around noon tomorrow." "How would I recognise you?" I said. "You don't have to," he said. "I will have a photo of you to go by. Just sit next to the window on the traffic side, not on the office building side, and have your back to the entrance." "Done," I said. So, the next day, I went to Mediterraneo, took a table to my left, that is, the traffic side of the restaurant, ordered a Fresh Lime Soda and waited for Romeo. Fifteen minutes went by, and I was fidgeting in my seat, nervous about getting involved with all these guerrilleros and their bloodstained secrets. May be my father was right. I was too immature to get into this cloak and dagger show. Then there was a slight tap on my right shoulder. I looked up and saw a scruffy looking individual, olive complexion, thick moustache, wild unkempt hair, horn-rimmed glasses, sizing me up in a kind of vague, absent-minded way. Completely inoffensive, I thought. "I am Romeo," he said and sat down in the chair across the table for two. It was when he started speaking that I was surprised. He had a thick American accent. He spoke non-stop for the next hour or so, never asking any questions about my class background, academic interests, or political philosophy. He spoke to me mainly about Proletariat, a trade union run by a few individuals, among them anarchists, Trotskyites, and people who spoke about Bhagat Singh. "Do you carry a gun?" I asked. He shook his head vigorously, and looked rather flustered. "No, no," he said. "I am not an armed member of the organisation. Some of them carried guns on them," he said, "but that was their personal matter. We are trade unionists, not guerrilleros. However," he said, "everything we say or do in public is noted by the police and the Intelligence Bureau. We are enemies of the state. But you don't have to think about all that." The work that he described Proletariat doing consisted of a lot of routine and very little adventure. One had to hold factory gate meetings, supervise the election of office bearers for the shop floor committees, doing propaganda. Putting up posters as required and arrange the May Day picnic. That sort of thing.'

'The police still following you around?'

'Of course,' she said, with a big smile on her face.

'They are watching us, right now?'

'It's possible. But I am not a high-value target. My activities are mostly overground. I am not involved in any illegality. But, of course, the Emergency has changed all that. Some of us have been trapped and arrested. We have our lawyers to take care of that; lawyers who are committed to the cause. But yes, I do feel threatened these days. It's not that instructions have been given about me. It's just the police mentality. They want to please their political bosses. So they will pick up a courier and call him a dreaded Naxalite heading an underground cell.'

'Have you ever had to deal with the police?'

'So far? No. But it could happen anytime now.'

'So how come you are going about your business as usual?'

'Just bravado, I guess,' she giggled. 'I don't know. There are times I feel scared even though Naxalites are popular with other prisoners. There is a feeling of solidarity. Of course, things might be different for somebody like me, somebody they'd like to make an example out of. Even inside prison, I might not enjoy all the support and fellow-feeling that others do. I look obviously rich.'

There was a long silence.

'Isabella Gondola is a curious name,' I said, trying to change the topic. 'Are you Italian?'

'No,' she said matter-of-factly. 'My mother is from Goa and my father is part Hungarian and part Sikh.'

'I am trying to fit you into my universe.'

'No problems. Happens all the time.'

I looked out through the glass front at the sea and gulls flying overhead.

'Freedom,' I said. 'That's a worthy goal. But I really don't think we should land up in jail for sedition.'

I was nervous. She could see that.

'You are nervous. At the very outset. No point in being scared if you are going to be a writer in life.'

I nodded without conviction.

'You are the first real writer I have met in my life,' she said, with that quick dazzling smile of hers. 'Not your usual two-penny college poet. You are definitely not going to end your life as a chartered accountant or a business manager.'

'What about you? What is a radical like you doing in a college like Sydenham?'

'My dad wants me to get into business after I graduate. I don't have the heart to tell him the truth. I guess I am a coward too, that way. So, tell me something about yourself, Sam, instead of interrogating me like a cop.'

'Me?' I said, suddenly finding it funny to be called upon to talk about myself. 'What can I say? I've never been asked this question before…'

'What do you believe in?' she said, helpfully.

'Nothing.'

'Nothing!' she exclaimed. 'What about your parents? Don't you love them?' she asked, drawing deep on her fifth cigarette in a row.

'No,' I said, truthfully. 'I wish they'd all die in a plane crash or something.'

Isabella Gondola laughed, a robust belly shaking laugh.

'You spoke like a true poet,' she said looking at me. 'Your father's a pilot, I heard.'

'With Indian Airlines. Very bourgeois, I suppose.'

'Did they come to see the play?'

'I didn't bother inviting them…it would go way over their heads. I haven't bothered telling them that I am wasting my time at Sydenham. My father would be furious. As it is, I have begun sneaking around him, trying to do things without letting him find out. It's like living in Hell, with a mask on your face all the time. It's suffocating.'

'Do you have a girlfriend?'

'No. That's shameful.'

'Are you a misogynist? A guy like you should have women crawling all over him.'

'I am pure and chaste, like driven snow. I can't afford to have a girlfriend. I wouldn't have the money to take her out for a movie.'

'Can I be your girlfriend?'

I felt my face go all red and hot.

'Okay, I am sorry, I shouldn't have asked that; I was

just forcing your hand a little.'

'You would be way too expensive for me.'

'No problem. I'll pay for everything. I've got money. My father is a rich businessman.'

'I don't want to be a freeloader,' I said, finding hidden veins of courage in my brain. 'Plus, I have dangerous habits. I smoke hash, drink like a fish…'

'So what? You are carrying your habits like some kind of badge of honour.'

She looked at me for a moment and saw that I didn't like that.

'Okay, I am sorry I said that. In Bombay, you start experimenting with all kinds of substances when you are in school.'

'I like getting intoxicated. It's a new feeling for me.'

She just looked at me, smiling away like nobody's business. I didn't have the faintest idea of what impact I was having on her.

'You are like Coke,' she said, finally. 'You are the real thing.'

Maybe I didn't look flattered enough to be hypnotised, not even by Cleopatra.

She scribbled in her notepad, tore off the last 1/3rd of it and handed it to me. It had her contact details, phone number and address (Cuffe Parade).

'Can I have your coordinates?'

'Sure,' I said, not having the courage to tell her that no girl ever rang me up at home and the moral police interrogation that my dear papa would put me through in case anyone did. I took the piece of paper she handed me and wrote my address and phone number.

'Would your folks mind if I just happened to drop by once in a while?' she said.

'Drop in whenever you want,' I said, full of bravado.

The conversation carried on for another few minutes, mostly around films and books that we had been seeing or reading in the recent past. I asked her to join the Gang for Friday morning shows at Sterling. She jumped at it.

'Your Gang is really something,' she said, 'urban legends who go around smoking hash in the canteen and they are all toppers. It's really intimidating. I am scared of being torn to bits.'

'They are not male chauvinist pigs, if that's what you want to know,' I said, licking my lips nervously. 'I am sure they'll be pleased to have you around even if you don't smoke or drink like us. They are not fearsome; they appreciate people who are standing outside the ranks.'

'Okay,' she said, 'I will see you Friday morning. At Sterling or at the canteen?'

'At the canteen.'

And then, she dropped me off at the college, where I was immediately accosted by Ram and Shah.

'Hey, Sammy boy, you bohemian dog,' said Shah, 'how did it go?'

'Red hot on her side, confused on mine,' I said. 'She didn't ask me to fuck her.'

Shah had a serious look on his face.

'Man, you've got a chip on your shoulders. That babe

is asking for you to park your cock inside her cunt.'

'I have problems that I can't talk about here.'

'Don't talk about it; just do it!'

'I don't know, I have an issue with my cock.'

'You've got gonorrhea? Syphilis?'

'No, no, not that bad, but it's a problem.'

'Why don't you take a sabbatical, y'know,' said Ram, as dead-pan as ever, 'and meditate on the Absolute until a replacement prick drops into your lap from Heaven.'

'I have invited her to the Friday morning show at Sterling,' I said, trying to appease Ram and Shah's sense of disappointment.

'Okay,' said Shah, 'you're going to have another shot at it.'

'She's welcome,' said Ram, no change of expression. 'We'll organise a consortium of lenders to finance your grand seduction of Isabella.'

'Why don't you sniff a few lines of cocaine, y'know,' said Shah.

I looked at him and said, 'I don't want to end up raping her.'

'Just for some courage, man!' he exclaimed.

At this point, Nero came and joined us, with a cup of coffee in hand.

'So, what happened Sam?' he asked, with a broad conspiratorial smile.

'She's a Naxalite,' I said.

There was a pin-drop silence at the table.

'Is she armed?' said Ram, finally. 'She looks deadly.'

'Wait a minute,' said Shah, 'do you have to be a member of Charu Majumdar's outfit to be able to screw her?'

'I don't know,' I said, 'but I remember reading somewhere that in some Latin American countries, you have to take prior permission from the Party boss before announcing your relationship publicly. No, not Latin America; it's the Burmese Party.'

'I don't see how the Party can keep tabs on a dazzling South Bombay beauty who's loaded enough not to give two farts for their opinion,' said Ram.

'Is that all she told you?' said Nero.

'No,' I said. 'She wants to go commercial with the play. She's willing to finance it.'

There was another lengthy pause at the table.

'Hey, man,' said Nero, 'she's really smitten…'

'No, this is serious,' I said. 'She said I made no concessions to the bourgeoisie. She's going to talk to her mother about it. She's also going to speak to the Prithvi Theatre.'

'Great man! Let's do it,' said Nero, raising his coffee mug as a toast.

7

I couldn't sleep. Every time I closed my eyes, my mind would conjure up the image of Isabella Gondola—smiling, looking at me with a frank desire, her hair windblown—the thing between my legs would stir itself awake and I would succumb to every sexual fantasy in the book. I was petrified at the idea of taking her along with the rest of the Gang to Sterling. I kept tossing and turning through the night, struggling to discipline my cock.

I was no revolutionary. I did want to place a bomb under the Bitch's desk, but I had no idea why one would want to overthrow the government; I thought my paradise would be both artificial and private. I wanted to get into bed with Isabella, but I didn't have my cock's permission outside singular fantasms. When exhausted, I finally managed to sleep for a couple of hours towards the morning; I had vivid dreams of being chased by two small, slithery serpents. I remember telling myself in the dream—I was never afraid of snakes before, why now?

I woke up the next morning groggy and unsteady. I jumped into the shower straight away and relished the impact of cold water slapping my skin and sending the blood coursing through my veins. On the way to college, I said to myself, I badly want to fuck that girl, anonymously, in my absence if possible, without a word being exchanged. However, my instincts told me that the consequences of having sex with Isabella might be incalculable. I suspected her commitment to subversion. How could a multimillionaire's daughter, who drove around in a Beetle and frequented five-star hotels, be a Naxalite? At moments, I felt these thoughts driving me around the bend. One fact, however, was ineluctable—Isabella Gondola was a woman; she had known other boys sexually. However, the idea of taking my clothes off in front of a woman filled me with shame. Plus, my prick was defective. I had to take it to a service centre and get it fixed. That would require money. Besides, how could it be done without my father catching on?

The other thing that I was thinking about was my play. I felt mildly thrilled at the idea of joining the big boys of the game. But at the same time, I had two questions bobbing up on the surface of my cerebellum: Would Naxalites, past and present, crowd the venue? If yes, would I then be asked to place a bomb under the Bitch's chair in exchange for all the ticket sales I would profit from?

At the College, the Shah of Iran came and tapped on my shoulder.

'Sam, we need to talk. Urgently.'

'About what?'

'Let's take a walk down the Drive.'

So we hit Queen's Necklace at 9 in the morning after picking up a pint of Old Monk from the local hooch joint.

'What's your problem, man?' Shah asked.

'About what?' I asked, the bitter shock of the rum hitting my chest like a thunderball.

'I mean, that chick is wetting her pants for you. Just grab her and fuck her, man! What's your problem?'

'It's my prick,' I said, utterly dejected.

'Your prick, your prick,' said Shah, 'I've been listening to this for the past two days. What's wrong with your prick? You've got syphilis? It can be cured, y'know. This is 1976.'

'No, more serious than that.'

'What could be more serious than syphilis?'

'My skin stretches too tight and tears up and bleeds at the slightest friction,' said I, shamefacedly.

Shah stopped in his tracks and looked at me.

'You don't have enough foreskin,' he said finally, fortifying himself with a large draught of rum. 'I know just the doctor for you…'

'I don't have the money,' I said. 'Besides my old man will blow a fuse if he sees me with blood bandages or anything of that sort.'

'You can shack up at my place for ten days.'

'What about your folks?'

'They won't suspect a thing; let me handle that, first we've got to fix up a doctor for you. Don't tell anybody else, Okay? This is just between the two of us, and maybe Nero. And, yes, don't fool around with that chick until you are back in shape.'

'Okay,' I said, miserably.

'Just cheer up, Sam, there's solution for every problem under the Sun.'

It felt pretty bad, but there was no way I was going to try and seduce Isabella Gondola with my defective virility. How could I even get around to explaining that to her? *Shudder*.

So, Friday morning, the Gang was at the designated canteen table, waiting for everyone to show up before pushing off to Sterling.

Isabella Gondola showed up with just a little eye makeup and lipstick. I had never seen a more beautiful girl in my life before. I introduced her to the rest of the guys. For the first time, she was coy and pert in her responses. She was actually a shy person, I realised. I found that touching. She took out a Marlboro and began smoking merrily even as Shah, Nero and Ram took turns to be gracious and welcoming to her. I could see she was nervous about being unduly frank, but she had this imperceptible Mona Lisa smile on her face which was completely disarming. Everybody assumed she was my gal.

'You realise, of course,' said Ram, 'that he hasn't done an honest day's work ever since he joined Sydenham.'

'That doesn't bother me,' said Isabella, 'I am used to the company of people who are misfits and broke. What's showing at Sterling today?'

'*One flew over the cuckoo's nest*,' said Nero. 'It's by Milos Forman.'

'Who's he?' said Isabella.

'A Czech director,' said Nero, 'he's very good. There's Jack Nicholson in the movie; he got an Oscar for this, if I remember correctly.'

'Oh,' said Isabella. 'I am not too up-to-date with the movie scene.'

'We're finding out too,' said Nero. 'No aficionados here.'

Just then, Feridoon landed up with a big, wicked smile.

'The eagle has landed,' said he as he settled down for some canteen tea. Looking directly at Isabella he said, 'Hi.'

'Hi,' said Isabella, smiling back.

'So, today's the big day, right,' Feridoon asked me.

I went red all over the place.

'Look at the son of a bitch, he's blushing,' said Feridoon, laughing.

'Isabella, Feridoon,' I said, 'Feridoon, Isabella. She's trying to expand her cultural horizons.'

'Cultural horizons?' said Ram. 'Is it something about the libido, or does it relate to the sixth five-year plan just announced by the Bitch?'

Isabella laughed, while I looked at her nervously.

'You've got to catch the snake by the head,' said Shah, merrily blowing smoke rings into the air. 'This slippery slimy bohemian dog doesn't know anything about life.

We were hoping you could put some sense into him…'

Finally, Chandra showed up too, looking like thunder.

'Who has been projecting this place?' he said. 'Who is despoiling the fair name of Bombay? Is it you, Sam, or the chick sitting next to you?'

'Chandra, Isabella,' said I, 'Isabella, Chandra.'

'You look as if you've been bungee jumping off the cliffs of the Malabar Hills,' said Chandra. 'Sammy, what's up?'

'We were discussing the movie,' I said, feebly.

'Have you changed your nappies?' said Chandra.

'You guys have a wicked sense of humour,' said Isabella, who had been smiling all along.

'Okay, I think we have a quorum,' said Nero, 'we should be off.'

Everybody got up and moved out of the canteen.

'How are we getting there?' said Isabella.

'On foot,' said Ram, 'like good Gandhians. We are consciously eschewing public transport.'

So, all the guys walked briskly, ahead of Isabella and myself, who brought up the rear.

'You are so shy!' said Isabella.

'With women, yes,' I said.

'But, why?!'

'I don't know. I guess I am unsure of my sexual status. Whether women find me attractive or not. That sort of thing.'

'But, why?! I am sure, plenty of girls would give their right arms to be with you!'

'I don't get any fan mail, y'know. Besides…umm…I think women are repelled by my brutality.'

'Are you a rapist?'

'I mean, verbally.'

'That's a side I haven't seen so far.'

'It's a defence mechanism, a disguise for my lack of romanticism. Or rather lack of experience in dealing with women as sexual beings.'

'You're pretty straightforward in saying this,' said Isabella as she lit another Marlboro. 'But listen, I've spoken to Prithvi; they said I could book the hall for 10 grand and that includes everything. We price our tickets ourselves. I've spoken to Alyque too…'

'You mean, Alyque Padamsee?'

'Himself, he said he would attend a few rehearsals and help you guys out if need be.'

'But he's into musicals and rock operas, *Jesus Christ Superstar* and stuff.'

'Listen, you don't have to commit yourself to anything right away. I am just exploring options, that's all. I just thought Alyque knows a lot about theatre and could give you the benefit of his experience.'

'Okay,' I said simply.

At Sterling, as everybody started bringing out their wallets, Isabella broke in and said, 'Leave this to me, guys. I am treating everybody here.'

'You're upsetting the code of chivalry,' said Ram. 'It will impact my coat of arms which already has a bend sinister.'

'I advocate women's lib, if you'd like to know,' said

Isabella, mildly. 'In my universe it's the woman who pays.'

'We'd all love to be in your universe forever, but meanwhile the deal here is that we go dutch.'

After a few more back and forths, it was Isabella who had her way.

Inside the hall, the seating arrangements were as follows—me on the aisle seat, then Isabella, the Shah of Iran, Chandra, Nero, Ram and Feridoon Cama.

Halfway through the movie, I realised that Isabella had slipped her arm through mine and was breathing heavily. I froze. I could neither withdraw my arm nor could I let it rest in that position indefinitely. So, I did nothing, said nothing, and did not even move a muscle anywhere. At the intermission, Isabella got up and bought us all packets of chips.

'Really,' said Shah, 'you shouldn't be doing this. Some of us are loaded up to the roof, y'know.'

'Next time you pay,' she said with a smile.

I relaxed. I thought watching the movie arm in arm was over. No demands were being made on my emotions. But no, as soon as the theatre went dark again, Isabella's arm was entwined in mine. I went stiff all over again. An affair was knocking at my door that I was ferociously trying to keep shut tight.

When the lights came on again, I freed my arm as tactfully as I could. But Isabella stuck to me like a leech. I couldn't figure out what to do next. Whether to loiter around the park or re-join the guys for a smoke and a drink at the Shamiana.

Outside the hall, Ram looked at everybody and said, 'What about some beer?'

'Great idea,' said Chandra, and we made our way to the Taj.

This time, I tried to keep up with the Gang's blistering pace, dragging Isabella along.

'So, how did you like the movie?' Chandra asked Isabella.

'I don't know much about American cinema, but the movie was great,' she said timidly. 'I thought Jack Nicholson was fantastic.'

'Wait till you see *Chinatown*,' said Nero.

'But the end was depressing,' said Isabella.

'That's reality,' said Ram, 'things end badly, more often than not.'

'I don't agree with that,' said Isabella, 'It's a question of probability. The hero should be walking away with the heroine at least half the time…'

'Art isn't necessarily about probability,' said Nero, looking serious, 'Just like life. There are always going to be more people who do not get what they want than the contrary…'

'In any case,' said Ram, 'in Hindi movies, God is always the backdrop to every action and every saying. The villain walking away with the heroine would be morally wrong, even if pragmatically correct.'

'Even so,' said Isabella, 'I think this movie is too pessimistic.'

'It isn't really,' said Ram. 'Murphy's spirit may be

broken, but the inspiration lives on, the Big Chief does throw the washstand against the metal bars of the hospital and make his escape; it's not all black, there is a ray of light at the end.'

'I don't know,' said Isabella, smiling a little and perhaps embarrassed. 'The only prominent woman in the movie is a torturer.'

'That's not a generalisation about love,' I said.

At this, Isabella jerked her head towards me—serious, focused and willing.

'That's true,' she said. 'But I found that a little misogynistic. I mean, not all psychiatric hospitals are run by women. On the contrary. Have you read Georg Lukacs?'

'Who's he?' I said.

'A literary theoretician. He thinks any narrative thought should be held together by typical representatives of their class or culture.'

'That's the Marxist point of view,' said Nero.

'That's correct,' said Isabella, 'but, I still believe that any narrative medium follows precise rules about representation, which is what their artistic success is built on.'

'So, a male sadist is closer to the truth than a female one in certain contexts?' said Shah.

'Yeah, I think so,' said Isabella.

'Perhaps,' replied Shah. 'I can't delve any deeper than that.'

'So, you have a confrontation between a macho rebel and a female sadist,' said Isabella. 'That's not typical.

All rebels are not macho and all women in responsible positions are not sadists.'

'A work of art is not necessarily about stereotypes,' I said. 'It could be about exceptions. The crux of the biscuit is their truth. And the truth is not always determined by sociology or psychology. It's about the imagination overwhelming our usual categories of thought. A work of art is not necessarily intelligence in the quotidian sense of the term.'

'Okay,' said Nero, 'time to return to college.'

And then, turning to Isabella, he said, 'Great to have you with us. Sydenham is not overfull with sexy political radicals.'

So, I drifted into Isabella's life attracted to her, both sexually and intellectually. It was only a year after reading Kafka's *The Trial*, but I had voraciously devoured whatever could be found at the British Council library, mainly plays by Pinter and Tom Stoppard, but also Graham Greene, Joseph Conrad, H G Wells, Virginia Woolf and E M Forster. Everybody thought she was my girlfriend, but we hadn't touched each other, not even exchanged a kiss. I was confused about my feelings for her. I felt overpowered every time I saw her, but I was also terrified of the emotions that a man could arouse in her, emotions whose responsibility I was either incapable or unwilling to take. I felt small when I was with her. I understood that she was a feminist and made a conscious effort not to fall into any sexual stereotype. She smoked, drank, drove her own car, used minimal make-up, just an eyeliner and no lipstick, and still looked gorgeous. It was because of her that I read Greer's *The Female Eunuch*, Betty Friedan's *The Feminine Mystique*, and Simone de Beauvoir's *The Second Sex* and found myself agreeing with a lot of stuff that they wrote about. She also introduced me to the poetry of Charles Bukowski, Joseph Brodsky, Philip Larkin and W H Auden. I badly wanted to be her boyfriend, to begin a romance with her, but the thought of saying anything intimate to her made me baulk. There was a hurdle in my mind that I couldn't overcome. And I knew what that hurdle was—it was my father's puritanism, his refusal to see his children as autonomous sexual beings, as adults, or simply as people who would be expected in any normal household to grow away from their family and make their own way through this world, sooner or later. All his dark forebodings about me, because I was the one doing late-night get-togethers, were influenced by what he read in the newspapers about how dangerous life could be in a city like Bombay. His mind would explode at the thought of a traffic accident, drug abuse and petty crime, and sexual promiscuity coming to grief and ruining lives. The more he read the papers, the more he cringed at the thought of me staying out late in the night with a bunch of people he had already recognised as a bunch of dropouts. And he was not willing to even broach the topic with me. Hence, I could never invite Isabella home for dinner or something of the kind. My father could become apoplectic at the mere thought. I did not know what to tell him. I also began accompanying

Isabella to her over-the-ground missions to Naxalite trade unions, more as an observer than a participant. I was amazed by the dexterity with which she dealt with labour issues. There were no fumbles, inarticulate sounds, or frantic last-minute consultations of notes and papers. She knew the subject and the Party's will on it. I loved to watch this lovely woman talk to the poor in such an unselfconscious manner, with so much simplicity and directness. It was also obvious that the workers respected her, more so for her class background and the spirit of sacrifice it connoted. They spoke to her as they would speak to one of their own. I saw in Isabella a great leader of people in the future and I totally admired her for that. She never asked me to join in or participate. I never felt any kind of danger. What I did feel was something desperate, something that came directly out of my guts, something viscerally powerful. Many people call it love.

One day, after over a year into the Emergency, I got a call from Isabella early in the morning. I think that was the first time she had called me at home. She said she wanted me to meet somebody, and would I be free in the afternoon around 4 pm? I said yes.

We got into her car and drove north, right up to Bandra, through Linking Road, up to Pali Hill. We whooshed into an apartment block called Pearl. The lift took us to the 15th floor and we rang the bell. The door said Dipankar Mukherjee, MA, LLB. The door was opened by a middle-aged man, with a broad face, head without much hair, and horn-rimmed spectacles, dressed casually in a jeans and a short-sleeved shirt.

'Hi, princess!' he said. 'I have been expecting you for the last hour and a half! Where have you been all this time? What are you up to? But come in, come in...'

'Dipankar *da*,' said Isabella, 'this is Sam.'

'Hi, Sam,' he said affably as we shook hands. 'Isabella has told me a lot about you.'

'Good things, I hope,' I said lightly.

'Mostly, yes,' he laughed. 'You are not very interested in politics, it seems.'

I shrugged, nervously. 'Some things do interest me,' I said. 'The anti-war movement in the West, for instance. But that's basically because there is some fabulous music coming out of it.'

'Yes, yes,' said Dipankar da. 'Please, sit down everybody. Shall I open a beer, or what would you like to have?'

'Beer would be fine,' said Isabella.

'Same here,' I said.

'Dipankar da has been working on a Bengali translation of *The Birthday Party* by Pinter,' said Isabella.

'Great play,' I said.

'Yes,' said Dipankar da. 'I am having quite a time getting it right colloquially into my mother tongue. Pinter is all about ears, y'know. But, tell me about the play you've written, Sam. Isabella tells me it's worth going commercial with it. What's it about?'

'It's very Beckettian, I feel,' I said shamefacedly. 'It's about two chess players whiling away their time playing chess while the world around them makes no sense. They are intermittently subject to aerial attacks by a person called Mack. It's about boredom interrupted by blue funk.'

'That sounds philosophical to me,' said Dipankar da. 'Nihilism.'

'I also like Artaud a lot,' I said.

'Aha,' said Dipankar da, as he placed a six-pack of Heineken on the centre table. 'You've been reading the right stuff, I see.' He opened a couple of cans and poured the contents into large silver beer tankards. 'Cheers,' he said and took a large draught of the beer.

'Where would you like your play to be performed?' asked Dipankar da.

'Prithvi?' said Isabella.

'That will take some money. Not lots, but some nevertheless.'

'I'll take care of the money angle.'

'You are going to borrow it from your dad?'

'No, no. I'll tap my mom and raise some money from friends and acquaintances.'

'You could also rent a college auditorium. It would turn out cheaper.'

'We don't want to be associated with academia. It would look amateurish.'

'What about actors?'

'The ones we worked with are wonderful performers. Professional quality.'

'That's good. Getting actors for anything that is avant-garde is one hell of a problem. About the money, I will see what I can do. I'll make a personal donation of 20,000 bucks, but I'll have to look at the script first, y'know, to make sure that the standard is right. Plus, you'll need to advertise the show. I know a few people in advertising. Alyque, he could do it pro bono.'

'That would be great!'

'The only other problem is politics. This regime is scared of its own shadow. You will have to get your script vetted by the cops. They are generally not a bright sort, especially when it comes to literature. Anything that looks like a deviation from the norm, y'know, anything they don't understand, is immediately suspicious. They are constantly on the qui-vive. But, I know a few people in the bureaucracy who can exert some degree of coercion on the police. But still, there is a fear of the unknown in any enterprise of this nature. The government is an irrational beast. It's totally unpredictable. Especially in the current situation, they are completely paranoid about dissent. Who will direct the play?'

'I will,' said I.

'That's another problem,' said Dipankar da. 'Don't mind; I am just playing the devil's advocate here. You are not a marquee name. I will try and get Alyque to plug the play, or to find a prestigious sponsor. The problem is that nobody understands the avant-garde in this country. They think it's nonsense, a waste of time and money. There might be a riot. So, you somehow have to get it across that this play is like nothing they've seen before.

It's experimental. Don't use the word abstract. It will keep the audience away. You will have to heavily emphasise the artistic side of the show so that we can get the intellectual and artistic elite to watch it. Then there's the media. Let me take care of that. I know most of the prominent drama critics; I'll put in a good word about you. But first, you have to let me take a look at the play. What would you need by way of props?'

'Nothing elaborate,' I said. 'It's very minimalist. Just two chairs, a table and a chessboard. Plus, dimmers and sound effects.'

'That sounds simple enough. Your play intrigues me. Anyway, so production costs are minimal. Costumes?'

'My actors wear whatever they are comfortable in.'

At this, Dipankar da grinned. 'Sounds better and better. Informal theatre. If we had café theatre in this country, your play would have been ideal. Like, in France.'

'Dipankar da,' said Isabella, 'worked for the UNESCO and was in Paris for eight years.'

'I was just a bureaucrat,' Dipankar da said modestly, 'it wasn't glamorous. But, I got to watch a lot of plays. Especially, Ariane Mnouchkine and Peter Brook. Also, Grotowski. Those are the big guys. Giorgio Strehler. But, the best part of Paris is that there is theatre everywhere—in cafes, small bars, in the street. There's this place called Beaubourg, where I saw this fantastic Japanese guy, dressed like a samurai, picking up people from the audience and making them go through the most impossible motions while declaring their love for a woman, for instance. It was hilarious and it was great theatre.'

'Did you watch anything by Beckett?' I asked.

'Oh, absolutely. There was a festival of plays by post-war dramatists—Beckett, Ionesco, Genet and a few others. So, I got to see *Waiting for Godot* and *Krapp's Last Tape*. I was blown away. You can see the poster for Godot on the wall behind you.'

I turned around and saw two silhouettes against a stark backdrop relieved by a tree without any leaves.

'You can take it if you want. I can always get hold of another one. I travel abroad at least once or twice a month. Would you like to have it?'

'Yes,' I said timidly.

He got up, took the frame off the wall and placed it tilted against the nearest wall.

'It's yours,' he said.

'Thank you,' I said.

'Most welcome. So what does the Party have to say about all this? For them, Beckett must be a decadent capitalist stooge.'

'The Party has nothing to do with this,' said Isabella, nonchalantly. 'This is my private affair. Dipankar da is an ex-Naxalite. He was there with Kanu Sanyal and Jangal Santhal at Naxalbari.'

'Did you kill anyone?' I asked with wonder.

'I was asked to kill a traffic cop,' Dipankar da said. 'I couldn't bring myself to do it. So, I ran away from Calcutta and took refuge with a relative in Delhi. They came looking for me right up to where I was hiding, but my uncle stood firm and told them they wouldn't be allowed in. It was tense for about two months and then Siddhartha Shankar Ray was voted, and he changed the game. He brought in Ranjit Bose as Commissioner, and the two of them went about killing every Naxalite they could get hold of. As a result, there was an exodus of talent and merit from Bengal and the state never recovered from it.'

'Jangal Santhal killed people,' I said.

'Yes, he did,' said Dipankar da. 'I saw some of that, but didn't have any qualms because the landlords were scum. It was the urban guerrilla that brought me to my knees. People being killed indiscriminately, literally for no reason, because people were given quotas to fulfil. It made me puke.'

'The Emergency is the first serious thing to have happened in my life, but I am a coward. I can't throw a bomb or even distribute literature. I wrote a play instead.'

Dipankar da smiled at me. 'That can be more subversive than throwing a bomb. But, it's good to be innocent. Only, innocence often means putting up with shit. I couldn't, I did have to compromise with my conscience. I fought back, not realising that killing and mayhem, no matter how justified according to the latest bull from Moscow or Peking, tears you up inside. It is often more ethical to just stay silent and suffer. I don't know. And then the rabble took over in the name of class credentials and all the brilliant people ran for their lives because the Party wanted a cultural revolution. It was madness. One Naxalite killed another under orders from

X, Y, and Z. In the end, people were asking who was in charge.'

'I have a certain fascination for that era of politics, although I was miles away from it. Beheading statues, in particular.'

'I know. Especially, Tagore. I was thrilled. I had never really liked Tagore. He had no notion of what a revolution in Bengal could mean. He has been recuperated by every regime in Bengal—the Congress, the Left, everybody. He called himself a parasite. Big deal. That didn't stop him from looking after his family's estates and eating out of silver utensils. You can't simply stand up and say, "I am revolting" and expect everyone to applaud. It must hurt you materially. People make a lot of noise about the quantity of written matter he left behind. Well, the collected works of Karl Marx run into 34 volumes, out of which no more than 10 per cent is readable today. So, I was thrilled when they beheaded Tagore's statue. It meant something had been understood somewhere. For me, Tagore's revolt should have been directed primarily at himself and his family, as representatives of the oppressing class, even in culture. I mean, anybody who finds acceptance as universally as Tagore does—rich and poor, Left and Right, men and women—must be doing something wrong. The quality of a great poet is to disrupt and disturb. Not to pacify and soothe. Tagore was a pacifier. There is this French novelist called Philippe Sollers. He says the vocation of the artist is to stand against the majority, not only those present and constituted but also against those to come, the majorities of the future. That's something, I believe. Anyway, all of that is gone. I still meet young Bengalis who say they want to end their lives in a hail of police bullets, but you can see romanticism in their eyes. For them, it is about poetry and student politics. Nobody is interested in shaking the foundations of this country's culture. It's either that or dreary nihilism. You're right, Sam, the world, indeed, makes no sense anymore. I mean, earlier they had God, and then they had Marx and Freud, now they have Pol Pot—petty, half-lunatic dictators who have a talent for genocide. Disgusting!'

'We are a myth-prone people,' said Isabella.

'Precisely,' said Dipankar da. 'I mean, there is a kernel of truth in every myth. But, at least the Hindus, as people, believe that the gods are intimately involved in the affairs of men—that is what makes the past interesting, and gives meaning to superficially human battles. We believe that Nature is a playfield of God or the Gods and we are so many puppets being manipulated by the Gods in furtherance of their schemes and purposes. All we can do, as puny human beings, is to execute rituals that intend to placate the gods and bring them over to our side. Hinduism is a transactional religion in that the relationship with the Deity is pragmatic. The worshipper says, "I want wealth," or "I want a son, for which I will sing your praises and sacrifice 500 cows for you,"—I am talking about the Vedic Hindus here— "so you will have to, at the very least, listen to me and do me no harm." Islam and Christianity are not like that. What the Muslims and the Christians say to their God is "We will follow your laws and ordinances, in return for which you will preserve a place for me in the paradise after I die, and protect me from Satan's designs." Whereas science believes that the Universe is a rational entity governed by laws that human beings can discover through observation and experimentation. And those discoveries can be used to make further discoveries, and then we come to a point where we know enough to manipulate Nature to our advantage. The Hindu gives a shit for this kind of reasoning. For him, reason is nothing. It can be overcome through willpower. The Hindu thinks he can transcend scientific laws and magically bring about or procure what he desires for himself. The problem is that this belief requires the majority to exercise its will in the same direction. It is then, and only then, that man can go to Mars and back, the weather manipulated, and social barriers between castes and classes broken. Supernatural! The only thing is that all this frenetic willing has brought us to a point where people can't afford one square meal a day, let alone two. If you ask a Hindu to explain the mess we are in, he will say it's due to the waning of religion; the individual will is being exercised at cross-purposes with other wills. That's why you have endless disruption. Do you know what the priest at the Gorakhnath temple has said recently? He says facts are not important. What people believe is important. What can you say to that? You can only debate if the facts are credible for everyone. But the Hindu questions your facts! No argument is possible. Take, for instance, all this pother about cows. Either the cow is just another animal, which you can eat if you want, or it's a special animal of divine nature. Okay? Let's have your case on the cow, get scientists to corroborate what you consider to be the facts about the cow and get a paper published by *The Lancet*, *Nature* or any of the prestigious scientific journals in the world, and if you win, it will be a great day for India. But, they are not stupid. My question is that if the cow is sacred in India, for objective reasons, it should be sacred for the whole world. That is palpably not the case. So, maybe only Indian cows are sacred? So, why not allow the rest of us to eat imported cows? One of the most traumatic things for the traditional Hindu is to grow up and find that his religion is not universal. It is believed by only people from the subcontinent. So, they deified geography. You are a Hindu if you consider this country to be your *pitrubhumi* and *punyabhumi*. That's Savarkar. We'll have to deal with him and a few other jokers in future, mark my words.'

'Aren't you being unduly harsh and pessimistic?' said Isabella.

'On the contrary,' said Dipankar da. 'I am just picking at the minor points.'

'What about the Left? Some of us would say we are growing, expanding even,' said Isabella.

'Let's see,' said Dipankar da, scratching his head. 'The Left is in a unique historic situation, that of being a player in a democracy. I am talking about the CPI and the

CPM. What happens to the idea of revolution? Because a revolution brings change on a permanent stable basis. What happens if the Left is voted in for a five-year term, at the end of which a Hindu right-wing outfit takes over and immediately goes about undoing what the Left had done? So…things are not so simple. The idea of revolution is the idea of a complete, systemic, total overhaul of everything overnight. Do you think the country will buy that? What about private property? How will you tackle things like Gandhism? The only thing that makes me root for the Left is its stance on religion in politics. It's hard secularism, no connection between the two. If there is a conflict between religion and science, between religion and the Constitution, religion will have to step down. That's forthright and brave. Instead of Gandhian mealy-mouthism—equal respect for all religions. It should be more like equal disrespect for all religions. God knows what's going to happen to this country! You guys hungry? I can rustle up some cheese balls and cocktail sausages… okay? Okay!'

He went into the kitchen looking busy and hassled.

'Is he a member of the Party?' I asked Isabella.

'Used to be, not anymore.'

'Is that possible? Can you quit the Revolution just like that?'

'That's why he went abroad. To escape being dragged back into the net or being hunted down and shot like an animal.'

'So, what does he do for a living?'

'He is vice-president of Risk Management with Procter and Gamble.'

'Big bucks.'

'He likes the bourgeois lifestyle. That's the only way to be satisfied in this country, according to him. Plus, he travels a lot to western Europe.'

'Married?'

'Divorced, has two kids, all of them in Toronto.'

'Loneliest loneliness says Nietzsche.'

'His wife and children come down in December every year. He goes to Toronto, but less frequently. What do you think of him, Sam?'

'He is an intellectual,' I said, not knowing what else to say. 'I have never thought about the things he's thought about. I don't even read the newspapers properly, even less these days than otherwise. So, I am not so well-informed. But, the way he says things makes a lot of sense. His logic seems to be crystal clear. I don't know. I don't have much of a head for these things. All I care to know is that my father is a peasant who is dead against pre-marital sex. And, he is scared of darkness and the things it breeds and allows to flourish. That's my only problem at the moment.'

'You'll grow, Sam, the more you go about the world, you will get to understand what this country is about. Maturity comes with time.'

'I am never going to grow up to be an adult as long as my parents are around. My life is like a bad Hindi film. Everyone lives happily ever after, except me. I stew in my own ignorance. Sometimes, I feel like running away from home. It's so suffocating. I am going to finish college, find a job and move out of my father's house as soon as possible.'

'I think you should. It will be sad if a talent, like yours, goes to waste because of your folks. I am there for you, Sam, all the way.'

Hearing this, I blushed. Does she know? Do I deserve to have her? I was so proud of being seen with her initially. She was easily one of the most beautiful women in Bombay, or even in the world. She had film star-like good looks. This is what held me together. Public opinion. Everybody thought she was beautiful. That made it objective and not subjective.

'Don't give up on your mind, Sam,' said Isabella.

'No, I will not,' I said. 'I don't know how to talk to people. I don't know what to say to them. Even somebody as intelligent as Dipankar da. I admire him, but I am not sure I can participate in a one-on-one discussion with him. I prefer talking to an audience of 200 people than to one or two friends. Except the Gang; they are different. Like me. But they are not into art. Most of them are going to land nice cushy jobs, wives and children and maybe an odd mistress or two. They think the same about me. They put all this theatre business down to youthful exuberance.'

'Sam, Sam, it doesn't matter, if people think like that. I know you. I know you have it in you to be a great playwright or a filmmaker. We will take on the world one arsehole at a time. Okay? Everything is going to be all right, don't worry. Give your script to Dipankar da. He is really well-connected in the theatre world and is genuinely very helpful.'

I didn't have the heart to tell her that in my world, the rich man is automatically a philistine. Had I been influenced by Isabella's politics? I don't know. But, this resistance towards collaborating with an element of what Isabella herself would call the class enemy, was deep-rooted. My father was someone who looked up to wealth and power and would humble himself before them.

'What do people like Tata and Birla do?' I asked him once out of defiance.

'They create jobs,' said my father, 'that take care of several hundred, thousand, families.'

My next question was going to be: What's so great about having a family? But then, my father might have had a heart attack if I said that.

At this point, Dipankar da returned to the living room with two plates full of cocktail sausages.

'Eat,' he told us with a broad smile. Here was someone genuinely fond of serving people, even the fake bourgeois like me or, rather, lumpen bourgeois like me. He handed us a silver toothpick each. The sausages, as I remember them now, were done to perfection, firm to the bite without feeling like a tennis ball. There were two dips, salsa and chilli ketchup. Then, he went back to the kitchen and brought back a big bowl of cheese balls with a bowl of mayonnaise on the side.

'So, Sam,' said Dipankar da, 'what do you want to

be? A playwright in English? There is no money in the theatre, except for a lucky few.'

'I don't know,' I said, suddenly feeling miserable.

'What is your priority right now?'

'Right now? Right now I don't want to live with my parents anymore.'

'That requires money. I don't suppose you will want to be a businessman, so that leaves the formal sector. You speak and write good English. That's enough to land a reasonable job for someone like you in Bombay. If you want, I can talk to a couple of people, y'know.'

'I would be most obliged. I don't know whether I am going to fit in easily.'

'Oh, you don't have to worry about that. I can fix you up as a trainee copywriter in an ad agency. I know Frank Simoes. He will give you a test and that's all. But I am guessing you are the shy retiring type.'

'I don't suffer fools gladly.'

'Mm. These cheese balls are really good. So, let me understand.' He took a deep breath and said, 'You would want to rent a room somewhere in Bombay. That is not going to be possible with your trainee stipend. You will have to find a place to stay. A paying guest sort of thing and even that costs some money. Can you stay with a relative?'

'I don't know. I haven't given it much thought.'

'The other alternative is to get a probationary officer's position in a bank. But, artistically, that's a desert. I wouldn't touch it with a barge pole. It will give you enough to rent a room and feed and clothe yourself in a city like Bombay. Do you know typing?'

'Yes, I do. I taught myself last summer.'

'That's great! You could find a job with a film studio as an assistant to the producer. Mainly clerical work, y'know, typing letters and following up with equipment providers, things like that. They'll pay you well too.'

'Okay. But I don't watch any Hindi movies.'

'That's not a problem. You know English. That should be sufficient. But don't be under any illusion. Life is hard in a city like Bombay. You'll be in a pigeonhole with an attached bath and a kitchenette. Plenty of people live like that. You'll have to commute by train, y'know, packed like sardines. There might be water shortages, waiting for the municipal tanker with a hundred people in queue. I don't suppose you know any cooking, right, so you have to find a place where you get a decent meal for cheap. It sounds horrible, but you'll soon get used to it. The main thing is that you don't let go of your talent. Keep writing. Expand your parameters. Read your classics over and over again. Once you get the hang of it, you will just sail through. But it will take time. You like Beckett?'

'Yes.'

'And who else among writers? Favourite novelists?'

'Joyce. Henry Miller. Kafka, of course. That's about it. I started reading serious literature only after joining college.'

'Not to worry,' said Dipankar da. He got up from the sofa and searched his gigantic bookshelves for something. He leapt up and picked up a thick paperback volume of Penguin Modern Classics. He returned and laid the volume on the table. It read *The Gift* by Vladimir Nabokov. 'Read this,' he said. 'It's worth your while.'

'I have heard of Nabokov, but I haven't read anything by him.'

'I am giving a free run of my library. You can come and take away any book you would want to read. I have a good collection of books on theatre that I keep at your disposal. You have to read and read and read.'

'That's for sure. My family is what you would call right-wing conservatives. Philistines. They don't have any time for books. The only books in my house are those on religion, the *Gita*, *Mahabharata*, or on Ramakrishna Paramahamsa and Vivekananda. You won't find a single work of fiction in any language. As for theatre, it's something you would do as a hobby, in your spare time. But, a career in theatre would mean that you would be going around in rags, smoking bidis, and keeping company with long-haired Leftist intellectuals. Strict no-no. I can't even talk to my brother about books. The only kind he reads are economics textbooks and comics. Nothing in between. My sister wants to be an air hostess; that doesn't call for me to pay intelligent attention to. The upshot is that I am secretive about literature. It's a clandestine pursuit that cannot be confessed to under any church. It's like dealing in illicit liquor. All my uncles are prosperous professionals who won't be able to spell Shakespeare correctly. And no one pays attention to me because they assume I would continue the family tradition. Get a good job, get married, start a family, put away money for your retirement and then spend the rest of your life talking about God and the purpose of human existence. Only, now, my father smells a rat. He has strong suspicions that I am going astray. He's trying to control me. Crackdown on evenings spent away from home. No nights spent out partying with friends. And, strictly no women. I have not dared to invite Isabella home, not only for the shock it will produce but also because I am ashamed to have the family I have. Evenings mean you have to sit in front of a TV and watch the occasional Hindi film video. I don't even have a room of my own. I have to share one with my brother who doesn't think much of me. He's the hero of the family: a brilliant academic record and a member of Bombay University's cricket team. It's not that he's hostile, or anything, but he looks at me as an inferior member of the human species. Somebody who doesn't want to be an accountant or a business manager which is what Sydenham prepares you for. I am totally frustrated in every conceivable way.'

Dipankar da heard out this tirade without interjecting or showing any emotion. He looked absorbed. 'I can understand where you are coming from,' he said after a moment of hesitation.

'I still feel there's going to be a revolution in this country one day,' said Isabella. 'It's bound to happen sooner rather than later. It's just that no one seems able to bell the cat of religion.'

'I share your belief, Isabella,' said Dipankar da. 'But,

I'll flee the country if it ever happens. Life is too precious to waste on world history.'

***

The same night there was a phone call from Isabella. She sounded flustered. My father was not in town and the rest of the family was watching TV.

'Listen, Sam,' she said, 'can you do me a favour?' Isabella said.

'Yeah, sure,' I said.

'I think my cell has been infiltrated. That's what the guys underground are telling me. There might be a police raid at my house any time now.'

'Really?' I was concerned. 'What can I do?'

"There are some pamphlets and literature lying about in my room. Can you keep it in your house for a few days, I mean, until this thing blows over.'

'Of course, I can,' I said, my throat parched, my heart pounding.

'That's really sweet of you. Is this a good time to come over to your place?'

'Right now?' I said, stupidly.

'Yeah, right now, it's urgent. It's a small rucksack.'

'Okay,' I said, knowing well that this was going to stoke my mother's paranoia about girls in my life.

'I will take an hour to land up at your place.'

'Okay,' I said, the dread growing inside me.

An hour later, there was a knock on the door. I jumped

at it before my brother or sister could get it. I found Isabella standing with a small rucksack in her hand. She handed the rucksack over to me, putting a finger to her lips to say shh.

'I'll see you tomorrow at the canteen, okay?' she said and strode purposefully to the lift. I closed the door gently behind me and walked to my room with it when my mother intervened.

'Who was that?' she said, vigorously puffing away. 'And what is this?'

Insane suspicion was wreaking havoc on her mind, I knew.

'Nothing, just some material related to the play we're putting up at the IIT youth festival.'

'At this time of the night?'

'It's a bit urgent,' I lied as best as I could. 'There are some posters that need pasting up.' I had half a mind to go for her jugular.

'Who was that?' my mother asked again.

'She's helping out with the production,' I said.

My mother looked at me intently.

'Ask her not to land up in the house late at night. Is this any time to go visiting people?'

Then, she sat on the sofa and resumed watching the rest of the show.

I took the rucksack to my room and quickly went through the contents. There was a heavy consignment of far-left pamphlets, essentially calling upon the police to disobey orders, plus a few brochures advertising the underground agenda of the CPI (ML). Explosive stuff! I quickly shoved the rucksack underneath my bed.

I couldn't sleep that night. Not because of the contraband lying under my bed. I was touched by the bravery of that girl, risking everything for her cause. I found the idea romantic and there was a faint quickening of the imagination when I thought about her. I gave myself up to the fantasies of love and danger that Isabella brought about in me. But then, I grew depressed when I thought about the state of my penis, unsuitable for sex except the auto-erotic one. Not that my dreams were sexual in nature. They had a purity that I found intensely romantic, like scenes from a Hindi movie, a spiritual love without any sexually meaningful physical contact.

At 4 am, the police came and took me away for questioning. The rest of the family were both terror-struck and amazed. My mother began to protest using a combination of threat and womanly sentimentalism. The cops just brought out the leaflets in the rucksack and showed them to her.

'Listen,' said my mother. 'My son is innocent. Some girl from the college landed up and gave this bag to him. He does not know anything.'

'Ma'am,' said the officer, 'this is dangerous leftist propaganda. The girl from the college you're talking about belongs to an underground cell of the Communist Party of India (Marxist-Leninist). Do you know what that means? These people were planning to blow up Bombay House.'

My mother raised her eyebrows, more surprised than fearful.

'We know our son; he would never do a thing like that. He's a good boy.'

'Your son is now an adult. He should know what is what. What he did is against the law. Anyway, all this is up to the courts to decide now.'

'The courts?'

'He is being booked for sedition and waging war against the state. Both non-bailable. The defence is sure to call you as a witness and you can say what you want to, in front of the Magistrate. You will be given a chance to tell your side of the story.'

At this, my mother flew into a rage.

'What are you talking about? I know my son. There is no way he could have got involved in something like this. It's about this girl who is playing around with him with her twisted guiles and politics. You can ask around in the neighbourhood. He is the most gentle person in the whole of Nepean Sea Road. You can conduct a background check of our family.'

The inspector would have none of this.

'Your son is accused of serious offences, and there is at least one person who will vouch for our side of the story. We're not dealing with emotions and sentiments here; we're dealing with hard facts. Compromising literature has been found under his bed. There is no way we can let him go. He might tamper with the evidence.'

'Do you know my family?' shrieked my mother.

'My husband is an airline pilot. He knows the Prime Minister's son. If you do this, you'll hear from very high up in the hierarchy.'

'We don't give a damn, ma'am. Our orders are to arrest anybody destabilising a democratically-elected government. Sorry.'

Then, he asked his men to handcuff me. He gave me a rough push and his men led me away to the waiting Black Maria.

As for me, I was on the point of liquefying. There was an unnameable dread in my heart. What would I tell my father? He would go to pieces, just like my mother. I had spoken to him the previous evening, minutes before Isabella landed up at my house. I had told him everything was okay. And everything was okay at that point in time. I could feel my world collapsing. I cursed myself for being so stupid when just a few moments ago I had been lost in wonder at Isabella's courage.

The police station was a dingy hole, with broken chairs and other dilapidated furniture. The lock-up was a tiny 7x3 feet dungeon, where you could throw a man and absolutely forget about him. There was no one else.

The inspector had a big smile when he saw fear writ large upon my brows.

He placed himself behind me as a flunkey quickly opened the grill gate of a door for me. Once the gate was open, he delivered a tremendous kick on my bottom, such that I was precipitated into the lock-up, losing my balance and falling on my knees on the rough cement floor.

'Take good care of him,' said the inspector, lighting a cigarette between his lips. '*Kalakar aadmi hai.*' ('He's an artist')

Everybody laughed.

I had never felt so lonely and physically threatened in my life. I looked around for a chair or a bench to sit on and realised that the lock-up was without any furniture. I broke down and cried, silently.

A constable came a few minutes later with some dal and three stiff chapatis.

'Eat,' he said.

I looked at him with tears in my eyes.

'*Pehle sochna chahiye tha*,' ('You should've thought about it earlier,') said the man.

I thought about Isabella; perhaps similarly placed in the Cuffe Parade police station. I wanted to cry out in rage and frustration but was scared that it would invite further humiliation and, worse, violence. Soon, mosquitoes started buzzing around my head and settling on my arm. It was 35° C and there was no fan. I was perspiring like a pig. I could see people coming and going, paying no attention to me. A woman constable came and looked at me as if I was some rare specimen of insect retrieved from the tropical jungle surrounding Bombay. She looked at me for a while and said, '*Isko kyon pakda*?' ('What is he caught for?')

A male constable going through some papers looked up and said, 'Naxalite.'

'*Bambai mein*?' ('In Bombay?') she said, with

wonder in her voice.

'Discipline *ka zamana hai*, madam,' said the constable, shifting his paan from one cheek to the other, '*ab kisiko nahin chhodtey.*' ('It's a matter of discipline. No one is spared now.')

The female constable sniggered.

'*Sharif khandan ka ladka hai,*' ('He comes from a decent family,') she said.

'*Koi farak nahin padta*, madam,' ('Doesn't matter, madam,') said the paan-chewing constable at the other end of a long table. '*Yeh log garibon ka khoon chuskar khoon kharabi mein lagey rehtey hain.*' (These people suck the blood of the poor and cause bloodshed.')

Then, he laughed uproariously as if he had said something really funny.

At 6 am, another miserable wretch was shoved roughly into the lock-up.

'Salaam,' he said, with a wry smile.

'Salaam,' I said, miserably.

'*Tere ko kyon pakda*?' ('Why are you caught?') he said.

I must have had a pleading expression, for he said, '*Maara kya?*' ('Did they beat you?')

I shook my head.

'*Poltical*?' ('Political?') he said.

I could barely nod.

'*To koi sharam ki baat to hai nahin,*' ('There's nothing to be ashamed of,') he said. 'Myself, thief. *Pachchis ghariya mili hain, mere makaan se.*' ('25 watches have been retrieved from my home.')

Then, he giggled.

'*Teen ghantey mein* Magistrate *ke paas jaana hai,*' (I'll be taken to the Magistrate in 3 hours,') he said. '*Poltical ko* bail *milna asaan nahin hai. Lekin* jail *me bhi nahin bhejenge.* Cigarette *peeta hai*?' ('It's not easy to get bail in political matters. But, they won't send you to jail too. Do you smoke?')

I nodded.

He brought out a packet of Charminar, offered me one and then lit it with what seemed to be an expensive imported lighter.

I took a deep drag on the cigarette and for the first time felt in tune with everything going around me. They were going to the Magistrate to ask for custody. I felt my heart sinking to the bottom of my stomach.

'Lawyer *hai*?' ('Do you have a lawyer?') the thief finally spoke.

I shook my head. In broken Hindi I made him understand that my family would arrange for one. I asked him about him. There was this very thin solidarity creeping into our exchanges now. Both of us shared an experience, if not a destiny, and there was incipient camaraderie.

'*Mera sardar ayega,*' ('My leader would come,') he said, grinning and showing a perfect set of white teeth. '*Chhura ke ley jayega.*' ('He'd bail me out.')

Then, he said, '*Jabse yeh Kuttiya ney mergency lagaee hai, poltical logon ki neend haram kar rakhi hai.*' ('The people in politics have lost their sleep ever since the Bitch imposed Emergency.')

At 8 am, I had two visitors—my mother and a lawyer called Shobha Gadgil. Immediately, I sensed a tightening of nerves among the constables in my vision field.

The lawyer had the lock-up opened.

'You call this food?!' She screamed. 'Just water and some rock-hard chapatis?'

'Ma'am, we didn't know he would be brought in so early, there was nothing else,' said the constable.

'I want home-cooked food for my son,' shouted my mother.

Shobha Gadgil raised her hand and then spoke calmly, 'I want to speak to my client, confidentially.'

She and I were quickly led down a corridor at the end of which stood what I guessed was an interrogation chamber.

The constable brought out some keys and opened the door. He was about to close the door when Gadgil exclaimed, 'Don't lock us in! We'll be through in ten minutes.'

The constable hurriedly put the keys in his pants.

'All right,' Gadgil said, turning towards me.

'Did they physically harm you in any way?' she asked.

I said, 'No, but the inspector kicked me in the butt.'

She quickly took this down on the piece of paper she had.

'Okay, so we'll mention that to the Magistrate. Now,' she said, closing her eyes momentarily, 'you've done a silly thing, son. They have the evidence to implicate you and establish a prima facie case in front of the Magistrate. We are going to argue that you were an innocent and gullible young man hoodwinked by this Kandala girl—'

'Gondola,' I said, suddenly realising that they, the police and the lawyer, would use me to damn Isabella forever.

'But,' I said, and immediately Gadgil looked at me sharply, frowning.

'But, it's not illegal to distribute pamphlets and Party literature…'

I didn't know where I found the courage to say such a thing.

'It is,' said Gadgil. 'Her Party is banned, and they have all gone underground…'

She could make out I was nervous.

She offered me a cigarette, State Express. When I took it from her, I noticed that my hands were trembling slightly.

'Relax,' said Gadgil, 'we are going to get you out of this.'

Then, she asked me how I knew this girl, what all had I done with her, for her, whether I was sympathetic to the Naxalite cause, whether I had ever been caught for any criminal offence previous to this and so on and so forth.

Then, she said, 'Did you know what was in those boxes recovered from your house?'

I said, 'I did.'

'Well, you are not going to say that in court, okay. You are going to say you had no idea what was in the box. You are going to say that you understood that the material was related to the play you were going to put up at the Prithvi. Understood?'

I nodded. I was miserable. I knew I would have to leave Isabella in the lurch, that our defences were going to be separate, and that I was going to stab her in the back. I did not have the courage to say that I was not going to lie in court, leaving Isabella to fend for herself and take the whole blame.

'Just keep your mouth shut for today. This is going to be between me and the public prosecutor, okay. You are not going to be asked any questions, except the Judge. You have the right to remain silent and not incriminate yourself in anyway.'

So, I was taken to the sessions court where I saw Isabella sitting with her lawyer and her mother. She looked faded and colourless, as if she had been gang-raped. There was a welter on her right forearm. I looked at her as I was brought in by the cops and huddled into the police enclosure. She did not even acknowledge my presence. She was weeping silently. I did not know it was love.

The police said I was a dangerous person, and that I was in cahoots with Isabella and the other criminals planning to blow up Bombay House. To which Gadgil argued that the defendant had no political background, that he only knew the girl because she had offered to put up his play commercially at Prithvi theatre, and that she had wilfully exploited her cleint's good reputation and his gullibility to plant pamphlets and leaflets because she had been tipped off by an informer that a police raid was in the offing. She demanded the dismissal of the case for frivolity and non-lieu.

The Judge sent me to police remand for five days for questioning. As I was being led away by the cops, I looked at Isabella hoping to catch her eye and somehow convey that I was not responsible for my defence, and that I wished her well, but she stood stonily staring into the void.

This time, they took me to the Arthur Road jail and placed in solitary confinement in a cell larger than the one at the police station and better furnished. There was a proper bed with relatively clean sheets, a table and a fan.

In the afternoon, Nero, Ram and the Shah of Iran landed up to speak with me. Ram was well connected politically and knew some great lawyers personally. They all said they would vouch for my good conduct and my innocence in this case.

'You made a mess of things, bohemian dog,' said Shah.

'I mean, late night parcels from closet revolutionaries, how dumb can you get, especially in the present climate,' (this was mid-1976) said Ram.

Nero was the only one who took a sympathetic view of Isabella.

'That girl is in love with you,' said Nero. 'And your lawyer is twisting the knife into her flesh.'

'I don't want to be in prison,' I said miserably, not daring to look at Nero. 'I have to go by what my lawyer tells me.'

'Have they begun your interrogation?' said Ram.

'Not yet,' I said, 'I am scared shitless.'

'Don't be, you have a fine lawyer and the police don't usually use 3rd degree on high-profile detainees like you.'

'They're calling me motherfucker and sisterfucker routinely,' I said.

'That's just talk,' said Shah. 'Have they done anything to you?'

'Not yet,' I said, somewhat exasperated. 'But, their intentions are clear; they are out to incriminate me.'

At this point, my mother landed up with a large tiffin carrier. The Judge had okay-ed home food for me.

'Your father is furious,' she said. 'You should have known better. Now, it's too late. Eat well and sleep properly. Don't worry, we'll get you out of here. Shobha tells me that in the absence of positive evidence, the court will have no choice but to release you.'

The next day, my interrogation began at 6 am.

There was one thin cop with spectacles called Pradip Goradia accompanied by another bulky individual who stood around aimlessly.

'Listen, son,' said Goradia. 'We know you are not a Naxalite, okay. If you cooperate with us and let us pin down the other detainees who are well-known Naxalites, you can walk out of this jail a free man.'

'I don't know much,' I said.

'You know Isabella Gondola,' he said.

'Only slightly,' I said.

'You have been seen around her for quite some time

in the last few weeks. My superiors have instructed me to wring any information out of you incriminating that woman. You knew she was Naxalite, yes?'

I nodded, barely. I resented being a police informer. I was determined not to say anything that could be used against Isabella, sedition be damned.

'What did she tell you about her Party?'

'Nothing much. She said she belonged to the CPI (ML).'

'Did you know that she was part of an underground cell in the Party?'

'No, I didn't. We didn't discuss politics that much.'

'So how did you come to know her?'

'She met me at the college and wanted to put up a play I had written for a commercial audience.'

'You called the Prime Minister a bitch.'

I was surprised at the triviality of the interrogation. I couldn't see what Goradia was getting at, except that he wanted to nail that woman down and take the mickey out of her.

'Many people call her that,' I said, surprised at my own resistance. 'They don't all land up in jail.'

'But, you hate her, don't you?'

'I suppose so.'

'Why? Because she represents the class enemy?'

'Nothing of the sort,' I said, finding words that I didn't know I knew. 'It's because she has taken away our basic freedoms.'

'You understand the situation in the country? There

are people who are being financed by foreigners to destabilise this regime. We could make out a case that you are an objective accomplice in potential terrorist attacks. You use Chinese money.'

'That is preposterous.'

'Not that much,' said Goradia, and he promptly fished out a dossier full of newspaper clippings about how the Chinese were implanting their influence in the country through their Red Army Factions. Isabella was in correspondence with elements belonging to the Baader-Meinhof gang in Germany as well as the Red Army Faction in Japan.

My heart sank to the bottom of my stomach.

'I had no idea. She was just another pretty face in college.'

'If you can testify that you knew of Isabella Gondola's connections with terrorist networks abroad, we'll let you go.'

'I have to discuss this with my lawyer.'

'Of course, of course. Think about it. Think of your future in this country. I'll come back tomorrow and brief you about the results obtained from the interrogation of your accomplice in crime.'

I said nothing.

Two days later, Goradia and another policeman in dark glasses came into my cell and said, 'Come, you and your sweetheart are going to be interrogated together.' I was bundled into a jeep and taken to the crime branch at police headquarters next to the Prince of Wales

Museum. I was ushered into a long rectangular room with a long table and teak chairs all around. The room was air-conditioned.

'Sit,' said Goradia. 'This is Prafull Mahtab, DIG crime branch, Bombay Police. Wait here, we'll be back in a few minutes.'

There was a knot of fear just below the diaphragm. When they brought Isabella into the room, I was in a state of shock. There were large dark rings under her eyes, which were swollen—from crying? She was dressed in a plain white t-shirt and jeans. As soon as she saw me, her lips went aquiver and tears streamed down her cheeks. I wanted to tell her everything was alright, that I hadn't sold her down the drain. But, I could say nothing. I was scared of incriminating her inadvertently. Suddenly, things didn't look as simple anymore. I had to be always careful not to say anything that might put Isabella in deeper shit than she was. It was the DIG who began the interrogation.

'Do you know Raghunath Laskar?' he asked, pulling on his pipe.

'No,' I said truthfully.

'He was the author of the pamphlet found in your possession. He's also accused in multiple cases of homicide and theft of weapons from the government arsenal.'

'I don't know who wrote the pamphlets,' I said.

I suddenly noted that the interrogation was being conducted under CCTV surveillance. I was shaken by this and it did not escape the attention of the men questioning me.

'Did you know that Miss Gondola was a card-carrying member of the Communist Party of India, Marxist-Leninist?'

'Yes,' I said.

'And yet you say you had no idea of what was in the box handed over to you by Miss Gondola. How do you expect us to believe you?'

I glanced at Isabella with a pleading look. She seemed oblivious to her surroundings. She was nervously fidgeting with her fingers.

'It's the truth,' I said. 'I had no idea what was in the box.'

The DIG then turned to Isabella.

'He says he had no idea what was there in the box,' he said.

'That's correct,' said Isabella.

She had lied to save my skin.

I felt like a worm.

She was now dry-eyed, seemingly resigned to her fate.

'So, what did you tell him when you asked him to keep the box in his house?'

'I said it was publicity material for the play,' said Isabella.

'Which play?' the DIG asked, apparently ignorant of this.

Goradia butted in to say that I had written a play called *The Players* which had been somewhat successful on the college circuit.

'Oh, I see,' said the DIG. 'You are an artist, are you?'

'I just wrote a play,' I said wearily.

'So you took the box on the understanding that it contained publicity material for your play?'

'Yes, sir,' I said, not looking at Isabella, too ashamed of confronting her morally.

'You didn't open the box to see the material?' said the DIG.

'No,' I said.

'Are you in sympathy with Miss Gondola's political cause?' said the DIG.

'I don't know much about these things,' I said.

'You mean to say that these people didn't try to indoctrinate you?'

'No.'

'How much do you know about communism?'

'A little bit. Vaguely.'

'Vaguely? Could you elaborate?'

'The usual things. They want to violently overthrow the government. No private property. Things like that.'

'Do you know what differentiates the CPI (ML) from other communist outfits?'

'They have an insurgency going in North Bengal.'

'Let me enlighten you. They believe in the annihilation of the class enemy.'

I said nothing.

'Class enemy includes people like you.'

I shrugged and said, 'We never discussed politics.'

'Okay,' said the DIG. 'What about your parents? Would they be sympathetic to the Naxalite cause?'

'No question of that,' I said, gradually becoming aware of where they intended to take this conversation.

'No question, you say?' said the DIG. 'How are your relations with your parents? Do they approve of your artistic ambitions?'

'They are against it,' I said.

Then, suddenly, Isabella broke in.

'Why are you dragging his parents into the picture?' she said.

'Okay,' said the DIG, 'let's talk about *your* parents. Wasn't your paternal grandfather a member of the Hungarian Communist Party?'

'He was,' said Isabella, sighing heavily.

I was flabbergasted by the way the police had gone about investigating this matter.

'So,' said the DIG, 'do you have any communist genealogy?'

'Not that I know of,' I said.

'Would you say that your relationship with your parents is conflictual? Your father is a well-respected member of the flying fraternity.'

'You could say "conflictual",' I said. 'But, nothing very serious. Nothing to make me want to become a Naxalite, if that's what you are trying to make this out to be.'

'So you don't have an iota of sympathy for the Naxalites?' said the DIG.

I said nothing.

'Aha, so you say nothing?' said the DIG.

'They are marginal,' I said, 'they live on the periphery

of society,' I said.

There was a smile on the DIG's face.

'Do you consider yourself to be a marginal? A peripheral?'

'Sometimes. But, I wouldn't have the courage to throw a bomb at anybody.'

'Aha. So, you think throwing a bomb at an innocent person is an act of courage?'

'I don't know, I guess I am confused.'

'Do you know that Miss Gondola thinks your play is in the revolutionary vein? That it is anti-bourgeois? Anti-people like you?'

'She told me what she thought of the play.'

'And she said it was revolutionary?'

'Not in so many words.'

'But, generally, that was the impression she gathered?'

They were trying to get me to inculpate Isabella, I could see that clearly now.

'More or less.'

'Why,' said Isabella, 'are you trying to use him to denounce me?'

'You will speak,' said the DIG sharply, 'when you are spoken to.'

'You are fascists, male chauvinistic pigs,' she shouted back.

At this, the DIG leaned across the table and landed a slap on her face.

'Shut up!' he cried. 'We know how to deal with fashionable communists like you who sit in their rich daddy's pockets and dream of revolution in air-conditioned bedrooms.'

He then turned to me, livid with rage.

'Did you fuck this woman?' said the DIG.

'W-what?' I stammered.

'Did you fuck this woman?' he repeated, viciously.

'No!' I said, mildly outraged.

'She's not exactly a *Sati-Savitri*, y'know,' said the DIG, now with a sly smile playing on his lips. Goradia laughed.

I said nothing. I was stunned by this naked show of violence. My heart was pounding. If they could hit a woman in the presence of someone she considered a friend, they could beat the shit out of me if it crossed their minds to do so.

'So, you two are just friends, is it?' said the DIG, in a jocular vein now. 'Revolution first, sex later, is it?'

I said nothing. I didn't want Isabella to shed anymore tears in front of these bastards.

'What are your feelings for Miss Gondola?' said the DIG.

At this, I looked at Isabella, hoping for a signal.

Tears were flowing down her cheeks, but her look was vacant.

'She liked my play,' I said. 'She wanted to put up a commercial show at the Prithvi.'

'That's all?' said the DIG.

'That's all,' I said.

'Well, son...we don't believe you,' said the DIG, matter

of factly. 'Here is the deal: you sign this statement…'

He pushed an A4 sheet in front of me.

'…and we will dilute the charges against you, you'll be let off with a reprimand.'

I started reading the statement. I couldn't believe my eyes. It said that I was an unwilling tool in the whole conspiracy to blow up Bombay House, that Isabella had hoodwinked me into keeping dangerous propaganda material in my house and so on and so forth.

'I have to speak to my lawyer,' I said.

'Okay, have it your way,' said the DIG, roughly taking the piece of paper away. 'You will be charged under the relevant sections of the IPC regarding sedition and waging war against the state. Maximum sentence, which is very much the flavour of the town these days, is death.'

At that, I felt the colour draining from my face. I glanced furtively at Isabella and saw tears running down her cheeks. She wouldn't look back at me. I was in Hell. So they took both of us back to the Arthur Road Jail and we went to our separate wards without having uttered a single word to the other.

The next morning, a burly warden turned up at 8 am, took out a bunch of keys and opened the grill to my cell.

I was taken to the superintendent's office where I found my mother and my lawyer sitting and chatting. The superintendent, a bespectacled man, affable and jocular despite his grim surrounding, looked up as I entered his office and smiled at me.

'Hello, Sam,' he said, with a broad smile never leaving

his face. 'You are a free man. We don't really have a case against you. There is some paper work which Shobha will take care of. You are free to go.'

I sat down next to my lawyer, trying to appear as feebleminded and contrite as possible. Next, we were led into a dingy window-less room with a single 40-watt bulb. There were forms to be filled up and signed and an 8-page statement saying I had no relations of any kind with Isabella Gondola, and would not try to contact or meet her in any way in pursuance of the legal matter under investigation, that I forgo all rights devolved upon me with regard to the production of my play, the licence for the commercial production of it would be cancelled in perpetuity—that was the exact language, that I was being let off for good conduct and in deference to the permission given to my parents to exercise the rights of guardianship over me, that I would not renew any contact, in whatever way possible, with the CPI (ML). Once I signed everything and handed over the bunch to a warden, the superintendent waddled into the room, belly thrust proudly out, and said, 'Be careful in the future, son, we will be watching you very carefully over the next few months. Behave, if not for your sake, then for the sake of your excellent family. Don't besmirch their name in public.'

At this, I smiled at him shyly and nodded vigorously at everything he said.

'You have a great future ahead of you, son, don't spoil it with these vile and pernicious writings of yours. Think of the nation first. Yeah? Okay?'

Then he lightly patted me on the back and addressing my mother said, 'He will make you proud one day.'

With that, we left prison. The only thing I had to look forward to was some food with the family.

At home, my father was waiting for me. He had a face like dark thunder.

Without any preliminaries, he launched into a tirade against me.

'So, you think your father is a poor airline pilot who wouldn't know his Bernard Shaw from Shakespeare. Who do you think you are? Where did you get this drivel of a play from? It's utterly disgusting. You should be in a lunatic asylum! I had to talk to Rajiv who pulled the right strings in Delhi to get you off the hook. You should thank your stars that you have a father like me who is well-connected enough to deal with situations like this. I don't want a son who is an anti-social drifter like you, bent on spoiling his future by keeping dangerous company and writing this gibberish for his intellectually fashionable friends. No late night parties! No bringing girls into the house! You understand?! Stop all this nonsense about art and stuff like that and concentrate on your studies! That's why you are in college! From now on, you will do exactly as you are told! We don't deserve this hassle! Now go to your room and think about your future! Understood?!'

The next morning, I was back at the Sydenham canteen where the Shah of Iran and Nero Gomes were having coffee.

As soon as the Shah of Iran saw me, he shouted out, 'Hey, Sammy boy, you bohemian dog! How come you are out? We'd almost given up on you.'

'The jail warden told us,' said Nero, 'that meeting you would be tantamount to aiding and abetting the offences with which you were charged. We got scared, man!'

'What about your chick? Is she out too?' said Ram.

'I don't know,' I said, feeling like a slime-ball. The cops had broken our spirit of solidarity, our comradeship. I couldn't tell them that.

So, I said, 'They made me sign on a piece of paper saying that I will keep my distance from dangerous, extremist, unpatriotic political formations and that I would not endeavour any further to push my play for a commercial production.'

'In other words, you sold out,' said Ram.

'The alternative was being hanged for treason,' I said, not looking at anybody in particular.

Everybody fell silent.

'It's all right, Sam,' said Nero Gomes. 'We understand.'

'I have been categorised as an anti-social under the Goonda Act. Every time something goes wrong, they will have the right to lock me up at the thana. My father has laid down a curfew, I have to be back home by 9 pm latest every day. Thank God for ganja!'

'That's the spirit, boy,' said Feridoon and slapped me on the back.

'Your daddy pulled strings for you to get you out?' said Shah.

I nodded glumly.

'Bad luck, man,' said Ram.

The bell sounded and everybody broke up for class.

A few months later, the Bitch lifted the Emergency and amnestied all political prisoners. It didn't register on my mind that Isabella Gondola would be free until I saw her walking down the corridor, looking heavenly in a faded pair of jeans and a white top. She had her head bowed and passed me by without uttering a word. I felt like a cad, but it didn't weigh on my mind much. I was, of course, overjoyed that the Bitch had been forced to withdraw the state of siege, and the Gang went over to the bar behind Eros cinema and had ourselves umpteen bottles of beer. People were out on the streets shouting 'Long live Democracy, Long live *Azadi*'.

The atmosphere was festive, electric. Even at home, my folks were happy. Dad had gone on furlough and we planned a trip to Goa. I couldn't see the point in travelling with the rest of the family, but I went along anyway, what the hell. We stayed at the Aguada and had a whale of a time on the private beach guzzling down cocktails like nobody's business. Everything was fine, except that I didn't have anything to say to anybody. But, nobody noticed, so taken were we by the general atmosphere of political excitement around us. Even the waiters said, 'Long live freedom, sir'. One of the first thoughts I had was that I could now write whatever my imagination suggested to me. This was the time I started going deep into the European avant-garde—Rimbaud, Baudelaire,

Lautreamont, Tristan Tzara, Alfred Jarry, Artaud and a few others.

Back at the canteen, they were offering free cups of Freedom Tea of which we partook copiously. Feridoon was throwing a party and had asked me to bring a girl along. But, soon I found out that my dad had no intention of relaxing the draconian curbs he had placed on my movements.

I told him that everyone was going and that this was just to celebrate our freedom. But, he would have none of it.

'Freedom doesn't mean anything goes,' he said. 'Especially, not with the company you keep.'

'What company?' I asked astounded. 'Some of these guys took the risk of coming and meeting me in jail.'

'I don't want you to be running around with women without knowing who they are and what they want. You don't know what's good for you.'

'So, you're going to tell me what's good for me?'

'You bet I am. You don't have enough sense to fit on a needle top.'

'I am going, and we'll see who stops me,' I shouted.

At this, my father looked stunned. But, only for a couple of seconds.

'If you do, nobody will open the door for you after 10 pm,' he said evenly.

'So I'll sleep out on the streets if that's what you want.'

'The discussion is over,' he said firmly.

I was in tears as I made my way to my room where

my brother was waiting to offer his two penny's worth of advice.

'You seem to be drifting aimlessly,' he said.

'I will, if that's what I want,' I said.

'Have you thought about pursuing a career? I mean, freedom is a wonderful thing, but the bottom line is you have to have money in your pocket.'

'I don't care, I will find something. Everyone does.'

'Don't you have any ambitions? Any dreams about what you want to do in life?'

I said nothing.

To say that I wanted to be a writer to my family was as tough as to say I love you to a girl. They would think I was mad, or worse, sub-human.

'What about journalism?' said my brother, sensing the edge of my silence. 'They pay pretty well nowadays.'

'I'll think about it when the time comes.'

'It might be too late to leave it till then.'

'I have another two years in college.'

'Suit yourself. As for me, I am not going to touch a penny from Dad after I pass out from Elphinstone.'

'It would be demeaning,' he said, after a pause.

'I don't care,' I said, bringing the conversation to a close.

So, I went to Feridoon's party. There were girls all over the place and I was petrified by the prospect of inviting one of them to dance with me. I didn't know anyone out there except a few members of the Gang. Nero Gomes was there and he was being piled upon by one of the women.

I sat by myself in a corner, guzzling Johnny Walker Black Label nervously. Ram turned up, lit himself a joint and passed it to me after a few preliminary puffs. I inhaled deeply, letting the toxin invade my lungs. 'I don't need a woman,' I told myself. I took some food, delicious Parsi stuff, ate it by myself and then went home without telling anybody. Fortunately, I was well within curfew time and my dad was in Delhi.

'You've been drinking again,' said my mother.

'Just a couple of whiskies,' I said.

'Did you meet that girl?'

'Which girl?'

'You know which one I am talking about, the one who landed us in a mess.'

'You mean, Isabella?' I said, surprised that the threat should linger after everything that had happened. 'She isn't into parties and stuff.'

'Don't you dare have anything to do with her again.'

***

'Isabella Gondola is back,' announced Ram Bhonsle. 'And, she isn't playing.'

Ram looked at me pointedly.

'What am I supposed to say?' I said.

'You sold her down the drain. You made separate peace with the Bitch,' said Ram.

'That's got nothing to do with me. It was my family—' I said.

'Your Dad went and licked Rajiv Gandhi's arse.'

'I am not here to defend my Dad.'

'Anyway, it's a good thing,' said the Shah of Iran. 'She's way too hot for you to handle.'

I shrugged. I was not in love with Isabella. But, deep down, the thought rankled. I didn't want to discover what lay there, deep down.

The question of the play and its commercial release came up.

'I think we should put it up at the Prithvi,' said Nero.

'That means big bucks,' I said. 'We don't have that kind of money.'

'We'll raise a fund. I am sure Jiten would only be pleased to help. We could touch the college for some money. Twenty thousand isn't an exorbitant amount.'

'It's a lot of money.'

'You could get Indian Airlines to sponsor the play,' said Ram.

'Are you crazy?' I said. 'My dad would kill me.'

So, we took the play to the youth festival at IIT Madras. There were five of us: Nero Gomes, Parag Trivedi, Ravi Sundaram, Rajiv Sahasrebuddhey and myself. I took five hundred bucks with me and a large-ish stick of hashish. We landed there on a Saturday and were immediately plunged into the thick of things. There was a short story writing competition for which we entered Parag Trivedi. The theatre contest was to begin the following Tuesday. We had enough time to acclimatise ourselves and to rehearse. Since Jiten hadn't come along, I had to fill in for the role of Flap. I was no actor. Only, without mikes we had to shout to be heard from the last row in the auditorium. That helped me to get into the rhythm and groove of the play. We came second. The local IIT gazette said they were glad to note that Beckett was alive and well in Sydenham. The campus was abuzz with rumours that five guys from Bombay were cleaning up all the medals in individual categories. We also went on a gourmet cuisine binge, lunching out at the Chinese restaurant next door to the IIT at Adyar or on Mount Road and the excellent Punjabi Dhaba we discovered there. I was also ogling at a girl called Renuka Reuben, a dark and beautiful specimen of womanhood who was smoking away nonchalantly at the cafeteria. Nero Gomes went over and asked her whether she would join us for drinks later in the day.

At exactly half past seven, we, the four of us, minus Sahasrebuddhey, turned up for our rendezvous with Reuben, only to find that she was not there. We were on the verge of leaving when we heard a strident 'Hello' behind us. It was Reuben dressed in a sheer silk kanjivaram saree. She had a triangular bindi on her forehead. We went and occupied a table just being evacuated by some local boys. I started rolling myself a joint. Reuben took out a packet of Marlboros and offered us some fags.

'So, where are you guys from?' she said, archly.

'From Bombay,' we said, in unison.

'Sydenham College,' I added, helpfully.

'That's a commerce college isn't it?' asked Reuben.

We said yes.'

Nero did the presentations. Coming to me, he said 'This is Sam, the bohemian dog.'

At this, Reuben smiled.

'Are you a model?' I asked.

'I have done some stupid ads,' she said, blowing smoke away from us. 'The money is useful.'

'So, where are you from, Renuka?' said Nero.

'Loreto College, Bangalore. You guys know Bangalore?'

'Not really,' said Nero.

'It's a one-horse town full of retired people,' she said.

'Madras is no better,' I said. 'You still have gender segregation in public transport. That's infantile.'

'Tamil culture,' she said blowing rings into my face.

'What are you here for?' said Nero.

'For the theatre,' she said. 'We put up Albee's *Who's Afraid of Virginia Woolf?*. Outside the competition.'

'Albee's interesting,' I said. 'But mostly college guys go for *The Zoo Story*.'

'That's easier to do,' said Reuben. 'You don't need props or anything; it's just two guys hanging out and talking.'

'Did you see our play?' said Nero.

'No, but I have heard a lot of good things about it,' said Reuben crushing out the cigarette in the large ashtray in front of her.

I lit my joint and inhaled long, hard and deep.

'Do you want some of this?' I said.

'Sure,' she said.

From her short, perfunctory puffs, I gathered she

wasn't really into this kind of stuff.

'Umm,' she said. 'This is good stuff, I have asthma so it helps.'

I had a big grin on my face.

'Are you guys coming for the big party on Saturday? You should, this place is full of geeks and nerds; we need some ordinary people around,' she said.

'There's the quiz tomorrow in which Sam is going to be our mascot,' said Nero.

'Sure, I'll come,' said Reuben.

We invited her to have dinner with us after the quiz.

She said yes to that too. But, she was looking directly at Nero when she said this.

'You don't look like a Bohemian, Nero,' she said, the first time she called any of us by our names.

'I am not,' said Nero. 'My big thing is a career in the private sector after I get out of Sydenham, next year.'

'Umm, business,' she echoed.

***

On Saturday, they had a big stage close to the deer park and a local student band called the Electric Frogs playing soul, funk and some classic rock 'n' roll. Everybody was moving in rhythm to the music with Renuka Reuben, sitting and staring at the whole scene. It was Nero who first proposed to Reuben that they dance to one of the slower numbers and Reuben accepted with alacrity. The rest of us sat around and watched her going crazy over the live music. Nero was having a hard time keeping pace with her. The next song was even slower and we saw Reuben clinging on to Nero for dear life.

'There goes your quarry,' said Parag to me.

'Man, she is not my private property, is she?' I said.

'You would give half an arm to lay her,' said Parag.

'Sure, but that's not happening, this time around, alas!'

Nero and Reuben were necking and smooching like mad by then.

After the number was over, Reuben and Nero decided they needed a break.

They came to where we were sitting and Nero plonked down on one of the unoccupied chairs and immediately, before everyone could realise, Reuben sat down in Nero's lap and straight away started caressing and planting kisses on his face, his eyes, licking his ears. Her big boobs were crushed against Nero's torso. I watched the show, overawed by Nero's capacity to arouse a woman's primal instinct without any help from hashish.

The evening progressed at a leisurely pace when suddenly the band started playing *Cocaine*. The whole place came alive suddenly. At first, people stood by tapping their feet to the rhythm and then started swaying to it, shouting out 'Cocaine' every time the refrain came around. We were no exceptions. We all stood up, singing along with the band, jumping up and down, revelling in the original guitar solo, looking at the sheer number of women up on their feet and adapting their bodies to the pace of the JJ Cale number. It didn't matter that we had no women to dance with or that the rest of us were too timid to ask a girl out to dance; we were just delirious with joy.

When the song got over, Nero and Reuben were nowhere to be seen.

'Nero boy is getting laid,' said Parag with a big grin on his face. 'What happened, bohemian dog, you were supposed to be the leader.'

'Fuck leadership,' I said, 'let's go and have dinner somewhere.'

And that's how the evening ended for the rest of us from Sydenham.

Next morning, Nero came and greeted us with a big smile.

We clapped in approval.

'How was she?' I said.

'Like an atom bomb,' said Nero, the smile never leaving his face.

'Did she refuse fellatio?' said Parag.

'No, she didn't,' said Nero. 'What about you guys?'

'We had dinner,' I said.

'That's not good enough,' said Parag. 'Nero, you lucky man!'

We had breakfast at the mess, cold idlis that gave you a headache with their lacklustre taste.

Then, we took the train back to Bombay.

The next day at the college, Feridoon broke the news.

I was sitting in the canteen having tea with the Shah

of Iran and Chandra, when Feridoon walked up to me and said, 'Bad news, Sammy boy, your girlfriend, Isabella, has had an accident. Her father is in hospital battling for his life; apparently his rib cage got smashed against the steering and your sweetheart took a shower of glass upon her face as the windscreen shattered to smithereens.'

And then, it suddenly struck like a hammer blow to my cortex.

I was in love with this girl. The light went out from my eyes.

Feridoon nodded at me, not smiling.

'She's at the railway hospital in Bombay Central. Visiting hours are from 9 to 11 in the morning and 5 to 7 in the evening. I suggest you go there immediately.'

I was feeling numb with pain; I was overcome with a melancholic lethargy. For the first time in many years, a prayer went up from my heart. It said, 'Please, God, don't let anything happen to that girl. I will die if anything happens to her.'

I got up from the table in a daze.

'Don't forget to take some flowers, you dumb, two-timing oaf!' Feridoon said.

***

I saw her sitting on her bed surrounded by her friends.

Her face lit up when she saw me approaching.

I placed a bouquet of yellow roses on her lap and said, 'How are things?'

Stupid, stupid, stupid! My heart was throbbing wildly, and all I could think of saying was how she was doing.

She lifted her hands to her face and said, '118 stitches.'

Her face had been done up like a patchwork quilt. There were threads all over the place.

Then, I noticed a couple of bearded guys with *jholas*, smelling of bidi smoke, looking at her intently, not saying a word.

She introduced me to them and said, 'Guys, this is Sammy, the famous playwright from Sydenham. Sam, this is Sauruv and Guddu. They are from the Party.'

I looked in their direction, but they were not interested in me.

I said, 'Hello.'

They said, 'Hello.'

Then, something terrible happened. For a flash, I was seized by vertigo. I was already terrified by my feelings for this girl. What was even more terrifying was her feelings for me. I was standing on the edge of a precipice and looking down at the rocks and the sea below. I didn't know what to say, how to say it or whether to say it at all. The boys from the Party intimidated me. I was cowed down by their presence. An image of my father crossed my mind. That image was saying, 'Beware.' But then, I had always been reckless.

'Sam,' said Isabella, 'we'll get to work on your play for a launch at the Prithvi as soon as I get out of this mess.'

'Okay,' I said in a small voice. 'I am more worried about you than anything else at the moment.'

'Please don't worry about me, Sam,' she said, obviously pleased at this show of concern. 'I will be out of here in a couple of weeks. How is the rest of the Gang?'

'They're okay, I suppose,' I said timidly. 'It was Feridoon who broke the news about your accident. How's your father?'

'He's in the ICU,' she said, her tone serious, 'his ribs are all messed up at the moment.'

I stayed there for another half an hour, till the visiting hours were over, chatting about this and that. I left the hospital in a state of deep depression. How to say to this girl that I loved her beyond anything else, and that I wanted to spend the rest of my life with her? I wasn't even aware that she would have to take permission from the Party before any kind of formalisation of our relationship. The dull ache never went away.

I was in deep doubt about how I was going about handling my emotions and the way the relationship was growing. I could see that to take this forward, I would have to tell her about my feelings for her and that is something that continued to terrify me. I was terrified about standing naked before her.

Two weeks went by in a flash. Her scars had healed completely and Isabella was back to being her beautiful self—beautiful not only physically, but also morally. I spotted her at a distance turning into B Street and I ran for my life. I didn't want to meet or talk to her or have anything to do with her. My only obsession was to mask my true feelings for her. Vertigo never let go of me entirely. I had difficulty believing that a girl like her could possibly love a failure like me. My father's presence loomed ever so large in my mind. He would just explode if I told him the truth. First of all, he would bring up religion. How can I marry a Christian? A cultural alien? But for me, part of Isabella's appeal lay in the fact that she was Roman Catholic. I conjured up images of a community living for love, where boys and girls weren't segregated, that had well-defined customs for seduction and courtship. I had no doubt that I would be very happy to be assimilated by Isabella's community. Only, and this is something I understood from everything she said about herself, Isabella had no religion.

She never went to church, she never prayed to God, and, contrary to what she believed, her father had always known of her membership of the CPI (ML). Her father had been a part of the League of Young Communists when he was a student in Delhi. He thought, Isabella told me, that this was a passing fad and that she would grow out of her radical Left convictions. From what I could gather though, this was not going to happen anytime soon.

Back at Sydenham, she suddenly came up to us and plonked herself next to me at 'our' table. Everyone welcomed her with open arms, asking about her health and her father's condition. She gave matter of fact replies.

'I heard you guys had a ball down south?' she said.

I looked at Nero and smiled.

Parag explained, 'He was the only guy to score with some chick called Renuka Reuben.'

Nero laughed at the thought.

'She's been writing desperate letters to him ever since,' said Parag.

'Not desperate,' said Nero. 'She wants to come to Bombay and settle down here if possible.'

'She has the hots for you Nero,' I said.

'Oh, c'mon Sam, it was nothing like that,' said Nero modestly. 'She just took a fancy to me, nothing long term about it. She wants to come to Bombay because she's dying of boredom in Bangalore.'

At that precise point, the Shah of Iran came and straightaway started rolling a joint.

'Hey, you guys,' he said, 'have you heard the news? The Bitch lost her election to her own seat and the Party has been decimated.'

'Chhotu!' shouted Ram Bhonsle. 'A bottle of coke each for everybody.' And then, turning to Isabella said, 'She was a creature from Hell.'

'Much worse, actually,' said Isabella. 'She's a very insecure person, psychologically. It was her son who was running the show all the time. Along with some religious Hindus.'

'Dhirendra Brahmachari,' said Ram. 'It seems they were fornicating together.'

'That may be Hindu right-wing propaganda,' said Isabella. 'But yes, she was up to her gills in Hindu shit, anyway.'

'Just shows that Hindu shit does not necessarily win elections,' I said.

'You never know,' said Shah. 'The idea of her leadership matches neither her rhetoric nor her ideological postures. People may, in fact, be holding back from endorsing her whole-heartedly. We'll see after five years…'

Feridoon was the next to amble into the canteen.

'Guys,' he said, 'my father is so kicked about the results, he gave me 2000 bucks to spend. I suggest we all go to Samarkand for some coffee and lemon tarts.'

'Yay!' was the unanimous chorus.

Some of us piled onto Feridoon's Cadillac, while Shah, Nero, Isabella and I decided to walk it out. It was a beautiful monsoon morning with overcast sky and a strong wind blowing across from the sea.

'Listen, you guys,' said Isabella, 'how soon do you think we'll be able to put up a professional, slick presentation of Sam's play?'

'One month,' said Nero.

'We'll need someone to handle lights and audio,' said I.

'I'll look after that,' said Isabella. 'I'll talk to Sanjana and see if we can get a booking for a dress rehearsal next month. You guys just look after the performance; I'll handle the production, okay?'

'Okay,' I said.

'Everything must go like clockwork,' said Isabella. 'Going from what I saw at the College, you guys were really good at the presentation. If you can maintain that quality we'll just sail through.'

'Shouldn't be a problem,' I said. 'Only thing, for me,

is to attract the public with an unknown work by an unknown writer which presents a number of difficulties relating to the understanding of the matter. How do you explain the Void in a commercial theatre context? And, we are dealing with minimalism here. No sets, no costumes, no conventional theatricality.'

'Sam,' said Isabella, 'just do the play as you did it on the college circuit and leave the rest to me. We have to attract a young audience, that's all, people who are just stepping into the world for the first time and discovering there isn't all that much to go by.'

'That's it,' said Shah. 'Not only is there not much to go by, you are being bombarded at the same time. The world is not an innocent by-stander while tragedy unfolds in front of it, because of it. It is an accomplice.'

'In your fight against the world,' said Nero, 'back the world. That's Kafka for you.'

'That sounds correct,' I said. 'I am a pessimist.'

'You guys get discouraged even before anything has been done,' said Isabella, trying to keep the wind out of her unruly, luxuriant locks. 'Let's at least give it a shot and then see what happens.'

'It's a lot of money to throw on something that we all doubt will appeal to a public, whether mainstream or marginal,' said Shah.

'Twenty thousand bucks,' said Isabella. 'My dad spends as much on whisky in a month.'

'Eh, Sammy, you lucky dog!' said Shah, 'how come you are looking crestfallen, you crazy bum?!'

I love this woman, said a voice inside my head.

'No-no,' I said, 'I am not crestfallen, I was just thinking that rationality is also some kind of an impasse, a cul de sac, y'know. At least that's what the play is about.'

'Sam,' said Isabella, smiling at me, 'you've got such a tremendous sense of dialogue, you should quit studying commerce and take up writing full-time.'

'My father will jump off the 7th floor if I told him that,' I said.

'Nobody is asking you to repudiate your family,' said Isabella, 'but you should make up your mind. For me, you are a writer and always will be one, no matter how precarious your financial situation. I could give you a stipend of 5000 bucks, y'know, just to spend your days and nights doing what makes you happy.'

'It was mind-boggling. I am not sure I'll write another play in my life. This one is a bit of a blast of inspiration. My head has stopped singing since I went to prison.'

At this, Isabella jerked her head away sharply and then back again. Her eyes, I could see, were moist.

I was pleased with the power I had over her. I was proud that I was her Chosen Man.

'What if I just took the stipend and bummed around boozing and smoking,' I said.

'You have an artist's conscience, Sam, you are the real thing; you are the only real thing I've met in life. I would hate to see you give up...'

'Hey, Sam, you bohemian dog,' said the Shah of Iran, 'you lucky dog, I would give my right arm for a deal like this, and you…you get metaphysical!'

'I just said I can write,' I said, 'I don't know if that is all it takes to be a writer.'

We swung into the lobby of the Sheraton and quickly made for Samarkand, the circular coffee shop with a glass façade facing Marine Drive in all her glory. They joined three tables together. Isabella and I took our seats at the left end and the others took their place around the curve.

'Anybody interested in having a bite?' asked Feridoon. 'I am ravenous. How about prawn cocktails and wontons?'

Everybody put up their hands.

When the prawn cocktails were served, Feridoon, joined by his steady girlfriend, a quiet Parsi girl called Aisha, raised his glass and said, 'Long live Freedom!'

'Long Live Freedom,' we roared after him. The other guests in the room looked in our direction and smiled at us. Everybody was in a mood to celebrate.

'God, how I love this place,' said I to Isabella.

'You mean Samarkand?' said Isabella.

'No-no, I mean Bombay. It's beautiful to look at, it's intelligent to talk to, it will always fight for its identity; it will never give up on its dreams.'

'You're a poet, Sam. 'I don't see Bombay that way at all. I see it as an exploitative entity that lives off the poor without giving much in return. What you had during the last two years were workers betraying other workers. There was no class solidarity; people just saw opportunities for the vile and the despicable and gladly took those opportunities. Would you like to go to one of our meetings in Lower Parel, within the compound of a cotton mill that's about to be closed down?'

'Yes.'

'Great! I'll get in touch with the Organising Secretary.'

'And you,' I said, trying to look shrewd, 'now that your cover is blown, of what use are you to the Party, except some moolah.'

Isabella shrugged, 'I guess I will go underground again; our cell is regrouping, but for the moment I can stick to overt actions like getting the unions activated, getting new recruits, distributing literature in public...'

'In public?' I asked, suddenly interested. 'Where exactly?'

'Kurla, Parel, Mahim, Dadar, Sion...the ugly part of Bombay.'

'I heard that the unions are all run by the mafia.'

'That's right-wing propaganda. But yes, elements from the mafia do arbitrate some deals, especially in real estate. But we are talking about textile mills, the lifeline of Bombay. They are all growing obsolete and outdated, while new players muscle in on the deal. There is someone called Datta Samant who is a rising star. He is not affiliated to any political Party. It's the parties who are running after him, trying to stake out territories for themselves. The big loser is the traditional left. Interested in politics, Sam?'

'Only superficially. Don't have the guts for it.'

'You should remain this way. Never change, Sam, not for anybody's sake. Your father's, least of all.'

'I'll have to earn my living at some point in time.'

'I was so ashamed of getting you involved with the Party. I didn't know my cover had been busted so badly…'

There were tears in her eyes.

I had no response to her emotions, especially in public when the Gang was around. They were all tough guys who didn't dance to anybody's tune. They would look down on me if they saw me getting all mushy and sentimental.

'It was,' I lied, 'an exhilarating experience. But, I felt like a worm following my lawyer's advice. They made me pour more shit on you than was warranted. How did it go in prison? I mean, if you want to talk about it, of course…'

'Enhanced interrogation techniques. They rarely hit me. Maybe once or twice. But, it was more about breaking down my resistance. They wouldn't let me sleep properly; they kept up an awful din near my cell. They would switch off the current on nights that were particularly muggy. That brought on the mosquitoes without coils or repellent creams. Solitary confinement. I asked for books, they flatly refused. Political prisoners are not your garden-variety criminals; their fate doesn't depend on the law, but on the whims and fancies of whoever thinks he has that kind of authority to wield. The cops are not told to do any specific thing; but they all understand, instinctively, what would please the authorities the most and they do it. That includes 3rd degree. You know, they got the bar association to pass a resolution that no traitor to the country will be represented. I didn't have a lawyer after the first week or so. And, the Party didn't help because they did not want to expose those whose affiliations were secret.'

'What was your worst moment?'

'A big, fat oily cop came to my cell, unzipped himself, took out his ugly cock and peed right into my cell.'

I was shocked beyond words and it showed.

Isabella just smiled back at me.

'What did they want, specifically?' I said.

'Names,' said Isabella. 'Names of the other members of my cell, the underground cadre.'

'Did you give it to them?'

'They tried everything to shake the information out of me by breaking my resistance,' said Isabella. 'The guy in the cell next to mine was criminally lunatic. He would be hollering obscenities all through the night. I had no access to radio or the papers. During my periods, they wouldn't give me any sanitary napkins. There was blood dripping down my legs. I was lying there like an animal.'

'What happened to your family? Did they get harassed too?'

'Everybody. My Dad was brought in for questioning, face to face with me. They tried to get him to incriminate his own daughter.'

At this, Isabella's lips began to quiver and tears flowed down her cheeks.

'That must have been the worst part,' I said, gently.

'They tried to humiliate him through me. They asked

him if I had kept count on my boyfriends. Did he know that I was no longer a virgin…stuff like that.'

I took out my handkerchief and handed it to her.

'But,' she said, wiping away the tears, 'the worst of all was their attempt to incriminate you. I said you were totally innocent….They asked me to sign on blank sheets of paper which they would subsequently fill according to their own requirements.'

'Did you sign any…,' I asked.

She shook her head.

'Did they get physical with you?' I asked.

'They got a lady constable to beat me up. She used her baton on me; she left me black and blue.'

I didn't know what to say.

'How did your family take it?' I asked.

'Dad was pretty cool about it. My grandfather was in the Young Communist League back in Budapest, during the war. Dad knows everything one needs to know about the cops and communists. My mother though was very upset that I hadn't told anybody about me joining the Naxals. She said how could I be so stupid? I couldn't tell her there were things more important than survival.'

'I feel terrible,' I said.

'Don't, Sam. It's all right now. I am free. The Bitch is out of power. I am going to be as free as I was before. My objective now is to put up a show for your play. Let's go to my house and discuss things. My family wants to meet you too.'

'Okay,' I said quietly.

She stayed in an apartment block called Horizon. We took the lift up to the 21st floor. I walked into an apartment that was at once simple and elegant. I could see that her parents, unlike mine, had a lot of taste backed by money, and that thought had gone into designing living spaces. We were greeted at the door by an attractive middle-aged Goan lady with short hair and a bewitching smile.

'Hello, Mrs Gondola,' I said as I shook hands with Isabella's mother.

'Hello,' she said, 'You must be Sam.'

I nodded shyly.

'Ma,' said Isabella, 'Sam is having lunch with us.'

'Do you eat beef, Sam?' Mrs Gondola asked me.

'Yes, I do,' I said.

'Okay,' said Mrs Gondola, 'we're going to have beef vindaloo and pomfret balchao for lunch. You guys just go and relax.'

I smiled shyly.

We went to Isabella's room which had one large poster of Che Guevara and another of Jimi Hendrix. The room had a view of the sea. There was an atmosphere to this room. I thought of the room I shared with my brother—so plain and ordinary, so lukewarm and bland.

'We'll put on some music,' said Isabella. 'Do you like Janis Joplin?'

'Yes, yes,' I said.

She fished out an album out of a rack which must have contained around 200 LPs. The album was called

Janis Joplin and the *Big Brother and the Holding Company*.

And then, just like that, I was tongue-tied. I had this stupid smile on my face, while my mind went, I love this woman. My heart was pounding wildly in my rib cage. Then, it started raining.

We discussed the play.

She said, 'Maybe we can get Naseeruddin Shah to play one of the characters.'

I didn't know what to make out of that. I had watched Shah and Benjamin Gilani play Godot at the Prithvi and had found them awful. I told Isabella so. I said I wouldn't be up to controlling Shah's native temper on stage and the eccentric liberties he took with the written text. Plus, the play went beyond the star system in Bollywood. I didn't want film actors on my play to attract the wrong kind of audience.

'Makes sense,' said Isabella, drawing long and hard on her Marlboro Light. 'So, no big stars, just Nero and Jiten.'

'They are the best,' I said. 'They know the play and they know what I want out of them. They're the only ones who would know the inner stagecraft mechanics of the action.'

'Okay,' said Isabella. 'Let's do the costing. Sanjana has read the play and found it very powerful. It's just the kind of play she wants to put up at Prithvi. She's willing to rent it out at ten thousand bucks per day. So, let's suppose we have two full dress rehearsals there, plus weekend shows with an audience, that comes to fifty thousand bucks.'

Just then, the phone rang.

Isabella picked it up and said, 'Hello.'

And then, she said, 'My God, is that really you Bobby? Where have you been? Swaziland? What on earth were you doing in Swaziland? Ha ha ha. Listen, why don't you come over…right now…I want you to meet someone… no-no-no, this isn't political…I want you to meet Sam, he's a budding playwright that I am sponsoring for a production at Prithvi…come over for beer and then lunch, okay?...Okay.'

I was staring hard at her, registering each and every twitching of a muscle. What she said next drove a stake through my heart.

'You must meet Bobby, he's a friend from school, he went off to the States to dabble in computers or some such thing…he's back in Bombay and wants to meet you. Bobby incidentally is a direct heir of the Maharaja of Peepli. He's very hoity-toity, very Doon School and St Stephen's and then Columbia and now he is in Fresno. You must meet him, he's quite a character. He's been around the world on a catamaran.'

I thought it best to smile. My father wouldn't let me out of sight within Nepean Sea Road, leave alone Swaziland. Suddenly, there was rage inside. Rage for what? For all the things I couldn't be for Isabella.

Ten minutes later, I was being introduced to Debraj Roy, Kunwar sahib of Peepli. He was taller than me, very handsome, with long gently curling locks, and was dressed snazzily in a black denim shirt from Pepe and a pair of Levis 501 that hugged his long slender legs and tapered off at the bottom. He wore a small padlock on a chain around his neck and had a small silver earring pierced through the lobe of his right ear. He and Isabella hugged each other. And then, she looked at him.

That is when I felt the first stab of jealousy.

Bobby Roy was all solicitousness and politeness in an indifferent sort of way towards me. He asked me several questions about my play and I tried my best not to sound pretentious. But, I wasn't intellectual enough to satisfy something in him that I recognised to be an inborn talent for simplification. My words were being jumbled up in his presence. I wanted to create a scene, walk out of the flat and go home, without having lunch. But, that would be like showing my cards at the very outset. Part of my mind said—to hell with these card games, let's walk out.

Bobby Roy took the news of our run-in with the law seriously. As I said, he was all solicitousness and considerate to the extent possible towards someone he had met a quarter of an hour before.

'I'll go get some beer,' said Isabella.

Had she had sex with him? The terrible thought flashed in my mind.

'So, you study commerce?' he said.

'Sort of,' I said cryptically.

'Sydenham is not a natural environment for budding writers,' he said, hitting the nail on the head.

'One makes do with what one has,' I said. 'I heard you went around the world in a catamaran. Who financed you? Yourself?'

It was his turn to say, 'Sort of. I had this gold necklace that my mum gave me and I sold bits and pieces from it, from time to time. And very often, I would beg for food.'

'All over the place?' I asked.

'All over the place,' he said.

That drove another stake into my heart.

'I suppose you like Hemingway,' I said.

'Absolutely,' he said with a broad grin on his face.

'Big game hunting, deep sea fishing,' I said.

'I like his larger than life personality, but I don't do everything he did,' said Bobby Roy. 'What about you? Writing plays is not very easy, I suppose.'

'I liked Samuel Beckett,' I said, 'Godot just kicked open the doors and windows in my mind. But then, he is a smaller than life figure. Larger than death, too.'

Bobby Roy looked long and hard at me, as if to say, what is a worm like you doing with a babe like Isabella? I didn't like it one bit—his staring at me.

Isabella came in with three tankards of beer balanced on a tray.

'Mom is going to make us some fritters,' she said.

Had they slept together? My mind said to me.

Bobby Roy said, 'Cheers to friendship!'

We said, 'Cheers!'

Then, Bobby Roy said something that instantly revived my spirit.

'How's the revolution coming along?' he asked Isabella.

A cloud passed over Isabella's face.

'Our cell got busted. They were pressurising me to bear false testimony against everyone they'd come to know had known me. Including Sam. That was horrible. I mean, he wasn't even in the Party, I had just asked him to keep some pamphlets and brochures in his room. They came and busted all of us the same night.'

For the first time in my life, I saw a woman feeling guilty for a man. Could that be love?

'So, how did you guys get out?' said Bobby Roy, not unduly impressed.

'Sammy's father knew the Bitch's family and got him out of jail within 3 days flat. Dad came and visited me every day. It was such a big shock to Mama to learn that I was involved with the extreme left. But, Dad had been a communist when he was young and understood my impulses. Dear, old dad. Well, to cut a long story short, the Bitch amnestied everyone after elections were announced. But, the cops were saying that didn't make a difference, they would be questioning me further…'

'You didn't say that to me?' I said, irritated at being kept out of the loop.

'That's because you're innocent, Sam,' she said, 'I wouldn't dream of seeing you in jail again.'

I was taken aback. Innocent in what way? I hadn't had sex with her, that's all, I hadn't had sex with any woman, thus far. What sort of innocence was that?

'What's the Party saying?' Bobby Roy said.

'My cover is busted,' said Isabella. 'I am pretty much on my own now.'

'They came and saw you at the hospital,' I said.

'The guys from the Party?' said Isabella. 'They have nothing to lose. Besides, I don't know about the violence, if that's the right way or not. The Party knows this.'

'I think you should stay away from these guys,' said Bobby Roy. 'Y'know, take it easy. I don't think the Party knows enough about your personal background. You should be "class enemy" to them.'

'There are guys in the corporate world who are members of the Party,' said Isabella. 'You can't kill the idea of Revolution just like that.'

'So, you'll continue?' said Bobby Roy.

'I suppose so,' said Isabella. 'Let's change the topic. I am trying to get Sam's play presented at the Prithvi. I'll send you an invitation when we are ready.'

'Most obliged,' said Bobby Roy. 'What's your play about, Sam?'

'Meaninglessness,' I said, brutally. 'The world doesn't make sense to me.'

At this, Bobby Roy laughed.

'Absurd theatre or something?' he said.

'Nihilism,' I said. 'Man wants to triumph over things that are not worth triumphing over. There is nothing to be triumphant about. Intellectually.'

'God exists, y'know,' said Bobby Roy.

'That makes it even worse,' I said. 'Physics has reached a stage where it can explain the universe without reference to God. Even if He exists, it doesn't change a thing. That only adds another dose of irrationality to something that is reasonably rational. It's the moral ambiguities that become difficult to handle after that, not the integrity of matter which science takes care of anyway. The existence of God is more monstrous than his non-existence.'

Isabella smiled broadly at this, as a teacher would at a bright student.

'Nihilism?' said Bobby Roy. 'That sounds terribly intellectual.'

'It isn't actually. It's about being trapped in a room to which you don't have the key. It's about gratuitously suffering, pretending that it adds dimension to your being. It doesn't. It's just plain old suffering without end or justice. God, if he exists, is a sadist, he takes pleasure in making people suffer.'

'That's a depressing point of view,' said Bobby Roy. 'Everything is not pitch dark. There is a small ray of light. You can call it love, friendship, the ability to communicate with people at a meaningful level. All these things are real. And, as a writer you should be able to tell us more about these things.'

I saw I wasn't dealing with a fool.

'It's not the answer to my question.'

'What's your question?'

'Why is there something instead of nothing? Love is not an answer to that question. Love only brings more pointless suffering into the world. My father loves me, but all he can do to express his love towards me is make my life hell over petty issues, like staying out late at night. He reads the newspapers minutely and notes all the things that are wrong in this world and then projects his own situation into that. It seems terrible things happen to people at night, so he's paranoid that all those things will happen to me. And it's true, terrible things could happen to me at any time, but that is no excuse for curbing basic freedoms. People are getting murdered every day—does that mean we stop going out? My father doesn't understand that. He doesn't understand that you have to engage with the world on its own terms, with all the risk that entails. But, finally, it just boils down to statistics. There is, for instance, a 50 per cent chance of me being run over by a late night-truck. That doesn't mean you stay cooped up in your hole for the rest of your days. He's a pilot, he should understand risk. But, he doesn't. He feels that if you are morally integrate, God cannot touch you.

That is a false proposition. I know several people who are morally degenerate and to whom God is doing nothing. The basic thing about life is that you are thrown into the deep end, especially if you don't know how to swim. My father was born in 1920. He thinks life for me will not be any more different than it was for him.'

'So, the suffocation is coming from the family. I can understand that. My own family wants me to play it safe. Only difference being they have small fortunes to play around with. They are status conscious. It's a different ball game. I am no revolutionary. I believe there are lots of things you can do nothing about and you have to live with that. Or else, you choke in pain. I think that's what's happening to you.'

'Not at all. I am just asking for a limited degree of freedom. Over my physical person, for instance.'

'Over your physical person? I don't understand.'

'The right to poison myself to death, if I so wish. That would shatter my dad to smithereens. He is one for taking this life seriously. He believes that it is everybody's duty to propagate the human species. Grow up, get a job, get married, have kids, settle down and then die. That sort of thing makes no sense to me. It's a waste of time.'

'You are just the sort of person the left would like to indoctrinate. Don't you love your dad?'

'I don't know. Sometimes, I positively hate him and his paranoia about his children.'

'You have siblings? How are they making do with your father's fears and obsessions?'

'They don't have a problem with that. They are good kids, they take their studies seriously, they know exactly what they want to be in life and they are, above all, obedient. They hold my father in awe because of his profession—he's a pilot with Indian Airlines—and because of his discipline. He doesn't smoke, drink or fornicate. And, he's pretty shameless about using his influence to get things done for him. He got me out of jail in three days flat, because he is a colleague of the Bitch's progeny.'

'And you resent that?'

'He wants something in return. Some concessions on my world-view, some going back on my desires. I am not willing to give in an inch. Worse, he suspects that I have no respect for his position, his reputation, in his immediate social circle. He keeps telling me that time and reputation never come back—once they are gone, they are gone for good. And, here I am, boozing and getting stoned on a daily basis.'

'You should join Isabella's Party.'

'I don't think,' said Isabella, 'he wants to see life through the narrow prism of a proletarian revolution.'

'I don't have problems with bourgeois values,' I said. 'But, I am going to resist being assimilated into the caste/class hierarchy tooth and nail.'

'He doesn't attend classes,' said Isabella. 'He just sits on the parapet outside, chain-smoking joints.'

'Is that so?' said Bobby Roy, and instantly produced a small pouch of good Manipuri grass from his denim jacket pocket. 'Let's have a smoke.'

He expertly crushed the marijuana between right thumb and left palm and rolled a joint in a State Express cigarette.

He gave me the privilege of lighting it and taking the first few puffs.

I lit the joint with a lighter and inhaled the fumes deeply into my lungs. I then passed the joint to Isabella who refused.

'I am not going into that stuff,' said Isabella. 'It's too expensive for me, as a habit.'

She was looking truly beautiful and I desired her physically, madly. And then, I was reminded about the condition my penis was in.

'I see a wave of sadness pass over you, Sam,' said

Isabella. 'What's the matter?'

'Nothing,' I said, 'I am just adrift in the ocean of experience.'

'But, you've written a fantastic play,' said Isabella. 'The theatre, that's your anchor.'

'Maybe, but the ship has to go hither and thither before dropping anchor somewhere. My ship is going nowhere outside my class experience.'

'You sound like a true communist when you say that,' said Bobby Roy.

'Class is a reality. My folks are also very class-conscious, in a crude, uninformed way. My father thinks that the Emergency was the best thing the Bitch has done till date. Trains running on time and all that middle-class blather. Things, like poverty, don't bother him. To each his own God-given station in life. That's how he thinks.'

At this point, Mrs Gondola peeped into the room and said, 'Lunch is ready.' We all got up and went to the dining room, adjacent to the living room where I noticed a large aquarium full of coloured species of fish.

Lunch was beef vindaloo and prawn balchao. After the joint, I was ravenous. There was bebinca for dessert. Bobby Roy was not a physical kind of person. He took small portions and nibbled at his food.

'So, tell me something about yourself, Bobby,' I said.

'Things are relatively simple at my end. I don't have to think about money. I'll inherit my father's domain after his death. Maybe, dabble a little in local politics. But, yes, I can understand you when you say that your fundamental desires are thwarted by your class situation.'

'Tell us about your catamaran experience,' said Isabella.

'Oh, it's nothing really,' said Bobby, 'it was just the four of us in Delhi, who thought we should expand our horizons a bit, literally. I always liked the sea; I was into stuff like surfing and sailing yachts. We used to participate in a few regattas, not to any good. We soon found out we didn't have the skills to win a major championship. So, launching ourselves on a catamaran was the natural thing to do. It was not competitive; it was just pure adventure. There were two of us, me and Jack Fearsome, a Brit who was crazy about sailing adventures. So, we got a catamaran custom built for us, right here in Bombay. And then, we sailed on 14 August 1973, me and Jack, and we made it across to the African coast somehow—nearly ran out of supplies—and then we hugged the coast up to Somalia, through the Red Sea and the Suez Canal and we first docked at Haifa. The porters looked at our sailing craft and laughed at the idea that we could go half-way round the world with that. Anyway, Jack knew some folks from back home in Tel Aviv and we bivouacked there for a couple of weeks, before setting out again.'

'And, you had your gold chain?' I asked.

'I had my gold chain and several other items of jewellery that I considered perfectly useless. So, from Haifa we went to Alexandria, where we parked the catamaran and went inland into Egypt.'

'Cairo?' I said.

'Cairo and down the Nile to Abu Simbel, Luxor, Karnak. It was mind blowing. Then, we went north to Turkey, Istanbul to be specific. We ate fish doner straight from the Bosphorus. By the time we came to Greece, the gold chain was almost gone and Jack was calling up his people in Manchester to send him some money.

We were stuck at the Piraeus for three days, waiting for the cash to arrive. We lived on guavas and cheese for about a week or so. So, anyway the money came through and we set out for Chios. I still remember our first experience with the Mediterranean in Greece. The water was really blue, blue aquamarine, y'know, and we could see right down to the floor of the shelf. We would park our vessel somewhere and go for a swim.'

'Tell him about Nisha Hadramawt,' said Isabella.

'Okay, so Nisha was a friend of mine from Oxford, on whom I had a massive crush and when we arrived at Athens, we were just crossing a square with a church on one side and I saw her parents waiting outside the church with bouquets in their hand. So, I went and said hello to them. They were really pleased to see us and said that Nisha was getting married and they were waiting for the bride and the groom to arrive. So, we went in. The church was really small, y'know, cosy and intimate and all that. And then, the bride was led in by her father. And then something happened. Nisha saw me standing a few rows behind the rows marked for the parents and relatives and close friends. She just left the altar and came running at me, hugged me and kissed me on the lips, with everybody looking on and wondering if the bride had gone crazy. So, that was that. We were put up at Athens by Mr Hadramawt and we had enough to eat and drink for a week. Then, we went north to Delphi and Olympus and it was really awe-inspiring, only, we were literally scrounging on our limited means. We were living on cheese and salami and boiled eggs and stuff like that.'

'How did you get visas for all these places?' I asked.

'Ah, that's another story. We were travelling on forged documents. The chap's picture on the passport had no resemblance to me, but nobody seemed to notice that.'

'That's a real adventure,' I said, suddenly feeling diminished. For me, adventure is to be able to spend the night at a friend's place. Anyway, so we disbanded from Isabella's place around 5 pm and I returned home, mellow with beer and sunshine, asking myself just one question: should I tell Isabella that I loved her, beyond any class arithmetic, to the point where I would be willing to lay down my life for her? All my courage would disappear in front of that girl.

I spent my time mumbling half-truths, disguising myself morally, feeling like a eunuch, trembling at the prospect of being turned down or some such shit. In hospital, I was sure that Isabella loved me, but now I was doubtful.

All I knew was that she had a larger than life presence in my life and I was not up to her social stature. I was pretty sure that she had slept with Bobby Roy and that knowledge cut me up into little pieces. Why should she be attracted to a lesser human being like me was beyond my understanding.

I roamed the streets of south Bombay like a nomad wandering in the desert, surrounded by mirages. I was trying to reason with myself about something that was beyond reason. Plus, there was this issue about my cock that needed urgent attention. An operation would have to be done clandestinely, but how would I explain the bandages and the blood to my dear Papa was also not clear to me. I finally decided to talk to the Shah of Iran about my problems.

'Something terrible is happening to me,' I said.

'Terrible? You look all right to me,' said Shah.

'It's not about appearance anymore. I am miserable inside.'

'Because of that chick?'

I nodded.

'What is she doing to you, man?'

'She's not letting me sleep properly. I have no appetite; I don't know whom to turn to.'

'You are in love with that chick.'

'I don't know. I feel wretched inside. She thinks I am a writer, whereas I don't know if I will ever be able to write another play or a book of any kind. Every time I sit down to write something, I go blank, it's like I am indulging in some kind of hollow pretence, that the real deal is telling her that I love her.'

At this, Shah grew serious.

'What's your problem, man? Just go and tell her. We'll

get your cock fixed, I swear.'

'It's not about my cock anymore. She is friendly with a guy who's an heir apparent to some throne and who's been halfway around the world on a catamaran with a forged passport. I am just a puny little snivelling guttersnipe who can't take on his father in a reasoned argument. Anyway, this is beyond argument. I think I am in love with that girl, but not sure that I fit the bill.'

'Hey, Sam, you bohemian dog. You are a coward. What are you scared of?'

'If she reciprocates my feelings. It's like jumping off a cliff and hoping to survive. I have vertigo man. I'd rather roam the sky like an eagle in the eye of a hurricane that's abandoned. I can't handle my own emotions leave alone the emotions of somebody else.'

'Have you asked her out for dinner?'

'In the first place I don't have the wherewithal to take her out for dinner. The main problem is that I am sexually inhibited. Saying I love her implies that I am willing to stand naked in front of her, fondling her breasts, putting my sad prick into her cunt. It's like leaping into the unknown. I may not remain a writer, I may be attracted to the idea of a political revolution or some such thing.'

'If you can't tell her directly, write her a note, explaining your feelings for her.'

'I am intimidated. She might think I am being presumptuous. I feel like crying all the time I am away from her. I am not her social equal. She's absolutely clear-sighted and I am a muddy soul. Leave alone circumventing the globe with a fake passport, I have to fight with my parents over whether I can spend the night at your place.'

'You need to go to a shrink, man. To sort out the mess inside. Your father has put a lock on your prick. Why don't you tell him?'

'He'll kill me. Firstly, it would be about religion. He doesn't see me settling down with a Catholic chick who, in his opinion, are all whores. And then, there is this revolutionary nonsense that I myself don't buy. My dear Papa would blow his fuse if he heard that. In Isabella's book, he is a reactionary. I can't run away from home, I need some shelter, and who's going to give me a job without a graduate degree?'

'How are you going to get laid if you can't speak two words of romance to a woman who wants it?'

'Don't be so crude. This is not just about sex. It's about living the rest of my life with this woman. I can't bear the thought of touching that female just to exploit her feelings towards me, if there are any.'

'That girl loves you, man. She wants to get into bed with you, I am certain.'

'That's the problem. Had it been any other woman, I wouldn't think twice about seduction. But, not with Isabella.'

'Why not?'

'I don't know. I feel wretched all the time away from her, but in front of her, I am tongue-tied. I am paralysed with fear.'

'What fear?'

'The fear of the unknown. What lies beyond.'

'I'll tell you what lies beyond—marriage and settling down.'

'Are you crazy? She's into things like revolution; she's against bourgeois morality.'

'Bourgeois morality? What's that?'

'She doesn't think much of marriage and stuff like that.'

'She wants to live-in?'

'Maybe. But, I am not sure. You can't rent a place in this goddamn city without a marriage certificate.'

'That's a problem. But, first things first. You've got to tell her about your feelings.'

'She'll think I am weak, some namby-pamby, washed out sentimentalist who can't handle a woman like her. The real problem is that I would have to cut off all family ties, no matter where I go with Isabella and that would impact my finances or my absence of it.'

'Don't blame your Papa if you can't tell a woman that you love her.'

I said nothing.

'So, how do you handle this non-relationship mentally,' said Shah.

'I fantasise about us. Romantic fantasies. Walking through the streets of Paris, hand in hand. Kissing her and holding her tight against me.'

'What about sex?'

'It doesn't enter my mind. My love for her, if this can be called love, is pure.'

'Fuck purity and all that Hindu nonsense. Man, you've got one hell of a twisted mind, which is going to take some time disentangling. Let me think.'

There was a lengthy pause in the conversation.

'Okay,' said the Shah of Iran, finally. 'What you have to do is to keep her company as much as you can, get to know her thoroughly…'

'I know she's involved with revolutionary politics. I know that she's slept around some. She's sexually more mature than I am. And, I am ashamed of my lack of sexual experience. I can't tell her I am a virgin, that she's the first piece of action in my life.'

'How old are you, Sam?'

'Nineteen.'

'In this country, I know forty-year-old guys who've never had sex in their lives and continue to live with Mummy and Daddy. Nineteen is okay for a first experience of sex. I was fifteen when I broke loose with a woman twice my age. What this means is that you are not going to be able to muster enough sexual initiative to take her to bed…'

'Yeah.'

'So, she will have to take the initiative. That's a tough proposition, man. Basically, women want to be sure that you love them enough, that she's not a fling or a one night stand. Why don't you begin small? Try kissing her for a start.'

'Are you crazy? Suppose she wants to have sex with me? What do I say? That I have a dysfunctional dick? She would know I am chaste as driven snow.'

'I don't think, machismo is the issue here. Not with this woman. She's sold on you. Even an idiot like me can make that out.'

I said nothing.

'Begin small. Hold hands, neck, smooch, that sort of thing.'

'She'll treat me like a kid. Right now she thinks I am a creative genius of some kind—smoking pot, not attending classes, a genuine free spirit. She might act pricey. Sexually.'

'No, no, no. She's not that kind of woman. I have a hunch about these things.'

There was another more or less lengthy pause.

'She's more hip than me. She listens to Jimi Hendrix and Frank Zappa. She has an expensive music system and owns hundreds of albums. I feel like a dumb peasant, in front of her.'

'Stay close to her. Keep talking to her, meeting her.'

'She'll simply notice that whenever she's on a one to one with me, I am numb with pain. That looks as if I am cold with her.'

'What's the problem, man?'

'She's so utterly beautiful, she could have any undergraduate in the University of Bombay.'

'Chicks are monogamous. Especially Indian chicks. They are all looking for that one man who will make their lives meaningful through something called love. But yes, given the scale of the problem, your response would be inadequate, whatever it is. You are surrounded on all sides by philistines. So is she, I suspect. That may be a basis for emotional solidarity. And, as far as I am concerned, I will bankroll your circumcision and you can shack up with me as long as it takes. Let's take it one at a time, okay?'

8

Ten days after my conversation with the Shah of Iran, I heard that Isabella had been picked up for questioning by the cops again. I was grief-stricken, almost bereaved. I didn't know which way to turn. It is only when you are on the point of losing something that you realise it may be precious. I had no appetite, went without a shave for several days and generally hung around the canteen with a dead look. I felt like a caricature, a cartoon revolutionary who would pick up a gun only to blow his own brains out. How could I explain this—that I was hopelessly in love with a girl who rejected middle-class norms and values—to my parents? Into what depths of cowardice could I sink at the prospect of telling this girl that I was hopelessly in love with her?

I went back to Arthur Road jail to pay a visit as a concerned citizen. She had just finished talking to her lawyer when she saw me and her pretty face broke into a smile of camaraderie and friendship.

'It's awful,' she said.

'Are they beating you up?' I asked.

'They haven't got physical as yet. They don't believe in discussing things over a cup of tea, information has to be shaken out of me.'

'What are they charging you with? Sedition?'

'And waging war against the state.'

'That's non-bailable.'

'I know. My lawyer is going to file a writ petition in the Supreme Court to have the charges against me dropped. I don't know if they are going to succeed or not. For the moment, I am stuck in jail. Also, Sam, don't come here to see me; they are treating everybody who comes to see me as a potential subversive.'

'To hell with them.'

'Don't say that. These guys are maniacs. They want names, addresses, functions, the whole jing-bang. They want me to back-stab the Party. They already have a lot of information about our cell, which is defunct in any case. This is just idle harassment. Dad is doing everything he can to get me out of this. I don't know what's going to happen.'

I wanted to tell her that my life depended on her, that I couldn't bear to see her in this miserable condition, that I would love her my whole life. But, the words got stuck in my throat; I was completely tongue-tied.

'What's the Party doing?' I asked.

'I am no longer in touch with them. In any case, openly defending one of their operatives will be tantamount to incriminating me. I am pretty much on my own.'

My admiration for her courage was inversely

proportional to my cowardice.

'You must get in touch with Sanjana,' she said, suddenly turning more serious. 'I have paid her the money for rehearsals. Just call her and fix the dates. I really want to see this thing through.'

This is not the time for altruism, I wanted to say.

'You must get out of here, first,' I said.

I can't bear to see you like this, I wanted to say.

'Don't worry about me, Sam,' she said. 'They want to implicate me in a plot to blow up Bombay House. They have no evidence against me. If there was a plot, I wasn't aware of it. I just distributed leaflets and brochures, that's all. I know nothing about bombs.'

How could she love a coward? I thought.

I said nothing, just sort of stared blankly at her, unable to believe that she would ever reciprocate my feelings for her. Can't she see that I was in love with her?

'Don't look so grim, Sam,' she said, 'I'll be okay.'

'We have to get you out of here,' I said.

The whistle went off and the visit was over.

'Don't worry,' I managed to say before she left to go back to her cell, 'we'll get you out of here somehow.'

I returned home, numb with pain. Dad was on his day-off and was pottering around his plants. He grew chillies in the balcony. He just looked at me and said nothing. I wanted to tell Mom that I wouldn't have any dinner, but was squeamish about facing the interrogation that would follow—what's the matter with you, etc.... I went straight to my room and lay down on the bed. I couldn't get Isabella's face out of my mind. There were no good books in the house, no good music, just volumes of the gospel of Ramakrishna Paramahamsa and a few books by Vivekananda. We were philistines. I was a class-enemy of the Maoists, a decadent by-stander, ready to be annihilated by the stray bullet or bomb. All the men in Isabella's life were larger than life figures, adventurers, pirates, revolutionaries, theatre people. I was just a puny little playwright whose father wouldn't let him run away from the darkness that prevailed in his home in myriad forms. I was halfway between a street urchin and a raving lunatic.

In college, everybody at the table recognised that I was not behaving normally. Only Feridoon Cama knew something about what was going on, I don't know how.

'Your girlfriend is in trouble?' he said.

I nodded.

'She's back in jail,' I said.

The rest of the table was having a conversation about the death of the Pope, so nobody paid any attention to what Feridoon and I were talking about.

'What are the charges?' Feridoon asked.

'Sedition and waging war against the state,' I said.

'That's death penalty stuff, if I am not mistaken.'

'It is.'

'She has a lawyer?'

I nodded.

'Appointed by the court?'

'No, her parents got her one.'

'What do you propose to do?'

'What can I do? Nothing. It's terrible what that girl is doing to me.'

'What?'

'She's pushing me to break off with my family.'

'She said so?'

'She said nothing. It's the whole situation. I feel like hitting my dad. They have no sense of aesthetics. Everything is so expensively ugly at home.'

'Don't do anything stupid, okay. My dad knows some ace lawyers. I could speak to him.'

'She's a Naxalite, for heaven's sake. Her own family is having problems defending her.'

'Is she willing to compromise?'

'She won't give in an inch.'

'That's a problem. What are the cops saying?'

'Nothing. They want names, addresses, code numbers. They want her to collaborate. Spill the beans, all of them.'

'And, she won't.'

'No. They are going to keep her locked up for good.'

'I thought that was the usual Emergency cloak and dagger stuff.'

'She's very serious about her political beliefs. And, she's not a snitch. They want a full and frank confession before a Magistrate. That's not happening.'

'Don't do anything stupid, Sam. Knowing these guys, they are probably keeping a track on you too.'

'They are, I know it.'

I looked at the cup of coffee that Chhotu had put in

front of me with distaste.

'I am in love with her,' I said.

At this, Feridoon looked at me with a solemn expression.

'So, tell her,' he said.

'I can't.'

'Why?'

'Something inside me is telling me not to. She's bigger than cocaine. I don't feel I deserve her.'

'Is she in love with you?'

'It is possible. But, she won't be the first one to say it.'

'Typically feminine.'

'Plus, she wouldn't want to drag me into her situation.'

There was a lengthy pause at this.

'I'll speak to my dad,' said Feridoon, finally. 'He knows some political people.'

'Okay. But, it looks pretty much hopeless. They've gone to the Supreme Court with a plea to drop all charges, but I don't know whether that can help. She's a Naxalite. Politically damned.'

9

The first time I learned that my father had put his thingummy into my mother's thingummy, I was shocked beyond words. I was 11 years old, looking at a college textbook that Rajiv Gandhi, the cricketer in my class, had procured from somewhere. I refused to believe in what the pictures and the text in the book were telling everyone—that babies weren't born out of kissing, as I had believed until then, that there was an ugly thing involved in fate. I chose to believe that unlike all other children, I was born out of kissing, that at least my Mum and Dad had not done anything dirty to have me. For the next week or ten days, I was walking around in a daze, unable to comprehend that life could come out of something so ugly.

Worse, soon after that, I stumbled upon the joys of masturbation. I found that if I held my penis under the falling jet of water from the shower, it grew hard with excitement and that if I held it long enough in that position there was a highly pleasurable crescendo of pain that ended with a climax. I couldn't link it to sex as yet, but I understood that it was something to be hidden. I next began fiddling with my penis in the classroom, my hands in the pocket, and lo and behold there was tumefaction. I persisted and felt my penis ejaculating. I knew nothing about semen and the rest of the stuff; it would take another year or so to actually witness the ejection of semen from my tool at which I was suitably horrified and fascinated at the same time. I couldn't talk to anybody about it, for I instinctively understood that it was something that you concealed from your friends and family. Only, my mother grew exceedingly irritated at the time I was taking to finish my bath (there was only one bathroom in the little West Delhi flat we occupied at the time). I barely understood that what I was going through had something to do with girls, but, yes, I was ashamed.

The prettiest girl in my class was a girl called Preetam Kalra. From the backbenches, I would cover one eye with my palm and watch her with the other eye. Nobody understood what was happening, otherwise, I figured, I would be lynched. I was not good at studies or in sports, the two realms where the male could shine forth and take his pleasure with the girls, any girl, in the school. During dance classes, the boys and the girls would form two rows facing each other and our dance instructor, a certain Mr Sinha, would order us, the boys, to pick a partner. I wanted to pick Preetam Kalra, but was powerfully inhibited by the fact that I was a nobody. I eventually and invariably settled for a dark nondescript Bengali girl called Keya. Cultural taboos and peer pressure prevented me from considering myself as an object of erotic desire. I was timid to the point of fainting and just stumbled across the precise point in the row where Preetam would be standing, unable even to conceive that I could ask her out to dance with me (besides which, I was no good at dancing either). I understood, dimly, that it had something to do with puberty and the awakening of my penis. Keya was safe, that way. She was too dark to be chosen as anyone's partner.

And so it went.

And, I also remember that I had studied hard at home for the annual examinations, just to see where that would lead me. I succeeded beyond my wildest imagination and stood third in the section with a first division (above 60 per cent marks), including general science, a subject that made no head or tail to me. The next time I entered a science lab, the other two students who formed the elite in class welcomed me as if I was one of them, as if I belonged. I looked at the instruments and devices in the lab with bewilderment. I couldn't put the two together—my passionate longing for Preetam and my high scoring sprint along the line. I dismissed the whole thing as a fluke and decided not to give up on my wanton and profligate ways. I still sat next to Keya and fiddled with my penis. Ashesh, who was good in studies and a renowned athlete, passed a snide remark in class—he's trying to stretch it in order to make it bigger. I paid no attention and bashed on regardless.

It was only in Bombay that Ravi Sharma first handed

me a copy of *Playboy*. I was dizzy with excitement and took it home safely ensconced among my books. What followed was a frenzy of masturbation—I would jerk off seven or eight times in a day. Worse, my penis seemed to have decided that it was somehow autonomous. It was in a tumescent phase practically all the time. I also found out that I was aroused by women with big breasts, they gave me an instant hard-on. That began my long affair with pornography. I located a lending library in the neighbourhood which kept *Playboy* and *Hustler*. I would rummage through the pile in uncontrolled excitement and take an issue home every week or so. I loved commodified women, women who felt no shame about their bodies and they were exquisitely beautiful. The result was that my romantic longing for normal girls decreased dramatically, whereas a fashionably dressed, well-endowed woman would give me a hard-on. The pleasure principle was shaking my being down to its bones, but I always knew where to draw the line. I knew that the women who posed for *Playboy* and *Hustler* wouldn't even discuss the possibility of a relationship without serious money being at the centre of the picture. Funnily enough, Isabella Gondola had gorgeous tits and was, what one could describe as, a voluptuous woman. With her, I didn't see myself as a sexually depraved person fulfilling his wildest sexual fantasy. I just wanted to gather her up in my arms and hold her tight against me. Instinctively, I treated her like I would an intellectual companion. I never found out what she read or whether she read at all; what was of consequence was that she was reckless, like me. She could put her life in line for her convictions, whether artistic or revolutionary. But, there was romanticism also. This was the time when I was discovering the French poets of Evil—Baudelaire, Rimbaud and Lautreamont, and I had this idea that I was going to be a great poet who would die of syphilis or a drug overdose. I was listening to the Rolling Stones, specifically two albums, *Goat's Head Soup* and *Beggars Banquet* and the song that would leave me breathless was *Sympathy for the Devil.* I would eventually grow out of that but those two albums remained my favourites throughout my life.

'Sam,' said Nero Gomes one day, 'you are ruining your life.'

'You bet I am,' I retorted. 'It's my life and it's nobody's business.'

'You'll need a job, one day; your dad's going to retire and move out of Embassy Apartments, Nepean Sea Road.'

I shrugged my shoulders. I didn't see his point. I was hell-bent on dying young, like Hendrix and Joplin. I was a megalomaniac already. Isabella Gondola fit into my scheme of things perfectly—a stunning beauty from an affluent family, imprisoned by the State on the basis of a lie. What could be more romantic? We both treated Death in a cavalier manner. Long after I had left Bombay, I would hark back to these moments of perfect happiness, when my life had ceased to make sense for me. My imagination was totally impervious to the impending catastrophe.

I would continue to visit Isabella in prison where

her physical condition seemed to have undergone some kind of drastic change. She had dark circles under her eyes. She looked unwashed and shabby. But, her eyes shone and her smile dazzled and that's all that mattered to me. Nothing of any consequence for my romantic or artistic life would be discussed. She spoke to me about the torture she was being subjected to—the noise, the lack of privacy, the interrogations at all hours of the day and night, the beatings by women constables—but the tone of her voice remained gay and insouciant. I had no words to express my admiration, my blinding love for this woman who was willing to lay down her life for her beliefs. However, I never exchanged a word with some of the bearded, *jhola*-carrying revolutionaries whom I came across at Arthur Road. I had nothing to say to them and Isabella, understanding my instinctive distrust of all forms of conformism, especially those that stemmed from ideology or political praxis, would never introduce me to any of them. I would just wait for them to finish before taking my place across the glass partition.

Her parents seemed unable to get her out of prison. The Supreme Court had turned down the plea for the charges to be dismissed, had washed its hands off the regime of violence and betrayal she was wilting under, which was breaking her down physically.

'What do they want?' I said to her.

'The same old thing. Names, addresses, phone numbers,' she said simply. 'They've already got many from their informers and other Party members. I know just one or two people who don't rank very high in the organisation. I prefer going down with my back to the wall rather than surrender to these animals.'

'I feel miserable,' I said, fighting back my tears.

She looked at me with the seriousness that a cancer patient deserves and said, 'Don't Sam, don't. I'll be all right in the end. They don't have a case against me.'

Soon, I started attending court on 'hearing' days. Her parents had tried to hire a top-notch lawyer whom they could afford to. But after a few sessions of counselling, Isabella decided that she would defend herself. The lawyer was apparently trying to broker a deal between her and the State and Isabella would have nothing to do with that. Also, I was ashamed that I had been bailed out of trouble by my well-connected parents, instead of fighting the authorities for what I believed in. I was not a Naxalite and would never be one, but I should have fought for the principle that you don't put innocent people in prison for things they haven't done and that wriggling out of a tight spot with the help of one's well-connected family was simply not done, it was dishonest.

The witnesses were called up, one by one, and they were all false—people who had been bludgeoned, induced, intimidated and cajoled into perjury. The Judge asked Isabella whether she needed legal aid, and whether the court could appoint a lawyer to defend her. She refused. But, and this was the miraculous part of the trial, all the false witnesses crumbled in front of Isabella's ferocious interrogation of their locus standi and their memory.

Most of the times, she had never met or otherwise known the faces that kept bobbing up and out of the witness box and, at least, two of them were cornered into admitting that they had never seen her or witnessed any criminal act being performed by her.

But, the prosecution was cunning. They had tortured some of her comrades into incriminating her and it was these declarations that gave Isabella the hardest time. At which point, Sadanand Patil came into the picture. He introduced himself before the court as a trial lawyer and sought permission to defend Isabella Gondola pro bono. The prosecution objected to the fact that Mr Patil was a card-carrying member of the Communist Part of India and would therefore subvert the due process of law by bringing extraneous political compulsions into play during the trial. The Judge looked witheringly at the public prosecutor and overruled his objection.

Isabella looked confused. Later, she admitted to me that Patil was indeed sincere in his desire to defend her, to put out her case as she thought fit. He straight away began by describing his client as an innocent cog in a revolutionary machine. He spoke about Isabella's grandfather who had been a member of the Hungarian Party who had suffered for being close to Imre Nagy. He showed that the communist ideal of fraternity and equality was deeply ingrained in her and that her membership of the CPI (ML), Charu Majumdar's Party, was born out of firmly held convictions. But, the truth was that she was a passive member of an underground cell and was used principally to distribute propaganda material and collect money from the better heeled members of the Party. Above all, Patil performed a miracle—the morale of the defence was lifted immediately by his presence and his impassioned rhetoric.

I went home relieved that at last something was being done to defend Isabella. Also, strangely, my head was buzzing with ideas. My mind was full of Isabella's situation and I saw, in my imagination, a 2000-word essay taking shape on Isabella, on the travails of an ordinary political cadre left in the lurch by her organisation which did not want to acknowledge that her plight was a result of genuinely held convictions. (I later heard that Isabella had been denounced by the state committee of the CPI (ML) as a snitch and a bourgeois counter-revolutionary who had jeopardised the lives of her comrades, and collaborated with the authorities, all of which was false). I was feverish with excitement as I wrote that article, words were bubbling around in my mind and sentences flowed fully formed from my brain onto the paper. It was entirely idealistic and non-sentimental. Once complete, I sent it off to *The Times of India*, even though I had the apprehension that it would be turned down because of its positive take on revolutionary politics. In the event, it was carried in the Sunday edition of the newspaper, not as an opinion piece but in the features section. The response, both positive and negative, was overwhelming. The SFI (Students' Federation of India) and the DYFI (Democratic Youth Federation of India) immediately swung into action and there were sit-ins in front of the court in favour of Isabella's release. Some of them managed to infiltrate the court room and raised slogans inside. They were firmly removed by the police. The prosecution went to town over these incidents saying it confirmed what they had been saying—that Gondola was a dangerous agent provocateur who, if released, would be a threat to society.

My visit after my article appeared was heart-wrenching. Isabella just looked at me and wept. She could hardly say a word. She had never looked as beautiful as she did to me now. She finally managed to put a sentence together.

'Sam,' she said. 'You'll get into trouble. These people are fanatics; they want us dead. Patil is doing a good job defending me. Don't get into trouble for my sake.'

I looked at her aghast and said, 'I can't help it, this is how I feel about you.'

This brought forth another bout of weeping.

'Don't worry,' I said to her gently. 'We'll get you out of here.'

She nodded, fighting back her tears. She was making an effort to smile, but it just wouldn't come.

I was in love with her, absolutely and with all the resources of my soul. But now, or so I thought, was not the moment to burden her with my feelings for her.

She asked me whether I had got in touch with Sanjana about the rehearsals.

I said, 'My first priority is to see you out of here.'

'No!' she exclaimed. 'The show must go on,

irrespective of whether I get out of here or not.'

I felt slightly ashamed at being free while she was in the pits.

I said the dates for the rehearsals had been tentatively fixed.

At this, she seemed to brighten up immediately.

'Really?' she said. 'That's great news. I so want to see your play at the Prithvi.'

I said she would. She would get out before the premiere.

And, we left it at that.

Back in Sydenham, the whole college was agog with the article in *The Times of India*.

Nero Gomes was the first to congratulate me.

'Hey, Sam!' he said, 'great article, man.'

'Blitzkrieg,' said the Shah of Iran.

'We are all Naxalites now,' said Ram Bhonsle, patting me on my shoulder with avuncular affection.

'Let me know if I can help,' said Feridoon, as solicitous as ever for the condition of other people's heart.

'What a chick!' said Benny Pathak, running his fingers through his curly hair.

I was a minor celebrity on the University of Bombay's college circuit. The next time we went to St Xavier's for the BOAC Trophy debate, people spontaneously came up to tell me how much they had liked the article. Everyone was following Isabella's trial with enthusiasm.

Also, I got the dates for the rehearsal confirmed with Sanjana who had read my piece.

'Great job, Sam,' she said to me soberly on the phone. 'I will spread the word among theatre people in Bombay. We are going to build a citizen's movement to free this girl. She your girlfriend?' she asked.

'No,' I said, shamefacedly.

There was love in that article.

I didn't know what to say, I just said, 'I am happy at the impact it is having on everybody.'

And then, of course, there was home.

My Mom read the piece and was shocked. My Dad was out of station on the day the article appeared, so there was no explosion immediately. But that there was some kind of family crisis brewing and spilling over into our lives, I had no doubts about that.

'What is this?' my Mom asked me as soon as I was back from college.

I was in no mood for a scene. I just kept quiet, hoping that would do the trick. But Mom was relentless.

'Have you become a Naxinite?' she shouted at me. 'Do you want to go back to prison once again? Don't you know that the rest of us have our lives to lead, without any harassment by the police? You should have thought about your father who's worrying himself sick over your future. Who do you think you are? A hoity-toity intellectual who doesn't have to earn his living and can make do with the crumbs off a political table? We gave you freedom hoping that you would use it responsibly, and here you go, splashing our name all over *The Times of India*. I have already ten people who have rung up and asked me whether my son is a Naxinite.'

'The word is Naxalite,' I said wearily.

'Whatever!' said my Mom. 'Do you know that they shot traffic policemen in Calcutta? Is that what you call courage? Why don't they go after the big guns, the Ministers and stuff? They won't because they are lily-livered.'

My mother saw that this was having no effect on me.

'Alright now!' she said. 'Have you been visiting that girl in jail?'

I could not hold my peace any longer.

'Yes, I have,' I said, defiantly.

'That's really brilliant! You give the police exactly what they want—a reason for picking you up and torturing the winkies out of you. And, what am I going to tell my friends? That my son is a Naxanite and wants to murder them in their sleep? Tell me something. Do you go to college at all? I don't see you carrying any books or bringing back any notes. What do you think you'll become without a decent degree? Do you want to be a vagabond?'

'Yes,' I said, anger getting the better of me now, 'yes, I want to be a vagabond, that's none of anybody's business.'

'So, how come you are eating and sleeping at your father's Nepean Sea Road apartment? Why don't you go and join your comrades in the jungle? Get bitten by mosquitoes at night and have some unearthly gruel for food. It's very fashionable to be sitting in an air-conditioned drawing room in south Bombay and discussing, I don't know what, how to liberate the poor.... Do you even know what poverty is like? Do you know how these people live? While you have scones for tea?'

All these were telling points and my mother knew that. Did I have the courage of my convictions? No. I was no revolutionary. The idea scared the living daylights out of me.

'I am just trying to help a friend who is in trouble,' I said. 'Plus, she's really interested in seeing my play performed professionally.'

'Oh! So, you think you are some hotshot playwright? Who's going to pay for lunch? That girl?'

'Yeah.'

'So, why don't you take your things and move out of here?' said my mom, hitting the nerve on its head.

I said nothing. I just stood around and stared helplessly at my surroundings.

'Okay,' said my mom, 'let your father get back. He'll know what to do with you.'

And she stomped back to her room. I was miserable.

At night in bed, I tossed and turned. I couldn't get Isabella's face out of my system. Then, I started praying to God, like a five-year-old baby.

The next thing I did was to get some books, whatever communist literature was available in the college library. I brought home the first volume of *Capital* and began reading it. After the first few pages, I put the book down. It was boring. The writing was average. Instead, I picked up volume 2 of the works of Antonin Artaud and my blood began circulating normally in a matter of seconds, as I read *The Theatre and its Double*. Everything Artaud said made sense to me—how to deal with nihilism, the essential meaninglessness of life. It was a brick thrown at the glass front of the cultural elite's head office. It shook me up. Once again, I was brought face to face with the fact that I did not have the courage to go down the path of self-destruction upon which Artaud, among others, had so boldly ventured.

Something else began working inside me. I began noticing the servants who came to our house to do the cleaning and dusting. They seemed happy to be able to work for a living, to earn a few bucks here and there. I noticed that the help who washed our clothes changed her own sari only twice a week or so. This is poverty, I said to myself. There was a slum, a big slum, carefully hidden behind the sky rises of Malabar Hill. What kind of homes did they live in? I wondered. In the newspapers, I had seen pictures—narrow, muddy shit-laden lanes, tarpaulin sheets, pukka houses with electricity, women washing clothes and bathing out in the open, people defecating on the rocky shore along Nepean Sea Road, the smell of shit wafting up to the 21st floor during low tide. On TV, I would often catch Kamleshwar, the writer, interview these people—maids, drivers, hawkers—and they all looked contented with their life, they knew money and love. I noticed that the man who came to clean the toilets wore a gold-plated wrist watch and held his head high. Were these the poor? Then, it dawned on me that these were the privileged among the poor—people who got to work for the fat cats of the Indian economy. They didn't look revolutionary to me, despite their willingness to stand shoulder to shoulder with their peers and demand the satisfaction of their needs. Where were the poor, if not in the slums? Where was the rock bottom of this well of frustration and despair? They did not lack money; they lacked status. There must be others, I said to myself, who were worse off than even these people—people who lived out on the streets, without shelter, without knowing where their next meal was coming from, people who routinely drank water to fill their stomachs before going off to sleep on the pavements, exposed to the elements. I realised that my parents didn't care for these people. They came into our house, did the job they were paid for and left. Their stories were muted, their desires unknown, their pain unacknowledged.

I asked my brother, the economist, what he knew about the poor.

'Well,' he said, with a thoughtful expression on his face, 'they live and die like flies. They breed and multiply and sink into even greater misery. They just add to the population without having any skills or anything. The best get to be like our toilet cleaner, the worst beg on the streets and spend the night next to an open drain, bitten by mosquitoes, overwhelmed by the smell of slimy decay.'

'What's the answer?' I said.

'We've got to control the population. We've got too many mouths to feed and we don't have the resources.

No matter which government is in power in Delhi, the numbers are beyond their control, beyond their calculations.'

'That's honest enough. Do you think we need a revolution?'

My brother put down the book he was reading, Ayn Rand's *The Fountainhead*, and looked at me.

'Socialism is not the answer. It hasn't succeeded in creating a wealthy society anywhere in the world. They had lifted people out of abject poverty, but that's where they stopped making progress, except in military technology. Just look at the Soviet Union, for a minute. They have enough bombs to blow this planet to smithereens twenty five times over, but that can't ensure a regular supply of toothpaste to their people. Capitalism at least feeds everybody, at least in America and western Europe. But, they don't have a crazy population figure that we do. Every step we take towards prosperity is neutralised by the birth of 1500 new-borns every minute.'

'Have you ever been to a village?'

'No. Wouldn't be caught dead in one of those awful places. It's like living in hell. No freedom, no food, no future. Only fornication and multiplication.'

'Are they ready to murder us even as we sleep?'

'Nah. Politicians come and throw them some money and liquor from time to time. That apparently works. Besides, hope springs eternal, as they say.'

'So, what are you going to do next?'

At this, my brother laughed. He reached for his

rucksack and fished out what looked like a brochure. It was the prospectus of Harvard University. As I flipped through the pages, I saw the beauty of the place—all green, students sitting around on the lawn, smoking cigarettes, chatting, laughing. It looked like paradise.

'That's where I intend to go,' he said, 'forever.'

'What about Mom and Dad?'

'What about them?'

'Who'll look after them, once they are old and decrepit?'

'Oh, don't you worry. Dad'll get his pension and other dues; they'll buy an apartment some day and everything will go on as usual. No fear of revolution in the next fifty years.'

And that's where the conversation ended.

I understood how generous and unselfish Isabella had been. Speaking to my brother was like speaking to a blind and deaf person. Isabella had woken me up.

10

On a rainy Sunday afternoon, Nero, Jiten and myself landed up at the Prithvi for a rehearsal. It was a small auditorium with a small proscenium which made for intimacy rather than grandeur. The acoustics were great, the actors could be heard even from the last row in the auditorium. We got down to business straight away. There was some pacing up and down to do and we decided that instead of walking in a straight line, the actors would describe a small arc. The crescendos came off beautifully. Sanjana joined us in a couple of hours. Nero and Jiten adjusted their parts pretty efficiently and everything seemed hunky-dory. Until, of course, the cops showed up. An SHO and two constables barged into the hall and asked to speak to me.

'Who is Sam, here?' the officer said.

'I am,' I said. 'Why?'

'Have you taken permission to put up this show?'

I looked at Sanjana, bewildered. I was completely innocent as far as legal requirements were concerned.

'We'll make an application tomorrow,' said Sanjana,

coolly, totally unfazed by the unwelcome intrusion.

'Do you have a copy of the script?' said the officer.

'You can have mine,' said Sanjana.

The SHO, with dark glasses on, took the script and pretended to read a few lines.

'What is this?' he said, 'some kind of abstract meaningless shit?'

'It's a play on the human condition,' I said, in a small voice.

The cop then changed his track.

'Are you the one who wrote that piece on Gondola in *The Times*?'

'Yes, I did.'

'Do you know she's a subversive wanting to throw the government of the day out of power through violent means?'

'I admire her for that.'

'Are you a Naxalite?' said the SHO. There was menace in that voice.

'No, I am not,' I said.

'Then, what is this play about? Are you trying to send out a subversive message through this shit?'

I wanted to say yes, but suddenly I was overcome by prudence and caution. Isabella had paid good money for these rehearsals.

'No, I am not,' I said. 'I don't want to overthrow the government. This play has nothing to do with partisan politics.'

The SHO looked at me through his dark glasses for

a while. He was dealing with an unfamiliar world; maybe he was confused.

'Okay,' he said finally. 'I am letting you off this time around. I want you to get permission to perform this play pronto and report back to me at the Juhu police station by Friday 6 pm.'

I said okay. The cop seemed appeased by the contrition and dejection.

After he left, I collapsed into a chair. The threat of arrest hung thick in the air.

Sanjana said they would place the play before the censors the day after and she would see to it that the matter was expedited. I said there was no need to hurry because as long as Isabella was in jail there could be no performance. I requested permission to go through with the rehearsals and permission was granted immediately.

In the evening, I received a call from Alyque Padamsee. He said the play must absolutely go through and that he would pull as many strings to help it along the way as he could.

'Don't let the bastards bully you into submission,' he said. 'I have spoken with Sanjana, and we've decided that all theatre people will unite in defence of your play, okay?'

I said I would do my best. I was a bit at sea with all the attention, but the possibility of being incarcerated once more weighed heavily on my mind. Another arrest and my family would cut me off for sure. Nero said nothing would happen, we would just sail through. I hadn't committed a crime by writing a play. On the following Friday at 6 pm, I presented myself at the Juhu police station, accompanied by Nero, Jiten and the Shah of Iran. I had smoked some weed to give me courage and to relax in front of the officer.

The SHO invited me to take a seat while he addressed some issues to do with the political rally the Congress was poised to hold within three days. After keeping me waiting for about 20 minutes, he strode up to his chair and straightaway started interrogating me about my politics.

'What do you think of Naxalites?' he said.

'Nothing,' I said.

'Then, how come you came out in defence of that anti-national bitch in *The Times*?'

'She's a friend.'

'She's putting up the money for the play?'

'Yes.'

'Red money?'

'I don't know? I think not.'

'You think not…'

'Even if it is red money, how is it germane to the issue?'

He correctly divined this to be an affront to his authority as a law-keeper.

'Listen, you whipper-snapper, let me decide what is legal or illegal. You have no right to spread sedition and subversion in this great country of ours. I can have you arrested in two minutes flat. But, I am sympathetic towards free speech issues. You are lucky to be having to deal with me, otherwise you might have been thrown into lock-up and beaten black and blue.'

I said nothing. The hashish was giving me great strength in my fight against the authorities.

'So, is this red money? Yes or no?' he said.

'I said I don't know.'

'You will have comrades and fellow travellers filling up the auditorium for you and the play will be judged to be a hit.'

'I'm not bothered about the size of my audience.'

'I have read your play. At least a part of it. Who is Max?'

I said I didn't know. Had I known I would have portrayed him differently. I said he represented the world outside.

'The whole world?'

'The whole world,' I said, not sure of my grounding anymore. I said, 'There are things in my play that I don't understand myself. It just turned out that way.'

At this, the cop sat back in his executive chair and swivelled around a bit.

'You should,' he said, finally, 'try to help people live their lives instead of piling this unholy garbage on their heads to demoralise them.'

I could have said that there were enough people out there doing that, my business was to understand what everybody means by life and whether we should be satisfied with our God-given condition.

'So, you don't believe in God?'

'No, I don't believe in God. Or rather, I wasn't sure about his existence, but if he did exist, then my question to Him would be how did He create such miserable circumstances that people in a poor country lived in. It wasn't fair.'

'You are a defender of the poor, are you?'

I said 'I didn't say that.' I said he had asked me a question and I had tried to give him an answer.

'Why don't you join politics?' he said. 'The country needs educated people like you to go into politics and clean up the system.'

'I don't understand politics.'

'But, you talked about the poor…'

'That's because their suffering is meaningless.'

At this, the SHO said nothing; he was looking at the air just above my head.

After a while, he spoke again.

'Listen,' he said, sternness creeping back into his voice, 'I will attend your play first day first show. If there is any law and order situation, I will close down the Prithvi for a month.'

I felt the colour draining from my face.

'Okay,' I said, in a small voice.

'You can go now,' he said, with a smile, savouring the fact that he had managed to scare me in the end. He held out his hand and shook mine.

'Best of luck,' he said.

'You did all right in there,' said the Shah of Iran as I came out of the SHO's office.

'I don't like it,' I said.

I called up Sanjana from a public booth and told her

what had transpired at the police station. She told me not to worry, she had spoken to Alyque and he had told her that there would be some voices in my defence at the censor's office. I told her I was slightly demoralised and she asked me not to be so; the play was good and there were enough people on the censor authority who understood good theatre and would speak up on my behalf. I said I was hopeful and we left it at that.

The following day, a Monday, I went to see Isabella at Arthur Road.

'I don't look great,' she said, with a wan smile on her face.

I said nothing.

'What's up with the play?' she said.

I told her what had happened.

She said the article had created a buzz among the authorities. They were paying her more unwanted attention than she could handle. She paused, she sighed.

I asked her what her lawyer was doing. She said he was sincere and was trying his best to help her get out of jail, but there had been a hardening of attitudes after the article. I was flabbergasted at hearing this. I said I was sorry that the article had backfired instead of helping her case.

She suddenly looked up at me with concern in her eyes. She said she had read my piece and was touched by it. She was afraid that the cops might start harassing me too, and that she didn't want to see me getting into trouble for her sake. I said she shouldn't bother about me;

she should think of beating the cops at their own game. They couldn't possibly have a case against her because the truth was that she wasn't involved with any communist conspiracy to overthrow the government. Any judge would see that, I said. She said she wasn't sure about that, that justice was often about perceptions rather than reality. She just wanted me to be okay with the law and not get into any more trouble for her sake. I said, I would always be on her side no matter the consequences. She was the bravest person I had come across in my life. She was glad that I thought so, but she didn't feel particularly brave and that she had doubts about 'ideological issues'. She didn't believe any more that annihilation of the class enemy was the correct political line. She didn't have the stomach for any kind of violence. As she said this, her lips quivered a bit and I felt her eyes welling up with anguish. She was devastated by what her parents were going through. I told her about my parents' reaction. She looked downcast. I told her I was okay with that, and that I was alienated from the family anyway and no longer had the desire to do what pleased them. I also told her about the conversation I had had with my brother, and that he didn't have any answers either and was bent upon running away. She said she wished we could all run away and find some real happiness somewhere else. I told her I didn't think happiness was the answer to my question and that it was more important to stand up for the truth with some dignity. She smiled at this, fleeting and wan. I suddenly realised she was utterly exhausted. I said I guessed it was very easy for me to say this since I wasn't in her position. She said she was sure that all visitors were being placed under surveillance. I said that didn't bother me. She said the cops were all vicious irrational beasts. At this, the bell rang and the visit was over. She looked at me with an intensity that was new. She said not to bother about her, she was resigned to her fate. I felt something choking my voice. I felt like crying. Her lips quivered again, and she looked down at her hands. Then, she was taken away.

When I got back home, my father was there and he looked at me with a stony silence. But, I was no longer intimidated by his presence. Isabella, through her suffering, was liberating me from all conventional constraints. I knew what my father would say if he found out what I was up to. I was no longer scared. I knew that my destiny was to be written by my own choices. I went to my room and lay down on the bed. But, I was restless. I couldn't get Isabella's tortured face out of my mind. I felt my life had been suspended by a love that I had no courage to articulate, that all my romantic fantasms didn't give me the moral force required to tell this woman that I loved her, loved her more than I loved my life. At times, Bobby Roy's face would bob up among the numerous images that my subconscious mind would thrust up to the surface. Then, I would feel hatred raging in my breast against my parents. They had raised me to be an overprotected nincompoop. I knew nothing about love. I wouldn't have the courage or the shamelessness to buy a condom in a pharmacy. I wondered desperately about the circumcision that my virile member required. I realised, at the same time, that my love for Isabella was not physical at all. I just wanted to kiss her and walk down Marine Drive hand in hand with her.

***

I told my family that I was going to spend seven days with the Shah of Iran in his suburban stronghold. I filled a tote bag with a few clothes and some toiletries and took the train from Churchgate. Shah hadn't attended any classes either over the last two years and this was his final term. He was poring over some books on accountancy when I walked into his parlour. He jumped up and embraced me and said, 'Sammy, you bohemian dog, you look as if you had suddenly seen a ghost.' I smiled at this, and said, 'I am all fucked up inside, man.'

Shah's face turned concerned.

'Is that so?' he said slowly, trying to comprehend the depth of my despair. 'You look fine on the outside. Come, come, man, make yourself comfortable.'

This was on the terrace studio that Shah occupied, a very cosy and intimate couple of rooms with a bathroom thrown into the bargain. His parents and his brother lived on the first two floors below. Every now and then, a train would go thundering past, whistling, beating out a military tattoo with its wheels. The night was black.

We settled down on the sofa and Shah said, 'Tell me,

Sam, what is the matter with you?'

'I don't know what the matter is with me,' I said. 'Am I crazy or am I seeing the true face of reality?'

There was a long pause.

'It's about that chick, isn't it?' said Shah.

'Partly, yes, even totally, from a certain perspective.'

'You are in love?'

'Desperately.'

'Tell her you love her.'

'No, it doesn't look appropriate under the circumstances. I don't want to burden her with trifles while she is in custody.'

'What are the circumstances?'

'She is being tortured by the police.'

A train rumbled past as Shah tried to understand the full import of these words.

'Beaten up,' I said, 'served rotten food, deprived of light and air, squalor, noise, all kinds of things.'

'She told you this?'

'Not in so many words, but she looks terrible. I got some details from the radicals who are sitting-in outside the prison. They've got people inside the jail who are providing them with this information.'

'Why are they torturing her?'

'They want her to denounce her comrades was what she told me explicitly.'

'And, she isn't squealing?'

'She has doubts about the Party and its politics. She said she is fed up with violence, she doesn't believe in the

Party line anymore. But, she doesn't want to spend the rest of her life as a snitch, as a collaborator.'

'It's not worth it, man. I think, she should just spill the beans, arrive at a compromise with the authorities and make a clean break with the past.'

'That's cowardly.'

'Does she want to live?'

'Absolutely. Her parents are going through hell. They are trying to pull as many strings as they can, to get her out of there. She also said she feels guilty about putting me in harm's way.'

There was another pause here as yet another train rumbled by.

'Listen,' said Shah, 'just tell her that you love her and that you want her outside the prison so you can spend the rest of your lives together.'

'It doesn't work like that,' I said. 'The Naxalites are no spring chickens, either. They usually have special plans for those who squeal and run.'

'You two could go abroad. But, yeah, it sounds like a lousy deal.'

'I don't know how long she's going to be able to hold out.'

'At least, tell her that you love her and want to spend the rest of your life with her. That might help.'

'Plus, her lawyer is adamant that there should be no deal with the Union of India.'

'I don't know what to say. You make it look hopeless, man. You know what's stopping you from declaring yourself? You are chicken.'

It was my turn to hold my tongue.

'Maybe,' I said finally.

'You don't want to get into trouble,' said Shah.

'No! It's not that....'

I took a deep breath in and then said, 'I don't think I deserve her. The kind of people she knows are not hoity-toity art cinema aficionados. They are larger than life.'

'And, you think they've all had a piece of her action?'

'I *know* they've slept with her.'

'You've got a massive chip on your shoulder, man.'

Another train thundered by.

'Tomorrow,' said Shah, 'I have fixed an appointment with the surgeon. We are going to get rid of your handicap.'

'Is it going to heal before I go back to Nepean Sea Road?'

'Doctor said it's going to take a while. Why don't you stay here for the rest of the month? I mean, until you are over and done with it?'

'I don't think that's going to solve any psychological problems, but, yeah, let's do it.'

At this, the Shah of Iran smiled and said, 'It's going to solve half the problem. The other half is up to you.'

We chatted for a couple of hours, talking about this and that, especially Chandra's break up with his girlfriend and the imminent departure of most of the Gang sitting for their B Com Part II exams in autumn 1978.

'I am going to miss you guys like hell,' I said. 'I am

going to miss all the wild times we've had.'

'Same here, man,' said Shah. 'Life is a bitch. Things get over even before they've begun. What are you going to do, Sam?'

'I don't know.'

'Get yourself a job.'

'I am not going to make it academically. I'll just do enough to pass the exams. I don't know what to do. I am not going to become a fucking pilot like my Dad.'

'What do you want to be in life, Sam?'

'I don't know.'

A train went screeching past.

'I want to be involved in theatre or something artistic,' I said. 'But, I don't see the road to that in front of me. I feel strong only when Isabella backs me. Without her, I am nothing.'

'You—' said Shah and then stopped.

I looked at him and said, 'You think I am a coward, don't you?'

'Listen,' said Shah. 'We guys are cool, even if we are not academic hot shots. But there is a trodden track for even failures like me. But, you, Sam, you've got huge issues to solve. You want to be an artist in a country where the best of us have to starve sometimes. You need money to eat and live comfortably. Where do you think that's going to come from? From theatre?'

'Alyque Padamsee—' I began.

'He's got a cushy job with Lintas. He doesn't do theatre for his bread and butter. Truth is, you've got no role models for what you want to be. If you succeed, you'll be the first.'

'I could go to the National School of Drama. But, my parents will refuse to foot the bill. '

'Why not join the Film and Television Institute in Poona?'

'They require a background in science.'

The Shah of Iran grew pensive at this.

'For me,' I said, 'to be an artist of any worth, something has to snap inside you such that you either practice your art or you die.'

'Let's have dinner,' said Shah.

***

The next day, we went to a clinic on Linking Road. The doctor was waiting for us and grinned broadly as we came in.

'Is it going to hurt like hell?' I asked the doctor.

'We'll be putting you under local anaesthesia,' said the doctor.

The idea of having a needle in my penis was terrifying.

'It will feel like a prick,' said the doctor, 'don't mind the pun.'

I took off my pants and underwear and lay down on the operating table. The doctor took out a long needle; I felt something like a jab at my penis and then it went dead. I closed my eyes and felt a knife being used to cut my flesh, but I felt no pain. It was over in half an hour.

The doctor put a large bandage around my penis and we were done.

'If you get an erection, the suture is going to come apart a little. Early morning blues, y'know. Don't worry, it's eventually going to heal. In another 3 weeks or so.'

The Shah of Iran paid the doctor and we left. I was dressed in a loose pyjama. I rang up home and told my mother that I would be away for three weeks, staying at the Shah of Iran's house. My mother sounded tense and suspicious, but didn't forbid me from staying away.

The worst thing was that early in the morning the suture would come undone. There was nothing to be done, but at the end of three weeks, the gash in my penis had healed substantially. The Shah of Iran offered to drop me home in his car. I said okay. I had had the sutures redone three days ago and my penis felt snug and comfortable now. Only, my exposed head was rubbing against my jeans and I was getting an erection every now and then.

I was not prepared for what was going to happen next.

My father got back from Bangkok the same night and the next day was his day off.

In the morning, he said, 'We need to talk. Urgently.'

He beckoned to me to follow him into the master bedroom. He locked the door behind me. My heart was jumping around like a monkey. I didn't like this one bit.

The first thing he said almost knocked me out senseless.

'You've got a circumcision done?' he said.

I just gazed at my father with wide-eyed surprise.

'How did you know that you needed one?'

I said nothing, sure that he had all the answers.

'You've been visiting prostitutes?' he said. I was speechless and outraged.

He brought out a large manila envelope, took out a bunch of photos and passed them on to me on the other side of his secretaire.

'Have a look at this,' he said.

I picked up the photos, numb with anticipation. There were pictures of me rolling a joint, walking arm on shoulder with Isabella, entering a whore house on Lamington Road, dozens of pictures with me and Isabella with or without the Gang, me and Chandraq seated on the parapet in our garden facing the sea and drinking straight from a bottle of rum, me, Nero and Jiten entering the Prithvi, me chatting with the OC, Juhu police station, and so on and so forth.

Then, he took out a cassette and played it on his small cassette player. I heard myself castigating him for his right-wing, conservative outlook. I heard Chandra making fun of my father and all the other guys laughing loudly. I heard myself and Shah discussing Isabella and this had happened just a few days ago. And, there were a whole lot of other pictures, each more damning than the other.

My mouth was dry with apprehension.

'So,' said my father, 'what do you think?'

I was so outraged that I couldn't find my voice. There was rage building up inside me.

'Y-y-you had me followed by a private eye?' I said, finally.

'You bet I had!' said my father.

And then, he just sat there, looking at me, frowning. The next thing he said brought my world crashing down.

'I am sending you to rehabilitation,' said my father. 'We've got to deal with substance abuse, first of all.'

'N-n-no,' I stammered. 'I will stop on my own. I am not an addict. It's just some recreational stuff.'

'Recreational?!' bellowed my father. 'You call this recreational?! You are taking this poison morning, afternoon and evening and you call this recreational? You are an addict!'

I tried to say something but couldn't find either my voice or the right words.

Meanwhile, the doorbell rang. My father sprang to his feet and welcomed two scruffy-looking men who walked into the room. They grabbed me by my hands; I felt a needle jab me on my forearms and then I went limp. They dragged me down seven floors, my father following them. They shoved me inside a waiting taxi and my father sat in front next to the driver. That was when I broke down completely; my mouth open in a soundless wail. My father looked back at me and I could just nod my head, as if to say, look at what you are doing to me. He gave me that dead pan, stony look. We arrived at a small clinic somewhere off Pedder Road and the two goons took me roughly by my arms and huddled me into a lift. My father stood outside waving me off.

I was taken to a large room with around 40 beds. Most of the people were asleep, a few sat with their backs to the wall, staring into the oblivion. But, it didn't bother me; whatever injection they gave me had rendered me indifferent to my fate. Worse was to follow. The assistants grappled me on to the bed and tied my hands to the bed posts and left me there like a Gregor Samsa cockroach on his back, unable to make a move left or right. Soon, I was asleep. I was woken up rudely by the clock in the ward, it was 2 pm.

'Lunch!' they said.

I said I wasn't hungry.

The guys took no notice of what I said or did. They untied me, lifted me out of my bed and roughly made me sit down on the floor along with a dozen other inmates. A thali was placed in front of me. I saw some dal, a mixed vegetables dish and some fish.

'You have to eat,' said one of the louts, 'before you are given your medicines.'

I picked at my food listlessly and felt exhausted. I swallowed it without chewing. Everything tasted like gruel. The guy next to me had his nose running and was shovelling food into his mouth nonchalantly. He asked me why I was there. I was too spaced out to give him an answer.

'I want to talk to my parents,' I said.

He looked at me without smiling.

'Visiting hours are between 6 and 7 in the evening.'

'I don't want to stay here,' I said. 'I don't like this place.'

I realised I was sounding like a little cry-baby.

The other guy sniggered.

'We all want to get out,' he said. 'That depends on your doctor and your guardians.'

'How long have you been here?' I asked.

'I've been in and out over the last 2 years,' he said.

'What's wrong with you?' I said.

'I broke up with my girlfriend and took to shooting myself with heroin,' he said. 'I was really out of control. And you?'

I didn't answer the question, just looked at the unappetising fish curry in front of me as if it was a mountain to climb.

'Drugs? Or, just plain old schizophrenia?' said the guy.

'I am not crazy,' I said.

'So, drugs,' said the other guy.

I said nothing. I didn't want to share my life with anybody in the room. Most of them looked as if they belonged to good families, but some of them, like my neighbour, with his snot covered runny nose, looked distinctly underclass.

'Where did you get the money for your habit?' I said.

'I stole my father's money,' he said indifferently. 'That's how he found out.'

'Your father must be loaded,' I said.

'He's a textiles wholesaler in Gamdevi,' he said.

'I want to call my parents,' I said.

'Sorry, no phone calls allowed,' said my neighbour. 'You'll have to wait till visiting hours.'

Suddenly, a quarrel broke out at the end of the row where I was seated. Somebody had hurled his thali against the wall. The two louts reappeared out of somewhere and roughly caught hold of the man and took him outside.

'Electroconvulsive shock therapy,' said my neighbour chuckling.

'Is this some kind of loony bin?' I asked incredulously.

'Partly. It's about 50-50. 20 rehab and 20 lunatics.'

Then suddenly, a guy with a vest and a lungi, started walking down the row, saying, 'I have been in the BSF, and have killed 30 people with my own hands. Anybody falling out of line will be singled out for merciless treatment. Is that clear? Either you behave, or you get taken to the machine and that costs Rs 6,000 per shot. Think about it.'

At that, somebody said, 'Why don't you just go and fuck yourself.'

The BSF man took out one of his chappals and started beating someone out of my line of vision.

'Are inmates allowed to beat each other up?' I asked. I was neither angry, nor fearful, but in despair.

My neighbour said, 'That man broke the collarbone of one of the nurses just two days ago.'

After lunch was over, a plump lady in a nurse's uniform walked in and suddenly all the inmates flocked around her. She had a little box with her. She called out a name and the person concerned stepped forward and took some pill or the other from the matron, popped it in his mouth and swallowed it down with some water.

My turn came. I said I wasn't sick. The nurse arched her eyebrows.

'This is for your own good,' she said and handed me a yellow pill. 'If you don't take it now, it will be mixed with your food the next time around.'

I took the little yellow pill and had it. After some time, I felt groggy, but it wasn't a drug high, just a little mind numbing.

'Methadone,' said the boy with a snotty nose. 'It's cold turkey management. They'll keep reducing the dosage until they're done.'

'I could've done this on my own,' I said, 'I am not an addict. I can give it up any time I want.'

'That's what everybody says,' said snot-face.

I went back to my bed and lay down. This time they didn't tie my hands. I lay there sprawled on the bed and suddenly Isabella's face popped up in my mind. This time I couldn't control myself. I wept bitter tears of sorrow and grief. I wondered whether someone would tell her of my predicament—it had been done so smoothly, so unobtrusively. I wanted to talk to her, see her beautiful face. Instead, I was raging against my father with all the strength left. I drifted off to sleep, merciful sleep which knew no boundaries and made all human desires equal.

In the evening, one of the assistants came into the room, to which access was barred by a collapsible gate, and hollered my name. I responded and came over to the gate.

'Step outside,' he ordered.

The collapsible gate was drawn and I stepped outside.

'Walk in front of me and not too fast,' barked the man.

I felt relieved. I rehearsed in my mind what I would tell my parents. When we walked down two floors, I was asked to make a sharp right turn and there were cabins separated by wooden partitions. The assistance, or rather the guard, shoved me inside a room and closed the door behind me. I stood facing a rather despicable piece of humanity, a small man with horn-rimmed spectacles busy writing something on his letterhead.

'Sit down,' he said.

I sat down opposite him. He continued writing on his letterhead, without lifting his head, without even looking at me. After about five long minutes, he stopped and looked up.

'You are in for substance abuse?' he said.

I said nothing. I meant to refuse any kind of collaboration with this fascist pig.

'What kind of substance? The photographs, I am afraid, are not very clear in this regard.'

I said nothing.

'Oh dear, oh dear,' sighed the doctor. 'You are one of those—'

He looked at me, rather wearily, I thought.

'If you don't cooperate, I will have to send your file to some other doctors who don't believe in gentle persuasion.'

I said nothing.

He said, 'Look, I want to help you get out of this institution. You don't look schizophrenic to me, that's one positive factor and you have some pride still left inside you. It's best you cooperate and go through the rigmarole.'

'Where are my parents?' I said.

'They've been advised not to get in touch with you for a few days,' he said. 'You'll get to see them once you start cooperating. See, if you don't talk to me, they'll assume you are a junkie, and will be tied to your bed morning evening and night.'

At this, I swallowed hard, but said nothing.

'So what was it?' said the doctor. 'Cannabis, barbiturates, cocaine, heroin?'

'Cannabis,' I said almost inaudibly.

'Okay, it's not as bad as I thought it was,' he said.

I said I detested this place and wanted to get out as soon as possible. I said some of the inmates were getting roughed up by the louts who ran the place.

'Restrain,' said the doctor. 'There are some pretty nasty customers up there in the ward. You are not one of them, I acknowledge, but, still, it is better to take precautions. How much of it did you take in a day?'

'A couple of joints,' I lied.

'10 grams? 20 grams?'

'10 grams,' I said, having no idea how much the stuff weighed.

'Okay, so 10 grams is not all that much,' he said, now smiling at me.

'I want to talk to my father,' I said. 'He's making a

mistake, I am not an addict. I can stop on my own. I don't like my ward inmates.'

'Yes, yes, I know you can stop on your own, but before that, we must get a grip on your dependence, your withdrawal symptoms, cold turkey as you call it.'

'I am not a junkie,' I said.

'Okay, understood,' he said. 'It's not as bad as I imagined it would be.'

'I don't want to be tied to my bed,' I said. 'I feel like an animal.'

At this, the doctor smiled at me.

'I will tell the sister to see to it that you are not tied up. Anything else?'

'I want some books, reading material.'

'You've got the newspaper.'

'I said books, not just newspapers.'

'All right, I will instruct the ward boys to get you some books to read. In English?'

'In English.'

'Okay, I am going to prescribe you a tablet of Methadone, twice a day, morning, after breakfast, and evening after dinner. These are mild sedatives and will prevent your mind from heating up unduly.'

'Also, I want to see my friends.'

'Ah, that's a different proposition altogether. They are all addicts as the detective said. It's better that you stay away from them, or else there will be a relapse and you will be back here in no time. There are people here, among your ward, who have been around for four years or more. Do you want to end up like them?'

I said nothing. I made up my mind to not utter a word more. But, my mind was in a whirl as I was led back to the ward by the louts as previously.

What hurt the most was that I couldn't see Isabella anymore. I silently cursed my parents for my plight. How could they be so hard-hearted, so callous, sending me to this dungeon, this hole for low lives? I wasn't an addict, I could stop on my own, I could leave this artificial paradise any time I wanted. I learned that everyone in rehab thought the same thing, no matter how habituated they might be.

In the evening, one of the louts brought me a copy of Oscar Wilde's complete works. This wasn't the kind of stuff I would normally read, but then, something was better than nothing. I tried reading *The Picture of Dorian Gray* and finding it unreadable, gave up halfway through. Then, all of a sudden, I stumbled on to *De Profundis*. I was immediately drawn in. I saw the miracles failure can perform. Each and every word was like an arrow aimed at the world. I particularly liked the part describing Jesus as a Man of Sorrow and how the inmates of the prison had helped him cope with the more brutal aspects of life in incarceration. I wholly identified with the author's misery and his new found faith in the God of the New Testament. Being gay under Victoria was the worst thing that could happen to a creative person, I thought. The prison he described was not much better than the loony bin thrust upon me by that unfeeling bastard, my father.

The methadone kept me quiet for a while, but soon I would be terror-struck at the thought of spending weeks and months in this hell. The bathroom door wouldn't lock and there was a rectangular window cut through the door which allowed the sisters and the other inmates to look at the bather's nakedness. I decided to bathe in my shorts. The bathroom was filthy with dry faeces stuck to the surface of the commode. Nobody ever cleaned this.

No sooner did I hit the sack at night than Isabella's face would once again bob up from the depths of my mind to the surface. I couldn't do anything for her anymore. What about the Shah of Iran, Nero, Ram, Feridoon, Benny and Chandra? Wouldn't they smell a rat? But, then I realised they had their exams coming up soon and must be preparing for them hard. They were all gifted students and many of them would launch themselves on brilliant careers shortly. Totally unlike me. I wondered and wondered and soon found myself slumbering away like a stuffed hog.

After 30 days of this torture, my parents came to take me away. My father embraced me and I noticed that his eyes were wet. This appeased me somewhat, but I told myself I would soon go and see Isabella and find out how she was faring.

'We have been given strict instructions not to let you out of sight for another 2 weeks,' said my father. 'Son, it's not too late, you can still get back into the groove if you make an effort.'

I said nothing. In my heart, there was only bitter

sorrow and nothing else.

Home felt different. It was like an extension of what I had seen and heard for the last 30 days. It was a prison where I was being held as a prisoner of war, against my will. When I walked into my room, I found my brother immersed in a magazine. He didn't look at me, he was deliberately avoiding eye contact with me. When he finally closed his magazine to look at me, it was as if I was a foreigner or something. I could see him struggling to find the right words to say to me. Knowing him, he must have been shocked out of his wits upon learning that I had a habit.

'Welcome home,' he said.

I said nothing. I was feeling tired and lay down on my bed immediately. My throat was parched and my mind was a blur. I couldn't focus on anything. All I could think of was Isabella.

My father walked in and, looking penitent, said to me, 'Son, this is for your own benefit, but the doctor has said you have to be kept under observation for the next three months. You can't leave house till you are absolutely okay. Okay?'

I said nothing. My thoughts raced wildly against each other. I thought about sneaking out and spending the night at some railway station. I could go to the Shah of Iran's house in Bandra, and shack up there. I desperately wanted to see Isabella.

'So, no going out,' said my father, 'and no phone calls.'

'This is a jail,' I almost shouted at my father.

At this, he seemed taken aback.

'It's for your own good, son,' he said, quietly. 'You can go anywhere you like after 3 months, accompanied by your brother or sister.'

'This is worse than jail,' I shouted at him. 'I don't need chaperoning. I am an adult, I can make up my own mind about things.'

'No seeing that female,' said my father sternly.

'I will,' I said, 'at the first opportunity I get.'

'We will be locking the door at night,' my father said, sounding weary and sad for the first time. 'Plus, an attendant will come and look after you from 8 to 8, tomorrow onwards.'

I said nothing. I was staring at the ceiling.

'Look,' said my father, almost pleading now, 'you are the flesh of my flesh. I suffer when you suffer. Think about your parents, we're old and defenceless people. Don't be cruel. God knows I've been tormented for weeks, worried myself to a standstill over your condition. Take your pills and listen to us and you will be free within 3 months.'

'You sent a private eye to snoop on me,' I said. 'What kind of freedom are you talking about?'

At this, my father looked away in embarrassment and sorrow.

'It won't happen again, I promise,' he said. He sounded abject and that touched my heart.

I said nothing.

'Get some rest and we'll talk in the morning.' Then,

he left the room.

As soon as he was out of sight, my brother turned over in his bed and asked, 'What was it like? The loony bin?'

'Awful,' I said, without looking at him.

'We won't talk about it, if you don't want to,' he said, with some exasperation. 'For God's sake, I am your elder brother. If you can't be frank with me, then I don't know who else you can speak to.'

I said nothing. For me, he was just another agent of surveillance.

Then he said, 'I've got a letter from Harvard. I will be leaving next month.'

'Good for you,' I said quietly. I didn't want to talk about Harvard, I wanted to know if Isabella was all right or not.

'If you want to talk to someone, I can arrange that for you,' he said. 'We have a cordless telephone in the house now.'

It was my turn to look at him.

'Never mind,' I said. 'I don't want any favours, especially not from you.'

My brother put his magazine aside and went and fetched something from the cupboard. It was a ghetto blaster.

He slipped a cassette into the machine and immediately the opening bars of *Gimme Shelter* began to play.

'Dad bought this for me in Singapore,' he said. 'You can have it after I am gone.'

The music made me feel a little better.

'I didn't know you liked the Stones,' I said.

'You think I am some old fuddy-duddy, listening to Engelbert Humperdinck and dreaming of escape,' he said.

'You didn't get into trouble,' I said spitting the venom from my mouth. 'I got into trouble. This is not wining and dining music, y'know.'

'You don't have to turn into a junkie to listen to the Stones,' he said.

'I am not a junkie,' I almost shouted at him.

At this, my mother came into the room, cigarette in hand.

She said, 'Son, have some food and go to sleep. Your brain is overworked, you need rest. That's what the doctor said.'

'I am not hungry,' I said.

'Forgive us,' she said, tears welling up in her eyes. 'We didn't know what to do with you. Sincerely. I won't have my child destroying himself under my nose. Please have your dinner and then you can talk all night long if you want. We only want you to be happy.'

'How can anyone be happy in a jail?' I said. 'You think I am some kind of a baby, don't you?'

'Your father is losing sleep over you. He's tired all the time. He's taken leave because he is under great physical stress and you can't jeopardise the lives of passengers. We only want you to become healthy and normal once again. That's all. Give up your filthy habits. Come back to us.'

I said nothing. I wanted to hurt them, as badly as I could.

'You don't have to eat with us, if you don't want to,' said my mother. 'I'll bring you some stew and a French loaf, you can have it in your bed.'

'Stop bothering about me!' I shouted at her. 'I don't love you people! Just leave me alone!'

At this, my mother broke down completely and started sobbing. She left the room.

The next morning, a burly, stockish man, obviously from the underclass, turned up at 8 in the morning and the first thing he did was to shave me while I was still in bed. I had slept badly and was totally exhausted, emotionally and physically. I had barely touched my dinner, having no appetite.

'My name Bala,' he said, exposing a perfect row of teeth with a gap between the incisors. 'I am attendant. You need cigarettes?'

I looked at him for a while and then said, 'A packet of Charminar.'

I looked around for my brother, but he had already left the house. The atmosphere must have been oppressive for him too.

Bala brought me the packet of Charminar and I paid him with whatever money was left over from my pocket money.

'My job, looking after you,' said Bala. 'You need something, I get it. Just tell, okay?'

I asked him to get the cordless phone for me.

'Sorry, not allowed. You want to brush teeth?'

I said nothing.

He got up, went to the bathroom and came back with my brush, toothpaste some water in a mug and a plastic basin.

I brushed my teeth, listlessly. After I had rinsed my mouth, he took away everything.

'Breakfast?' he said.

I said nothing.

'You want egg?'

I said nothing. I didn't want to touch anything coming from my parents.

'I want to go out,' I said, finally.

'Sorry, not allowed.'

I turned over and went back to sleep.

I don't know how many minutes later this happened, but someone was shaking me awake. I opened my eyes and found my father standing beside me. He looked terrible. He hadn't slept well either, but this touched no chord in me.

He handed the receiver of the cordless phone over to me.

'Call who you want,' he said.

And then, he and Bala stood there, staring at me.

'I want some privacy,' I said.

'Sorry—' went both he and Bala.

'Not allowed,' I said. I hurled the receiver against the wall.

Dad went and picked it off the floor and put it to his ear.

'It's working,' he said. 'You can make any call you want, but in our presence.'

'Is this the Iron Curtain?' I said.

'It's for your—' my father stammered.

'I know what's good for me,' I snarled at him. 'This house is a fucking prison.'

I was showing them the real me, outside the bounds of respectable fiction.

My father quietly left the room, holding the phone in his hand.

'They suffering,' said Bala.

'I am not their son,' I said, bitterly.

'No, no. They love you.'

'Fuck off. Get out of my life. I don't want anything from you.'

Bala looked down at his fingernails briefly.

'You are mental.'

'Fuck off.'

I had hot flushes, my brain seemed unwired. I was nervous and distraught. I was having trouble focusing on things. Everything was a torture, even shifting positions on my bed. My head felt light and airy like a helium-filled balloon, I couldn't think. There was only one word going through my mind: Isabella, Isabella, Isabella....I decided I would get out of this prison somehow or the other, even if I had to wander the streets of Bombay naked and hungry. How to get rid of this baboon with a one track mind and the only English words he knew was, 'not allowed'?

I said, 'I want to go to the loo.'

'Okay,' said Bala.

I got up without much difficulty, went to the attached bathroom and locked the door behind me. I took my throwaway Gillette razor from its stand and slashed my wrists with it. The cut wasn't deep and all I could get was a thin seeping and oozing of blood. I put my wrists into a bucket of water and watched the blood lazily leaving my body. Within 30 minutes, the bucket had taken on an orange hue. My mind was in a daze; at this rate it would take me a whole day for all the blood to empty out of my veins.

I must have lost track of time, but at some point there was a loud banging on the door. I could hear my mother screaming out, 'Open the door! Open the door!' The banging on the door went on for some time. I could hear my mother bawling her guts out. My head was drooping and it felt light, I was having trouble connecting the dots.

Then, there was a change in tactics. Somebody, perhaps Bala, was trying to force the door apart from its hinges. He finally succeeded and everybody, my father, my mother, my sister and Bala were staring at me sitting on the bathroom floor with blood in the bucket. It didn't register at the time, but at some point my mother fainted. At some point in time, an ambulance was called and I was rushed over to the emergency ward of Breach Candy hospital. At some point in time, the doctor looked at my wrists and said, 'It isn't serious. I will do the dressing, he should be okay in a couple of days.' At some point in time, I was taken back to the house, to my room. All sharp objects were removed from my room. The door to the balcony was padlocked. I wasn't allowed to lock the door of the bathroom when I used it. My reaction to all this was refusal to touch food. When Bala brought me my breakfast, I threw the glass of lukewarm milk on his face.

After this, my father walked into my room with the cordless phone in his hand and said, quietly, 'You can call who you want, son,' and then left the room along with Bala. I was sensing victory. I immediately called Isabella's number. Her mother picked up the phone.

'Aunty,' I said, 'how is Isabella?'

'She's on a hunger strike,' she said. 'She is being fed intravenously at the prison hospital.'

My heart sank when I heard this.

I asked about the progress of the case.

'The charge sheet has been filed and a date has been fixed for opening arguments.'

'Is she allowed visitors?'

'No. She is in hospital, under 24x7 surveillance. They fear she could harm herself.'

'Does she have reading material?'

'No. She is not allowed anything. The lawyer is going to petition the court on this and other matters.'

She asked how I was doing, and I made some vague remarks about being ill and bed-ridden.

'Take care of yourself, son,' said her mother.

'Okay,' I said.

And that was that.

I called for Bala and he came and took the phone away from me.

'Feeling better,' he said with an uncertain smile on his face.

I said nothing. I didn't even look at his face. I was tossing and turning in bed, I was in hell.

A doctor came in mid-morning and gave me a shot of sedative. That calmed things down a bit, my mind went from being a chaos of desire and violence to numbness. I was constantly plotting and scheming about getting out of here, but I couldn't see how. I could go and shack up with the Shah of Iran for a while, but what after that? I had no answers as far as my future was concerned. Also, my father said he would be sleeping in my room and my brother would take the couch in the living room.

I said, 'I wanted to listen to some music.'

Bala brought out the ghetto blaster and a drawer full of cassettes. I slid in *Déjà vu* by CSN&Y. In a few moments, I was calm again.

I wanted to die.

11

And then suddenly, after 3 months of torture, I was a free man once again. Or, somewhat free.

My father said, 'The cops will be watching you.'

'Let them,' I said.

Then, he said something that resembled a torpedo.

'I have asked for a transfer out of Bombay. I have asked to be posted in Calcutta.'

I just stared at him, my mind blank, unable to grasp the full extent of my misery.

'I am not going to Calcutta,' I said.

'Where will you stay? Who will look after you?'

'I have friends.'

'I mean, for the rest of your life.'

'I'll find a job.'

'Who will give you a job on the basis of your mark sheet, assuming that you sit for your B Com exams?'

'I'll find something.'

'You will have to earn enough to be able to stay in a decent locality, pay your bills and for your food, transport, clothes. Will you be able to manage that on your own?'

'We'll see.'

'Son,' said my father, very solemn now. 'Life is not a joke. You can shout freedom from the roof tops all you want, but nobody's even going to look at you unless you have some money in your pocket. You have no idea how tough things can get. The best thing for you is to give up your romantic foolishness and come with us to Calcutta.'

'But—' I tried to say something.

My father raised his hand, frown on his face, 'I have tried disciplining you. It's been a failure. I have decided that you are on your own if that's what you want. You want to throw away your life because of some dumb girl somewhere, that's entirely up to you. But, from my experience I can tell you, life is cruel and unforgiving. Think about that.'

And, the conversation was over.

The first thing I did was to take a bus to Arthur Road prison. I found out that the chargesheet hadn't stood up under judicial scrutiny and that Isabella had been granted bail and would be out of prison the next day at 4 pm. After that, I went to college. There was no one. Our table was empty, the Gang had been dissolved; they were all presumed to be studying hard. I decided to take a train to Khar and go see the Shah of Iran.

'Sam, you bohemian dog, where have you been?' said Shah.

I told him the whole story. He listened in complete silence, I had never seen him looking so serious ever.

'You are in deep shit, bohemian dog,' said Shah. He

thought for a minute and then said that I could stay with him as long as I wanted, as long as it took me to find a decent job.

He picked up the phone and spoke to Benny Pathak whose uncle ran a famous advertising firm. They had a brief conversation during which I heard Shah saying whether I could go over and give a test the day after. Then, he turned to me and said

'If you get your degree, you could land a job with Frank Camoes's agency. I have fixed up a test for you within 3 days.'

'How long can I stay with you?' I asked.

'Forever,' replied Shah with a smile.

And then, looking at the scepticism on my face, he said, 'Look, we'll cross that bridge when we come to it. Just give the test, and we'll see what happens.'

'I'll have to deal with my father. He thinks you guys and that chick are ruining my prospects.'

'To hell with your old man. If he isn't giving you any money, he doesn't have power of life and death over you. First things first, you have to get your degree.'

'That will take some doing. I haven't learnt a shit in the past two years, y'know.'

'Do the minimum necessary.'

'Okay,' I said. I was dejection personified.

'Hey, cheer up, bohemian dog, your chick is out of prison tomorrow! We'll celebrate that with some weed.'

'I can't. I am being watched by the police. That's what I have been told, unofficially.'

'Okay, booze then.'

I nodded and looked away.

'Look,' said Shah, 'pick up a few things and come over tomorrow. Tell your folks you are going to spend the week with me, studying.'

'They'll laugh at that.'

'Let them,' said Shah, dead serious now. 'It's a question of life and death, man. Just pick up some books and clothes and shift the capital of Bohemia.'

'You've got your own studying to do.'

'Don't worry about me, Sam. I'll be fine.'

'I'll try, but I can't guarantee success.'

'Try. Your life depends on it.'

The next day, at 4 pm, I was in front of the gates to Arthur Road prison. Isabella's parents were there too, and they were delighted to see me.

'Hi, Sam,' said her mother.

'Hi, Aunty,' I said.

'Where have you been?'

'I was having my own set of problems to solve at home.'

'You look fine,' said her father, a Marlboro hanging from the corner of his mouth.

'Isabella really missed you,' said her mother. 'She was constantly asking about you and we couldn't tell her anything. I am glad to see you hale and hearty.'

I managed a smile. My heart was thumping. I wasn't sure I would be able to handle what was going to come through the trapdoor built into the prison gates. They had begun letting out prisoners in dribs and drabs. At around 5:30 pm, someone with frizzy hair, thin as a reed, with a colourless face stumbled out of the trap door.

'Isabella,' shouted her mother.

She looked at us and immediately her whole face brightened. She came running over and—she embraced me first.

'Sam, Sam, where were you all these days?' she said, half sobbing, 'I've missed you so much.'

I was on the point of going stiff and awkward all over when I mentally adjusted myself and put an arm around her back and said, 'I have missed you, too.' That was factually correct.

'Darling,' said her mom, 'you are looking terrible. Never mind, let's all go home and get a bite to eat. You coming, Sam?'

I nodded shyly.

Her parents had no problem with me.

On the way, we chatted about life in prison. Isabella, looking worn out, said there were cockroaches in her cell and mosquitoes, too. They would give her tube of mosquito repellent once a week. That made her feel sticky and sweaty all night long. She had no contact with any other prisoners. She was not allowed to leave her cell for the evening recess for the fear of contaminating the other prisoners with her poisonous ideas. Interrogations were rough with female officers hitting her and manhandling her in the most callous way. They would just slap her around and make her head spin with dizziness. Her lawyer couldn't do a thing about it, the police just denied everything. The Judge was sympathetic but wouldn't budge without evidence. She finally decided to refuse food to stop the beatings and they had to take her to the dispensary, tie her hands to the bed and put her on a saline drip and feed her through her nose. I had spent 3 months in a loony bin myself, I could relate to her predicament, but I said nothing in front of her parents. I had this stupid smile on my face which conveyed the nothingness of my moral being. There was no doubt in my mind anymore that this beautiful woman was in love with me. This should have made me happy. But I wasn't. I wasn't sure that love was the answer to my question, or that love was strong enough to conquer the world of happiness.

'First things first,' said Isabella's mom as we entered their spacious Cuffe Parade apartment, 'you must take a bath. Then, I'll have some coffee and biscuits for you two.'

Isabella beckoned to me to follow her into her room.

The room was bare now, the poster of Che Guevara was gone, and so was the red flag of revolution. Her bookcase had been tampered with and there were large sections missing. Grief stricken, Isabella went over and peered at her books, what remained of them.

They've taken away Bakunin, Mao's little red book, Sartre, all of it. Isabella was almost in tears.

'Those books are hard to come by,' she said. 'They are like my friends.'

I fetched out my handkerchief and gave it to her.

'It's all right, Sam,' said Isabella. 'I'll get over it. These guys have almost taken away my life.'

The word processor, too, was missing.

'They were trying to rape your mind,' I said.

Isabella turned to look at me and smiled radiantly.

'That's exactly it,' she said, 'Sam, you are so good with words.'

And then, she disappeared into the attached bathroom and soon I could hear her singing *Let It Be* under the shower.

She came out after half an hour. She didn't look like her former self, she was colourless and exhausted, but her eyes looked refreshed. She took off the towel wrapped around her head and started blow drying her hair.

'So, tell me, Sam, why didn't you come to see me for 3 months?' she said. 'Did the cops pick you up for questioning? Or something like that?'

I shook my head.

'Much worse than that,' I said. 'I was in a loony bin.'

'What?!' she said, looking shocked.

I told her the whole story.

'Jesus,' she said, when I had finished. 'Sounds much worse than a prison. In prison, they at least respect your physical mechanism beyond a certain point. They never poison you with harmful chemicals.'

'I survived,' I said.

Then, I said, 'My dad's asked for a transfer to Calcutta. I am expected to follow the family.'

Isabella held her breath and then said, 'Oh no!'

'I've spoken to Shah, he's fixed some kind of a copywriting test at Frank Camoes. He says I can shack up with him for as long it takes to settle down in Bombay for good. He thinks this can work. What the hell am I going to do in Calcutta? I've been there twice before, and I hate the place.'

Isabella took my hand in hers and said, 'God will find a way…'

'What's God got to do with this? Do you believe in God?'

'Yes, I do. Mao believed in God.'

'How can you reconcile the idea of God with the idea of revolution?'

'Revolution is also a manifestation of God's will.'

'Do you think he looks like Durga or something?'

'No,' she said, suddenly downcast, 'it has nothing to do with religion. But, Jesus was a revolutionary…'

I shrugged. I had stopped believing in God since I was 13 or so, when I looked at the idol of the goddess and said to myself, God can't look like this.

'What does the cadre think?' I said.

She shrugged.

'Does the Party know about your change of heart?'

'They know. I told them that I have my doubts about this annihilation business. People love their parents and their siblings, and vice versa. Annihilating the class enemy also means that the most deprived are shot dead because they happen not to understand the Party programme when it comes to the family.'

'Would you settle for an arranged marriage?'

'Never! That's a different ball game altogether. I don't want to be described like a cow for sale in some goddamn newspaper.'

'There you are. This family nonsense has its limits. You have wonderful parents who understand ideas, like freedom and equality.'

'Sam, Sam, Sam,' said Isabella all of a sudden. 'You mustn't go to Calcutta. Your life is here, in Bombay. You are going to be a playwright or a film-maker. That's your vocation in life. You can't do anything else, corrupt your soul, or become a commercial zombie of some kind. No! I'll take care of you. I have a cousin who's looking for paying guests. I'll talk to her and she can take you in.'

'Who'll pay the bills? You?'

'Yeah, me!' she said eagerly. 'What's wrong with that? We're not into some bourgeois client-patron relationship. All you should do is think about writing. I'll take care of the rest.'

I looked down at my fingernails. I was embarrassed and didn't want to show it. I was not equal to Isabella's passion. I didn't measure up to her love. Besides, I had doubts I would ever write anything meaningful ever again.

'What is the Party saying?' I asked, trying to change the focus of the conversation.

'They've forgotten about me. I am on my own now. That's for the best, I think. Besides, my conscience is clear. I didn't denounce anybody, I didn't collaborate or anything, I am not a snitch. That only means that the cops are going to come down on me like a ton of bricks. They can't forgive me for not squealing like some of the other comrades who sold themselves out. Like Judas. I am through.'

Then, Bobby Roy loomed at the door to her room.

'Bobby!' cried Isabella. 'Where *have* you been? I was just thinking about you!'

'You're not looking good, kid,' said Bobby.

'Oh, I'll be okay in a few days,' said Isabella. 'You're looking great though.'

'Just back from the Serengeti,' said Bobby casually, as if going there was the most ordinary thing in the world. Money pushes your horizons further, makes conquering things normal. It is people like me, the excluded, who think that climbing the Everest is a heroic deed.

'Hi, Sam,' he said, as if taking notice of me for the first time. 'How have you been?'

'Okay,' I said, with a smile.

'When is your show coming up at Prithvi?' said Bob.

'I don't know,' I said, looking at his huge 6 and a half feet frame.

'Sam's father wants to take him to Calcutta,' said Isabella. 'Don't you think that's awful?!'

'They have 8 hour power cuts, the traffic is always in a mess, there is garbage lying all over the place. And then, you have Bengali superciliousness to deal with. Y'know, our culture is the real thing, all the others are spurious off shoots motivated by prosaic middle-class aspirations.'

'I know,' I said. 'But, I might not have a choice. Can you get me a decent job somewhere, which will allow me to pay my bills and eat with what's leftover?'

'What about working in a newspaper?' he said. 'Wait a sec…I can call up Khushwant and ask him if he can accommodate you somewhere.'

'You mean Khushwant Singh?' I said.

'Yes,' said Isabella. 'Editor of *The Illustrated Weekly of India*. My dad knows him, too. That's a pretty good idea, Bob. Let's do it.'

Isabella got off her bed and went over to the secretaire in her room and fetched out a diary from the drawer.

She flipped a few pages until she found what she was looking for. She dialled a number from her diary and said, 'Hey, Bob, you do the talking…'

I didn't want to be beholden to Bob for anything in my life, but I said nothing.

'Khushwant?' said Bob, into the phone. 'How are things with you, you old rake? I am fine…just got back from Africa…a rally, that's right…how's the magazine coming along?...listen…there's this friend of ours who's looking for a job, you got anything?...okay…okay… okay…he's right here…here, Sam, talk to Khushwant.'

I took the cordless receiver from him and said, 'Hello, Sir.'

'What exactly are you looking for, Sam?' said Khushwant.

'Anything that will allow me to keep body and soul

together in Bombay,' I said. And then, I added, for good measure, 'I don't know what are the possibilities in the media, I don't follow politics too much.'

'We could put you in the features section,' said Khushwant. 'You could do human interest stories with the occasional interview with a film star thrown in. Would that interest you?'

Had I been alone, I would have said humans don't interest me that much. But in Isabella and Bobby Roy's presence, I said, 'Sure.'

'Come over next Thursday morning, I will give you a small test and then we'll take it from there. By the way, are you the one who wrote that piece on Isabella for the TOI?'

'Yes,' I said, flushing pink from neck upwards.

'It was great, I liked it enormously,' said Khushwant, 'if you can write like that consistently, then you'll have no problems finding a place in the Weekly.'

'Thank you, sir,' said I.

'Thursday morning, then, okay?' said Khushwant. 'I will tell my secretary to expect you around eleven-ish. Okay? Bye.'

And, he put down the phone.

'That was short and sweet, wasn't it?' said Bobby Roy.

'I'll have to take a test coming Thursday morning,' I said nervously.

'You'll sail through, Sam,' said Isabella. 'I mean, you are the only person I know who can really write.'

'Did he say anything about remuneration?' said Bobby Roy.

'No, nothing,' I said. 'I guess, it is a little premature.'

'That's right,' said Bob. He was looking smug and complacent about it.

Problem was, I didn't know whether I respected Khushwant or not. I had come to distrust people who thought that politics was an instrument of self-advancement and living the good life. I didn't know much about politics, especially Party politics, but for me, the battle was a battle for ideas, for how we wanted to live in this world. Writing was, for me, a way of changing my world, of creating more lebensraum (that dirty word) for maniacs like me. Plus, I didn't want to become a hot-shot journalist, rubbing shoulders with the high and the mighty and ending up as an editor-in-chief, or something. That was not my ambition. I was afraid that in a professional set up I would just get pushed upward on the strength of my work and gradually give everything up for the cosy comfort of an upper middle-class existence. Khushwant Singh may not like my brand of politics.

'Drinks anyone?' asked Bobby Roy.

'Just hang on,' said Isabella, 'I'll get some beers from the fridge.'

'Excellent!' said Bobby Roy.

I wondered distractedly whether Isabella and Bobby Roy had slept with each other. It was painful thinking about it. Maybe it was just puritanism, sex as something secretive, clandestine. Somehow, I couldn't hold it against Isabella, Bobby Roy was a gorgeous specimen of manhood. Any girl would give half her arm to sleep with him. Plus, he was royalty, scion of the royal house of Peepli. His mother was an inspiration for several masters of the Bengal School. He was well-connected worldwide. I wouldn't want to see myself as a rival for Isabella's affection. Next to him, I was a blubbering middle-class idiot. Then, I thought about my parents and was driven crazy with hurt and despair. They were peasants. So what if my father was a pilot and my mother a chain-smoker. They would ferociously defend middle-class norms and values. They were pious, conservative and tyrannical. In my eyes, they suffered by comparison with Isabella's and Bobby Roy's parents. The only thing that separated me from them was that I had written a play that challenged, obscurely, middle-class norms and values. They thought being in Sydenham was a big deal. I would sit for my exams, come out with flying colours, get a cushy 9 to 5 job, get a woman to fuck, produce children and then fade away into the gentle night of the believers. Whereas I, to be absolutely frank, I was satanic in my aspirations, I wanted to break everything, flout every norm, exclude the superfluous and be left with enough mind to enjoy it. What could I write about? My experience was so narrow, so hedged in from all sides, so devoid of poetry. What did I know? Nothing. The only thing I knew was that I couldn't fit in with my parents' scheme of things, be a faithful replica of their own selves, struggling every day to maintain themselves in their position in the world. All the rest was just literature. People didn't read books to change their world; they read books that were amusing, informative or edifying. Whereas, I had opened, with considerable help from intoxication, a trapdoor which led to the other side. And, what was there on the other side? Isabella and bliss? I wasn't sure. My inspiration had all dried up. Or, so I thought. I had tried to write a radio play for a contest run by the BBC; it was a hopeless effort and I petered out after two or three pages. It didn't come to me naturally. That was a bad sign.

Plus, I was alone. The Gang would pass out of college in another six months and be scattered abroad by life. I would be on my own, without the crazy voice of the Shah of Iran, and mellifluous artistic elucubrations of Nero Gomes or the witty sarcasm of Ram Bhonsle, to see me through. What could I be without them? Sure, I had a couple of hard contacts with reality coming up. How would I face up to them? I would have to twist myself out of shape to produce the kind of normative crap that filled our newspapers and magazines. There was nothing creative about journalism or copywriting. They were just professions that allowed you to think about money, mostly other people's money. What could I say about soap or lampshades? It was the worst way to make money, in my opinion.

So, we finished lunch and I took my leave. Isabella looked worn out and listless. She accompanied me to the door and said, 'Sam, look after yourself, will you.'

At home, I went straight to my room and lay down on the bed, hoping to think furiously about the future.

The first step towards revolt is the revolt against

parental authority. That's not something I had learned from the Gang or even from Isabella, all of whom were socially well-adjusted people. That is something that had come to me through reading, through something deep within me that had stirred my soul. I got my ideas about freedom from Kafka, Joyce, Beckett, and Henry Miller. It didn't correspond to anything in my lived experience, which was a struggle against repression, especially sexual repression. How to tell my father that I had had a defective penis that hadn't allowed me to pursue a quarry in any meaningful way? And, the question about money was a genuine one. I just couldn't think about going to work like my father and contenting myself with what fate had in store for me. Maybe I overestimated my own capacity to endure the kind of hardships that poets and philosophers in this country routinely went through. Without having a reasonable chance to succeed, to beat the world at its own game. I dreaded the word 'future'.

What was surprising about my father coming back from Calcutta was the change of tone. It was a complete departure from his usual demeanour. He was all sweet reasonableness.

'Look, Sam,' he said to me. 'Your brother is off to the States in two weeks and I don't think we are going to see much of him in the immediate future. Your sister will be married off in a few years from now. We, your mother and I, will have no one to look after us, no one but you. I have three years to go before I retire. Who will care for us when we are old and infirm? Think about that. We've brought you up as best as we could, we clothed you, fed you, took care of you without making any unreasonable demands. All I am saying is that you have some duty towards your old parents. I don't mean money, we have enough to live out the remainder of our days in this world. I mean, someone who cares for us, someone who will render those infinitesimal services that old people cannot provide by themselves. Because they are old. Calling up a doctor, liaising with relatives, being present at family gatherings, reinforcing our life-support systems, if you get what I mean.'

Then, there was a significant pause.

'I am not having any private eye following you around and spying on you, or anything of that sort. I understand that it is demeaning for you and for us. But, be a little responsible. Think of what your actions will mean to your old parents. I am not suggesting that you stop meeting your friends, even though I dare say some of them are very bad company and you know that, too. That girl you are obsessed with, she is no good. She'll ruin your life in no time and make you end up in jail, just like her. I don't want to see you running for your life from the police like a petty criminal. Let's be practical. We can't take care of you indefinitely. You will have to stand on your own feet, just like the rest of us. I am not suggesting for a moment that you give up on your writing. But first, you must eat. Where will that come from? The theatre, everybody says, is not a paying proposition. Your attitude is, how shall I say, absolute, it's all or nothing. It may work in the West, where they have solved all economic issues, cultural issues, where a writer does not have to beg for his next meal. This is India. It's a poor country. People starve to death over here. And, don't think just because you are my son that you will escape misery. Over here, anything can happen. Anything. You have to take life's hard knocks to understand this. I wanted to study law and be a lawyer. But, I also had to think about earning a livelihood at a very young age, at your age. So, I became a pilot and I don't regret anything because my life hasn't turned out to be as miserable as I felt it might at one point. I have done well for myself. You, too, might discover the happiness that comes from being like everybody else. You must try, Sam, you have to give life a shot. Nobody becomes an artist just by roaming the streets and looking hither and thither for something creative to do. You have to live, meet other people, strike up friendships, experience betrayal and injustice, taste the joys of living. This is a free country, you are free to be what you are. But, you can no longer ignore the consequences of your choices.'

There was another pause. I could see he had been rehearsing what he meant to tell me all the way back from the city of the Black Hole.

'So, what do you say?'

'I don't want to go to Calcutta,' I said.

'Okay. You want to stay back in Bombay. Fine. How are you going to meet your expenses?'

'I'll get a job.'

'A job that will allow you to live decently in this

expensive city. Where are you going to find that, if I may ask?'

'I have a couple of interviews coming up.'

This took him aback a little. Then, he smiled.

'Good. May I ask, where?'

I told him about Khushwant Singh and the copy test Benny Pathak was arranging for me.

He looked at me seriously now.

'They'll pay you a stipend, provided, of course, that you get your way. Will that be enough to take care of your board and lodgings?'

'That's my lookout,' I said, defiantly.

He looked downcast.

'I don't have the right to ask you how you are going to live in this town?'

I said nothing.

'They are going to pay you a pittance before they confirm you. I know because I have been through the rigmarole myself. I had a helluva time looking after myself and your mother in Ludhiana on a salary of Rs 50, which, at that time, was a reasonable middle-class one. I had no luxury. I had to pay for the flying school with a little help from your grandfather. Otherwise, I wouldn't have been able to make it. I would still be slaving away as a clerk in some godforsaken place barely making my ends meet.'

I said nothing. I had no answer to his question.

'I am your father, Sam,' he said gently. 'I have a right to be bothered about you. Your Principal spoke to me the other day about you, that you don't attend classes, and that you are always outside the college up to your own tricks. I am worried, frankly, about you getting a degree out of all this.'

'I'll get my degree.'

'I will be delighted if you do.'

There was another pause, a lengthy one this time.

'There are opportunities even in Calcutta, y'know,' he said, finally. 'You will get to like the city once you've made a few friends there. I know Subroto Sen of Clarion. I could recommend you to him. And then, Calcutta is a place for theatre, for being a writer…'

'Not in English,' I said cutting him off abruptly. 'I don't know any Bengali.'

He let out a sigh.

'Okay, I won't press you any further. Make up your own mind. But, do consider what I have just said. Don't be carried away by the attention that you are receiving from that girl. She doesn't know a thing about life. She has a rich father and she thinks she can play at Maecenas with you.'

This made me mad.

'She knows more about life than you do,' I said, raising my voice a little.

'Okay, okay,' he said, backing off. 'She may know more about life than I do, but I can tell you that she's looking for a parrot in a cage, somebody, an artiste, to patronise and condescend to.'

'No, she's not,' I said, furious. 'She has morals, she's a decent human being who genuinely cares about what's going on in this country! She's not some escapist looking to start a family and settling down in life, oblivious of the general misery surrounding her. She doesn't think that paying your taxes absolves you from any duty to the oppressed and the downtrodden.'

'My, my. Those are very big words. So, you want to be a revolutionary?'

'I didn't say that,' I snarled back. 'But, I am not going to live my life like a frog in the well. I want to know what's what. I want to know how people exercise their authority over others, what values they ultimately represent, whose side they are on. And, I might as well tell you, I am on Isabella's side and that's not going to change, no matter what!'

He was crying, my father.

'Don't you have any respect for me?' he said, piteously.

I said nothing.

'Am I some sort of a bourgeois monster who thinks life is all about money?' he said, wiping the tears away discreetly. 'I know money is not everything, but it is also true that you cannot do without it.'

'I am not interested in playing games. I want the game to change. I don't want to play by other people's rules, I don't want to live other people's lives. And, if you are so interested about me, let me tell you that Isabella represents freedom, the kind of freedom that I never enjoyed anywhere else, not even among you!'

My father heaved another sigh.

'Okay, Sam,' he said. 'Have it your way. There is only

so much I can tell you. I can't force you to do something you don't want to do. It's been pretty much like this all your life, right since you were a child. Just know that I want what's best for you. That's all.'

And then, he returned to his study.

At night, I dreamt of Isabella and wept like a baby, while my father snored away in his bed next to mine. I wept for my broken life, I wept for the love I was unable to express, the love I dared not claim for myself because I was a dirt-poor playwright who didn't know whether he had a future or not.

12

On a desolate, rain-driven Monday morning, I landed up at the Times of India building and went straight to Khushwant Singh's office. His secretary asked me to wait in the antechamber. A few moments later, I was ushered into his room. Singh was looking at proofs, checking them with a Mont Blanc ball-pen in his hand. He beckoned to me to take a seat and then went right back to his proofs. This lasted quite a while. After he was finished, he rang a bell and a factotum came in and took the proofs away. Singh put the Mont Blanc in his pocket and turned to me.

'Splendid piece on that Gondola girl,' he said, smiling, revealing his betel stained teeth. 'Problem is we're looking for hacks and not writers. We also need people to man the desk.'

I falsely said I would be glad to do anything that was available, for I knew I could never be a hack.

'What's your idea of journalism?' he said.

'I have no answer to that question. I haven't given it much thought.'

'You must have some idea. What does it mean for you? Fame, money, or just another livelihood?'

'Just another livelihood.'

'You don't sound desperate.'

Then, I told him about myself, how I didn't want to follow my parents to Calcutta, how I wanted to work in the theatre, here in Bombay, and be close to the people who cared for my talent.

He looked at me, kind of shrewd.

'Give me your CV,' he said.

I fetched it out of my trouser pocket and handed it over to him. It was slightly crumpled.

He looked at it at some length.

'I see you've been a debater for Sydenham and you've put up a play.'

'I wrote the play.'

He perused me silently for a while and then said, 'You know, going to work is about boredom. You think I am really enthusiastic about all the stuff that goes into the Weekly. I don't give a fuck. Only, from time to time, you get to tell the truth. I don't know if that compensates for the boredom, but it is reason enough for me to continue editing the Weekly. Are you prepared to be bored?'

I didn't know what to say. Actually, I knew what I wanted to say, but couldn't find the words that would have been tactful enough to cover up my absence of thought on this subject.

'Yes,' I said because I figured out that's what I was expected to say.

But, Singh had an uncanny compass for hypocrisy.

He looked at me and said, 'You are saying that because you want the job.'

'No. I am willing to give it a try, I have nothing to lose.'

'You are not desperate. Anyway, we'll give you a test and then we will see what happens. Okay?'

'Okay,' I said, relieved.

He picked up the receiver and called his secretary.

'Sandra,' he said, 'show Sam into Gupte's room, and give him some sheets of paper. I will be preparing a test for him, so…Sam go with Sandra.'

I got up and left for Gupte's cubicle which was a few metres away from Singh's office. She gave me a few blank A4 sheets and a ball-point pen and asked me to wait. I waited for half an hour before Sandra returned with a question paper neatly typed out and some galley proofs of stories that would appear in the following week's edition. I had to edit the proofs for grammar, spelling, punctuation, syntax and structure. I was also to write a 1000 words on why I wanted to be a journalist.

I got the proofs done in about 15 minutes, but no sooner did I confront the blank page for my little essay on journalism, than I went blank, totally blank. That was because I didn't really want to be a journalist, I wanted the money so that I could live an independent life in Bombay. I couldn't say that, I was scared shitless. So I wrote the first thing that came to my mind. I said journalism is about changing the world around us, it was a potentially revolutionary vocation, one couldn't approach the profession with a merely mercenary attitude, how does one look at reality when one knows that reality is looking right back at us, and by revolutionary I meant not throwing the current government out of power, but standing up to the majority, the one that would control the police and the army, it was sophisticated subversion, and so on and so forth. I was through with that in another half an hour or so. Once I had finished, I picked up my papers and gave them to Sandra.

'That was quick,' she said.

'Really?'

'Really,' said Sandra. 'Just give me a sec,' and, she went into Singh's office with the papers and was out in a trice.

'Leave your phone number and address,' said Sandra, 'Mr Singh will get back to you.'

I left, knowing in my heart of hearts that I wouldn't get the job.

I went over to Sydenham and found Nero Gomes and the Shah of Iran sitting quietly at the table, nursing their cup of coffee.

'I thought you guys were deep into studying,' I said.

'We are,' said Nero, with a smile, 'we're just checking out the joint one last time.'

'How's your chick, bohemian dog,' said Shah.

'All beaten up and bruised. She's out on bail, she can't leave the country and has to report to the local police every Thursday.'

'Watch out, Sammy boy,' said Shah, 'the police are mean and lawless, they might pick you up for questioning if you see her too often.'

'I don't give a damn,' I said.

'I've got a copy test fixed up for you with Benny Pathak's uncle Frank Camoes,' said Shah. 'Should be a breeze for you.'

'I just gave a test at the *Illustrated Weekly*,' I said.

'How did it go?' said Nero Gomes.

'Badly,' I said and described the encounter with Singh. 'Couldn't bring myself to fudge things and cater to the reigning philosophy at the TOI. Plus, I am a big zero where current affairs are concerned. I don't spend hours reading the newspaper, like my dad. Anyway, my folks are shifting to Calcutta in about six months.'

'I know,' said Nero seriously. 'Shah told me about that. You shouldn't go.'

'As my dad tells me, where am I going to stay, what am I going to eat?'

'We'll work something out,' said Nero. 'How's your old man?'

I told them about the private eye and the rehab, everything. They looked on in horror.

'Don't worry, man,' said Shah. 'We'll find a way to keep you in Bombay.'

'I want to go abroad. Like my brother who's leaving for Harvard the next month.'

'You'll have to finish college before that,' said Nero. 'Getting a job in Bombay should be an easier proposition.'

'Can't stand this country,' I said. 'I feel like smashing everything to bits all the time. I want to go somewhere I feel at home, where they will let me be…'

'To study what?' said Nero. 'I don't see you making it to some lousy business school where they teach you about corporate ethics, if such a thing can be said to exist. What are you doing about the play?'

'I'll have to talk to Isabella and Sanjana. Can't concentrate on the immediate stuff. I am too absorbed by the long run.'

'In the long run, we're all dead,' said Shah.

I sniggered at that.

'Keynes can go to hell,' I said. 'If they don't beat me up now, they'll beat me up after the play.'

'Who?' said Nero.

'The cops.'

'Why should they? They know you're not a member of the Party.'

'Listen, Sammy boy,' said Shah, 'that girl is really in love with you. I would walk a hundred miles barefoot to be with her.'

'Have you told her about your feelings for her?' asked Nero.

'I am petrified by the idea. By what will follow.'

At that, in walked Isabella Gondola.

'Hi, guys!' she said.

'Hi, Isabella,' said Shah and Nero in unison.

'What's happening?' she said.

'I just gave a test at the *Illustrated Weekly*,' I said. 'I don't think I'll make it. I can't write rubbish on command. I deal with reality through fiction. It's hopeless.'

'Don't be such a pessimist!' said Isabella. 'It's just a job so you can keep body and soul together. It's no big deal!'

'Try putting some sense into this bohemian dog,' said Shah.

'You're looking great,' said Nero.

'Thanks,' said Isabella. 'Actually, I don't feel all that great.'

In spite of the impression of physical frailty, she still looked beautiful.

'How's the case going?' said Nero.

'I've heard that they are going to drop all charges against me. I can't see how. I was up to my neck with the ML. However, I was not part of any conspiracy to blow up Bombay House. I've a great lawyer who's doing all he can to see that I don't go back to jail. The cops hate his guts.'

'I'm sure things will work out for you,' said Shah.

'Hopefully. You guys been studying hard? We're all going to miss the Gang, you guys really put Sydenham on top.'

And then, the conversation drifted to more mundane issues.

I couldn't get my head wrapped around my feelings for Isabella. I was desperately in love with her and spent all my idle hours devising ways to talk to her about emotions, hers and mine, but the moment she appeared on the scene, everything boiled down to the trite and the banal. Was she really in love with me? Was she waiting for me to take the initiative? Was she too expensive for me? 'Rich girls don't marry poor boys,' said Scott Fitzgerald. But, I couldn't, no matter how hard I tried, run away from the fact that this girl had some feelings for me. Whether they amounted to love or not was the agonising question I was up against. I couldn't make any commitments till I found a financially secure way of staying on in Bombay. Does love calculate? It probably does in someone else's dictionary. Everything seemed hell-bent on crushing me—my family, my college, everything, except the Gang, or at least the Shah of Iran and Nero, and Isabella. That didn't amount to much, as far as the future was concerned. I had no answers, none whatsoever. The entire problem lay in coherently articulating my love for Isabella, a love that vanished as soon as she appeared in front of me, physically. I felt no lust for her, I didn't want to physically possess her, but I knew that somehow, in some crazy, weird way, my imagination depended on her.

'Care for a coffee at the Shamiana?' said Isabella, after the guys had left.

'Yeah, sure,' I said.

'I have something to tell you,' she said mysteriously.

My curiosity was instantly aroused and I racked my brains for an answer. Zero. At the Shamiana, we sat facing the Gateway to India and the sea beyond. Isabella ordered two cappuccinos and I looked at her and said, 'Tell.'

'Bobby's asking me to marry him,' she said. She was looking at the table cloth, as if her fate was etched out on the house linen.

It was like receiving a punch to the face.

Isabella looked at me and smiled.

'I am through with Bob,' she said. 'My parents think he's a great catch, but Dad was categorical that the decision would be entirely mine, no matter what.'

'Your Dad is really sweet,' I said, my heart racing; I must have looked pink with embarrassment.

Isabella just went on smiling at me, until I wondered whether that was all.

'What's so funny?' I said finally.

Then, I was hit by a brain wave.

'You guys have slept with each other, haven't you?' I said.

The smile vanished from Isabella's face in a trice. She wouldn't look me in the eye. I guessed right that she had.

'It was nothing,' she said with a tremor in her voice. 'He just tore my clothes off and screwed the shit out of me. He knocked me up and then I had to have an abortion. You are the first person I am telling about this.'

Suddenly, I felt the pain. Isabella, the revolutionary, was not strong enough, she was vulnerable, insecure and probably traumatised. My heart sank at the thought, and then, I felt angry. Why was she unburdening herself thus? Was she looking for sympathy? I was not a shoulder to cry upon. I felt anger building up inside me, against my father and against Isabella who couldn't deal with sexual emancipation, who was proclaiming sacrilege with a view to enlisting me in her cause. I resented that. I felt like hurting her.

'So, what's the big deal,' I said, 'lots of men are like that.'

'He says he loves me,' said Isabella, again avoiding eye contact. She was crying.

I hated her for being so shattered about a sexual accident. I wanted her to be strong and free. Instead, she was snivelling around like a *pavitra bharatiya nari* (chaste Indian woman). Very obviously, Bobby Roy had counted for something in her life. I was the nice gentle, emotional physician who would cure her of her disease of sentimentalism. Or, so I surmised.

'Was he the first man in your life?' I said, not knowing what else to say.

'No,' said Isabella.

'When did you lose your chastity?' I said.

'When I was fifteen. With a guy called Indrajit Hazra, who played cricket with me.'

I felt rotten inside. I refused to take Isabella's bait, I refused to provide her with a harbour against the storm. This was her problem. I had nothing against Bobby Roy, except that he wanted to be my father, the indulgent one, the one who understood the pain of being sexually immature at the age of nineteen. I wanted to hit out at somebody.

Then, I said something really cruel.

'I don't know why you are making such a fuss about small things?' I said.

'Why should such things bother you? You are a modern—'

'You think rape is a small thing?' said Isabella.

'But, he continues to be a friend.'

'A friend, yes.'

There was a lull in the conversation as the waiter placed our cappuccinos in front of us.

'There are a lot of things I admire about Bobby Roy. He's genuine, he's not phony, he's not putting it on. He really means what he says.'

'Why does he want to marry you?'

'Because he loves me.'

'And, you? Do you love him, too?'

Then, she said something that shattered my illusions for good.

'I used to,' said Isabella, looking me in the eye this time around. 'But, now, I don't know. He's so reckless and irresponsible.'

'He cannot be a father to your child?'

Isabella shook her head.

'He is a predator.'

Then, I displayed my utter lack of sexual maturity, my utter lack of knowledge about what might go on between a man and a woman.

'So, why don't you seek your pleasures elsewhere?' I said brutally.

Isabella's mouth dropped in astonishment and she stared at me as if I were a stranger.

'I am not like that. I know lots of men, my age and above; I don't go sleeping around with them just to get even steven with my boyfriend. Oh, Sam! You don't know the first thing about love!'

This cut me to the bone. It was a direct nuclear hit to my heart.

It was my turn to look away, in embarrassment, shame and rage.

'How do you know I know nothing about love?' I said finally. I mean, I worshipped that woman and I was not even a pretender for the throne.

She quickly realised it was a risky avenue to tread upon.

'Of course, you have women falling all over to get to know you. You remind me of Stavrogin.'

'Who's he?'

'He's somebody in Dostoyevsky's *Devils*, an absent minded killer of women.'

Frankly, I was flattered by that description of me as a homme fatale.

'You don't get to see lot of women in Sydenham. I am not a prince of Peepli, or something like that. I am not royalty. I was trying very hard to hide my sexual innocence, my shame at being so ignorant about the ways of the world.'

'Sam, Sam,' said Isabella, with passion, 'you are a writer, you are a creative person. You are not Bobby Roy, and you'll never be, I mean, you are so cold! Don't compare yourself with Bob, you are different, there aren't too many men like you in this world.'

She had understood that I was jealous of Bobby Roy, that I wanted to be like him, casual and callous in love, someone with money. She had understood that I had an inferiority complex about men like Bobby Roy. She sounded disappointed with my reaction. I had an imagination, a very rare thing among English-speaking Indians.

'So,' I said, feigning indifference, 'will you marry him?'

'No!' she said, and suddenly, it was clear that something had changed in her ever since she approached me that night after the play, something had been uprooted in her, that there was a yawning abyss under her feet and that she would sink without my emotional support.

'No, Sam!' she continued, 'I can't even think of settling down with him and have children and all that nonsense. At bottom, he's a creep.'

Should I have said I loved her at this precise point? I don't know. What I do know is that after this point, there could never be innocence between Isabella and me, that I now had power over her, for she had surrendered to me. I felt nauseated. Had I said I would marry her, at that point, I could have said goodbye to my ambitions of being a writer. Castration would come into play massively, the pleasure-principle would take the back seat with reproduction, propagation of the species taking the wheel. Isabella, then, was an ordinary woman, with no aim in life independent of her paramour; she was ready to be moulded into any shape I wanted, she was like putty in my hand. Nausea.

'Excuse me,' I said, 'I have to go to the men's room.'

I rushed into the toilet and disgorged my entrails out. Vomit. Waves of vomit that shook my body and my mind. I quickly washed myself and went back, to find that Isabella had paid the check and left. To say I was dejected would have been an understatement. I was shattered.

That night, as I lay in bed, listening to the gentle snoring of my father, something started to speak in my mind. I knew I had to take it down, but I couldn't put on the lights without waking my father who was, like me, a light sleeper. I went fumbling in the dark and found a writing pad and a ball-point pen on my brother's desk. I started taking dictation in the dark, hoping that it would be legible when I woke up. Something, discourse, poured out of me and went on for about an hour or so, after which the source dried up. I woke up the next morning and read what I had written. It was a love story in 2000 words, not realistic, partly nonsensical, but beautifully put. I called the story *Quixote* and handed a type-written draft to Cristobal Colon who was editing the college magazine that year. After reading it, he looked up at me and said, 'This is a masterpiece man. You can really write. I'll carry it in our annual number.' So, that was how I started selling myself cheap, not realising the value of the writing, desperate to just see it appear in print. Nero Gomes was the second person to read the story.

'It's wonderful, man,' he said, thumping me on the back. 'A love story rooted in the Absurd. Not a whiff of nihilism anywhere. Truly Nietzschean.'

Colon wrote a very nice introduction and it was

published in the annual number of *Rapport* and got me the Best Writer's trophy of the college.

Soon after this, I got a call from Khushwant Singh. He said he had liked what I had written about the profession, that it was very idealistic and true, and that he appreciated the forthright manner in which I had tackled the ethics of the profession. Also, I had done a good job with editing the article submitted to me. He said he could offer me the job of a feature writer, but first I would have to complete my graduation. In the meanwhile, he said, he would be glad to carry any freelance stuff I could produce. And that was that.

Another Thursday, and I was to sit at Frank Camoes for a copywriting test that Benny had fixed up for me. I went there one afternoon, and was dazzled by the number of beautiful women who worked for him. I asked myself if I could be a part of this world and then decided I had very little choice. I was given a short product description of a mobike and asked to produce 150 words on it. I didn't know then that copywriting was not about literature, not about fine writing, but about selling the product. I wrote a poetic, florid, and ultimately, neurotic piece that I was very satisfied with. Lily, Cameos secretary, told me her boss would get back to me in a few days. I had only one thing on my mind, Isabella. Soon, college was closed for winter and the Gang was busy appearing for their exams. I lay locked up at home, furiously reading whatever came to hand. I was soaking in literature and it felt great.

Then, suddenly, my father came up to me one

morning and flung the newspaper at me.

'Read this,' he said, roughly, pointing to an anchor piece.

I read and read and my horror grew with every letter in that piece. The police had rearrested Isabella Gondola for involvement in a plot to assassinate the Chief Minister of Maharashtra. They had secured 3 days remand. I instantly knew they were going to torture her. There was a picture showing her in handcuffs being shoved into a Black Maria full of petty criminals. It broke my heart.

My father came back and looked at me, without saying anything, from a safe distance.

'So, what do you think?' he asked me finally.

'I don't know,' I said.

'You don't know? You don't know. They are going to pick up everyone she's met in the last six months, since she got bail in the Bombay House case. And, this is twice as serious, this is about bumping off a major politician.'

'I don't think she is involved in any way,' I said, determined not to be bullied over this. 'She will be found not guilty because that's the truth.'

'How do you know that's the truth?' my father almost shouted at me. 'She's some rich kid mixed up with Naxalites just for fun? She doesn't care about how many lives she's wrecked with her goddamn political views. And, you say she's innocent? How naïve can you be?'

My head was spinning slightly and I had difficulty in focusing.

'I'm going to meet her and ask her,' I said, diffident.

'She's in remand. She's not allowed any visitors. They are going to interrogate her. Don't you know anything about the law? I wonder how her parents put up with all this.'

'Her parents are very understanding and sympathetic. Her grandfather was a lieutenant of Imre Nagy.'

'Who's Imre Nagy?'

'Somebody who led an uprising against the Soviets in Hungary in 1956.'

'Two years before you were born. So, she has political pedigree. This is India, my son, and you don't know what police can be like.'

'I don't think Isabella could ever be involved with killing someone in cold blood,' I said, not knowing what else to say. 'She's been having doubts about her Party's politics. The Party didn't help her the last time round.'

'Because that would have been tantamount to establishing the police's case, you idiot,' said my father. He was clearly worked up about this, desperate to make me see the grim reality of the whole thing. I may have been naïve, idealistic and plain stupid. But, I loved that girl and my heart sank when I looked at the picture in the newspaper.

'So, what am I supposed to do?' I said, rather pointlessly.

'I'll tell you what you should do. Cease having any kind of contact with that girl. She spells trouble. You will be lucky if the cops don't come around seeking remand against you. You've been so thick with her over the last few months. Don't you dare go see her again. We will be shifting to Calcutta in a few months, and I want your bags packed and done. That's my final word. No arguments, no buts, nothing. You don't know what's good for you.'

'I have a job offer from *Illustrated Weekly*,' I said, and immediately realised it was a mistake.

'Did that girl put you on to it?' said my father. 'Did she?'

I said nothing.

'So, she did. She has this dream about making you a star of the theatre, she wants you under her wing. Bloody nonsense. How much is Khushwant Singh willing to pay you?'

I said I didn't know and in any case I would have to graduate before taking up that proposal.

'What is the starting pay for a trainee at *The Times of India*, do you know?' said my father.

I said nothing.

'I'll call up Burman, he's personnel manager there, he should be able to give me a fair idea.'

My father was well-networked through the Willingdon club. He could pick up a phone and talk to the Chief Secretary of the government of Maharashtra.

'Give me a second while I talk to Burman,' he said, and left the room.

He came back after a few minutes and said, 'Huh, seven hundred bucks a month! Will you be able to eat anything? Leave alone paying rent and electricity bills!'

I must have looked dejected.

Suddenly, my father stopped bullying me and tried gentle persuasion.

'Look,' he said, with all reason and grace, 'if you come with us to Calcutta, I will put you in touch with Subroto who's the boss at Clarion. You can have a decent career and stay with us until you arrive at a decent salary and settle down in life. Don't destroy yourself over some stupid girl. You don't know where you are going to land up with her. Jail is a nasty place, it turns thieves into murderers. It's not what your romantic imagination makes it out to be. Do you really want to sacrifice your life for the revolution or some such shit? Give it a thought.'

And, he left the room.

My first concern was to get in touch with Isabella's parents, but I couldn't talk to them over the house phone. I would have to use a public telephone. I put on my slippers and made for the door.

'Where do you think you are going?' said my mother.

'Downstairs,' I said, 'to buy some cigarettes.'

'Oh, so you're openly smoking now? Is it?'

I shrugged. I didn't give a damn. The girl I loved was in distress and it seemed paramount to me to stand by her. It is what any decent human being would do in my place.

My father came out of the bathroom with lather on his face.

'Be back in 15 minutes, or else,' he said, glaring at me.

I must have looked at him with utter contempt, for he brusquely said, 'We're saying this for your own good.'

I went to the public booth across the road, dropped a coin and dialled Isabella's number. A maid servant picked up the phone. I said I wanted to speak to Mrs Gondola. Maid said they were at the hospital.

'Hospital?!' I said. 'Why hospital?'

'*Chhoti memsahib ko maara hai*' ('Isabella has been hit'), she said.

Suddenly, everything fell into place. Isabella had been seriously tortured and she had been taken to the hospital.

'Which hospital?' I asked frantic, and out of control. My hands and feet were going numb with grief.

'Lakdawala,' said the maid.

That was in the Bombay Central area, not far from Nepean Sea road.

I hung up in a daze. I had no money on me. I couldn't take a bus. I decided to walk it out. Something inside me was going to pieces. I couldn't think of anything but to be with Isabella. The traffic went past me in a blur. It was a delicious winter morning and Bombay was warm without being oppressive. The world was inhabited by my pain, and I didn't know why everybody was so indifferent to my plight. The most routine gestures looked extraordinary to me. Any world that could contain so much pain had to be absurd. Beauty was being massacred. After about an hour's walk, I finally reached Lakdawala. There were cops everywhere. People were being frisked. I, in my khadi kurta and jeans must have looked more like a Naxalite than not, and I was abruptly detained by a burly constable.

'Where do you want to go?' he asked gruffly.

I told him.

'Not allowed,' he said.

'I want to talk to Isabella's parents.'

'Why?'

'I am a friend of the family.'

'Are you a Naxalite? How come they haven't taken you in for questioning?' He called out to his officer, who strode up to us and said, 'What is it?'

'This boy is saying he wants to meet that Gundola girl's parents,' said the constable.

'Why?' said the officer, looking suspiciously at me.

My courage was deserting me.

'Nothing,' I said, timidly, 'just wanted to know how they're doing.'

'How do you know Gondola?' he asked.

I said we went to the same college.

'What did you say your name was?' said the officer.

I said my name, more and more uncertain of myself.

'Wait,' the officer ordered.

He went back to his jeep and spoke to someone over the walkie-talkie. I could see him nodding once or twice. He took out a packet of State Express and put a cigarette between his lips, lit it and took a deep breath.

Then, he strode back at us.

'We are taking you in for questioning,' he said. 'You have been seen with the suspect on numerous occasions in the last three months. You must be knowing something about her political activities.'

I said I didn't know a thing about her political

activities, but it was evident that they were not interested in listening to my side of the story. They knew their side of the story and they wanted me to endorse it anyhow. Or, so I conjectured. I felt my heart sink inside me. What would I tell my father? Would these animals put me through third degree too? I was now shaking with fear.

The burly constable took me roughly by my arm and led me to the officer's jeep.

'I want to talk to my father,' I said, my voice soft and yielding.

'Later,' said the officer, 'after we've dealt with you.'

They took me to the Colaba police station where I was ushered into an interrogation chamber. They took down my details, name, father's name, address, phone number.

The officer finally put his pen down and sighed.

'Look,' he said, 'we don't think you are linked with the plot to assassinate CM sahib, but we want some information. About who she frequents politically, who are her other friends, where she goes, where she gets her money from, any information that could be useful for our interrogation.'

I said, truthfully, that I was not well-acquainted with her political associates, even though I had seen a couple of them the last time she was in jail.

'Can you give us their names and addresses?' he said.

I said I had no idea who they were and where they figured in the Party hierarchy. I only knew that Isabella was part of some kind of cell.

'Aha,' said the officer. 'What kind of cell?'

I said, truthfully, 'I had no idea of how the Naxalite Party hierarchy functioned. There was some talk of blowing up Bombay House, but I had never had any discussion with Isabella about this.'

The officer reached for his file and took out a newspaper cutting. It was my TOI article.

'You wrote this?' he asked.

'Yes, but it was only to help as a friend. I was not a member of the Party, or anything like that.'

'But, you sympathise with them,' said the officer.

'No, I don't,' I said. 'I had just spoken to them once or twice about her life in the prison, since they seemed to have people inside the jail who were informing them about her condition.'

'Can you give us their names?' said the officer.

I said I had no names.

At this, the officer lost his temper.

'You think we're going to buy this?' he said. 'You consort with her, visit her house regularly, are involved in some kind of drama contest with her, and you say you know nothing about her associates.'

I said it was an implicit understanding with her that we wouldn't talk politics.

The officer looked at me, a sort of stare with a sullen look on his face.

'You are not going to leave this police station without giving us the information we want,' he said.

My throat was dry. I asked if I could get a drink, or something.

'Later,' said the officer. 'What are you so nervous about if you haven't done anything wrong?'

I said nothing. But, I could feel the blood draining away from me. My courage, the little I had, the little that my parents had nurtured in me, was deserting me.

'Are you willing to stand in court and say that Isabella Gondola was involved in a plot to kill CM sahib?' said the officer.

I was amazed. I said, 'I know nothing about any plot to kill CM sahib.'

'You are lying,' said the officer. 'The last time around, we seized some of your books and there were copies of Karl Marx and Bakunin and Mao among them.'

I said, 'I had got interested in these authors for Isabella's sake. I didn't like them too much.'

'Ah, so, you are some kind of Romeo, is it?'

I said nothing.

'We know how to make you talk.'

One look at my face, and he knew he had scored a direct hit. I wouldn't be able to stand up to third degree. What came next, took me totally by surprise.

'Your brother is leaving for Harvard next month? He'll need immigration clearance from the police.'

I could hear things coming crashing down all around me. They would go after my brother who wasn't even remotely connected to the case.

'He's innocent,' I said miserably.

'Everybody is innocent until proven guilty,' said the officer with a laugh.

Then, he looked at me for a second, with a totally blank, vacuous expression.

'A bright boy like you, ruining his future over some silly girl he happens to like, over a drama contest,' he said, vaguely.

He beckoned to the constable to fetch him a paper and pen.

'How old are you?' said the officer, after the constable had left.

'Twenty,' I said.

'Twenty! My goodness! You have your whole life in front of you,' he said, smirking beneath his moustache.

The constable returned with the paper and pen.

The officer took some sheets and the pen and slid them across the table to where I was sitting.

'Describe your life with Isabella Gondola in your own words. We want names, addresses, phone numbers, whom she met, any friends of her you'd happened to have met. The head, the tail, the whole damn thing. You've seen *Jaws*? The movie? We want you to describe the great white shark, its habitat, its habits, its acquaintances, its activities, especially political ones. Solid evidence,' and he beat upon the desk with his knuckles. 'Solid as concrete.'

'I know nothing.'

'Come, come, you are not the one to die for the revolution, you are just the son of an Indian Airlines pilot. You are not a martyr for the oppressed and the downtrodden. Deep down, you care for your parents, especially,' at this he sneered at me 'your brother who is bound for an American paradise. Cooperate and we'll let you go. Or else, I will be forced to arrest you and produce you before the Magistrate within 24 hours and seek 14 days remand. And, you better know what that means.'

I started crying.

'Aw,' he said, 'come on, yaar, all you have to do is write three lines—that you know Isabella Gondola, that you know she is a member of the Communist Party of India (Marxist-Leninist) and that, to the best of your knowledge, she was involved in a plot to kill the CM of Maharashtra. Simple! You might be called up as a witness, all you have to do is repeat those three lines ad infinitum ad nauseam. Understood?'

I looked at the blank sheet of paper in front of me, not knowing what to do. I couldn't think straight, I was so scared. This would be like plunging the knife into her back. I would be a snitch for the rest of my life, I would have to live with this. The alternative was to see my brother's future jeopardised for good. I wanted to talk to Isabella. I realised all my strength came from her. I couldn't do it.

I said, 'I can't do it.'

The officer reacted without anger. He stood over me calmly and said, 'We might use this bit of paper, and again, we might not. It all depends. One way or the other, you will be a part of this trial and it could be a long and nasty business. You know our courts? It takes 20 years for a verdict. You might be arrested on a non-bailable charge, and I hope you know what that means. Don't fuck with the police.'

I said, 'I want to speak to my father.'

He looked at me for a while, examining the disaster I had turned into.

'Okay,' he said finally. 'We'll have to arrest you and demand 14 days remand.'

I was much calmer now. I said nothing. I had crossed the Rubicon.

'Lock him up,' he ordered the constable.

I was back in a cell. I knew my father would throw a fit, but I couldn't give a damn. I was not on his side. I was on Isabella's side.

There were two other people in the cell, one of them obviously a Naxalite—beard, kolhapuri chappals and khadi kurta. He cheered up as soon as he saw me.

'Gondola's boyfriend?' he asked, without curiosity.

'Friend,' I said. I was suddenly feeling very tired.

'They want a confession?' he said, with a friendly smile.

I nodded. I was in no mood for a conversation.

'They'll put us through, what they call, enhanced interrogation techniques, a euphemism for torture. They believe evidence is to be shaken out of us. Have you had lunch?'

I thought the question was weird. Who could think of lunch in this place?

'They are obliged to provide you with all meals while

in custody,' he said, his friendly, affable manner never leaving him.

'I am not hungry,' I said.

'I'll order some biryani for us. You have to keep body and soul intact for what is to come.'

He called out to a constable and said, 'Bring us some biryani.'

I was surprised to see the constable agree without a murmur.

'Perks,' said the Naxalite with a laugh.

My father landed up at around 3 pm.

'I have come to take you away,' he said, his face looking like thunder. 'Enough is enough.'

I must have looked stupid.

'I have spoken to the CM's private secretary and he has agreed to order your release on compassionate grounds. This is your last chance. If you make a mistake after this, there'll be nobody to bail you out of this business.'

'I am not coming,' I said stubbornly.

At this, he appeared flabbergasted.

'You mean to say you are willing to put up with third degree?' he said, incredulously.

'I have chosen my side,' I said, trying to sound even and calm even though I was trembling inside.

He threw a fit.

'You think you're going to die for some goddamn revolution? You think this is glamorous? They will break every bone in your body. They mean it. Look, just come with me now, your mother is frantic with worry, think of your old parents. I am doing this for your own good. You are only twenty, goddamit. I am trying to put some sense into that bird brain inside you. This is serious business, not a play. This is the real thing.'

I said nothing, not even looked at him.

'Listen,' said my father, and his voice grew plaintive, 'come with me and I promise not to interfere with your coming and going if you stay away from this woman.'

'I hate you,' I said.

It was his turn to look away. He didn't know what to say.

It was to be the finest moment in my sordid little life.

Just then, a constable came running in with a bunch of keys and opened the lock-up door.

'Get out,' he said. 'Your girlfriend is dead.'

'You killed her,' I said. Tears rolled down my cheeks.

'Get out,' said the constable. 'We have other horses to flog.'

He took me by my arm and shoved me outside.

I went, my head bowed with pain and grief, but there was something deep inside me that was exulting. I hadn't given up, I hadn't gone down on my knees, I hadn't been a traitor and a snitch.

I was looking forward to the headlines in next day's newspaper, but there was nothing about Isabella on the front page. I flipped the pages and on page 6, bottom right-hand column, there was a short write-up saying that Isabella Gondola had her intestines ruptured and that she died of a multi-organ failure. They had shoved a metal object up her arse during her interrogation. Some human rights organisations had taken up the matter with the High Court. Nobody contacted me, not even Isabella's parents. She was being turned into a statistic. Apparently, custodial deaths were a dime a dozen in this country. Human life was cheap, there was so much of it being wasted through apathy and carelessness.

But, I hadn't told Isabella how much I loved her. I was, ultimately, a failure.

EPILOGUE

'Love', 'art'—these words were too big for me. I had been found wanting in my ambitions. I didn't have the stature. Love was like jumping off a cliff—either I would dash my brains out on the rocks below or dive clear into the deep, blue sea. It was too much of a risk, the risk of losing myself, the risk of routine. Fame. That was another big word. I was just Sam, the bohemian dog from Sydenham, who had to now look for a profession in the alien city of Calcutta. I was just an ordinary dog. Like other dogs, I dreaded the unknown. It had defied me and I had thrown in my towel, like the rest of them.

In Calcutta, I sat for an exam for the recruitment of probationary officers in a public sector bank and cracked it. I was called in for an interview. They asked me several political questions to which I gave carefully rehearsed answers.

What do you think about Bob Dylan? Do you agree with his political views? Do you think we let Pakistan off cheaply after the Bangladesh war? Shouldn't we have settled Kashmir once and for all? What do you think about the civil rights movement in the US? What do you know about the Black Panthers? Are Naxalites traitors to the government and the country?

I knew what they wanted to hear and gave the suitable replies.

I got the job.

I married Deepika. She was chosen by my parents. She is beautiful and caring. She takes care of me, keeps my surroundings nice and tidy. We have a daughter, and we take pleasure in seeing her grow up.

I have ceased to be a writer, I have closed my book. I had also made peace with God. I wasn't overly religious, that would have been bad form. Let's say, I was mildly participative on religious occasions, like Durga Puja. I had no real convictions, politically and ideologically. The world still didn't make sense to me, but I had consumed my pain, I had been transformed by it, I couldn't go back.

With Isabella, there would have been no defeat. I would have known despair and longing and love and fighting hard for my beliefs. I would have been authentic and whole. Fate had decided otherwise.

I wasn't unhappy.